I0552570

FACE OFF

Maureen Ulrich

Book Two
in the *Jessie Mac Hockey Series*

A Wood Dragon Book

This book is a revised edition of the previous book under the same title published by Coteau Books in 2010.

Typeset by: Christine Lee
Cover photograph by: Wanda Harron
Cover art by: Callum Jagger

Library and Archives Canada Cataloguing in Publication
Ulrich, Maureen, 1958-
ISBN: 978-1-989078-26-6

Issued in print, audio and electronic formats

Wood Dragon Books
Post Office 429, Mossbank, Saskatchewan, Canada, S0H 3G0
www.WoodDragonBooks.com

Maureen Ulrich
Box 53, Lampman, Saskatchewan, Canada, S0C 1N0
Contact: maureenulrichwrites@gmail.com

What is a Faceoff?

In ice hockey, a faceoff is used to
start or restart play.

An official drops the puck between two opposing
player's sticks, and the players battle for possession.

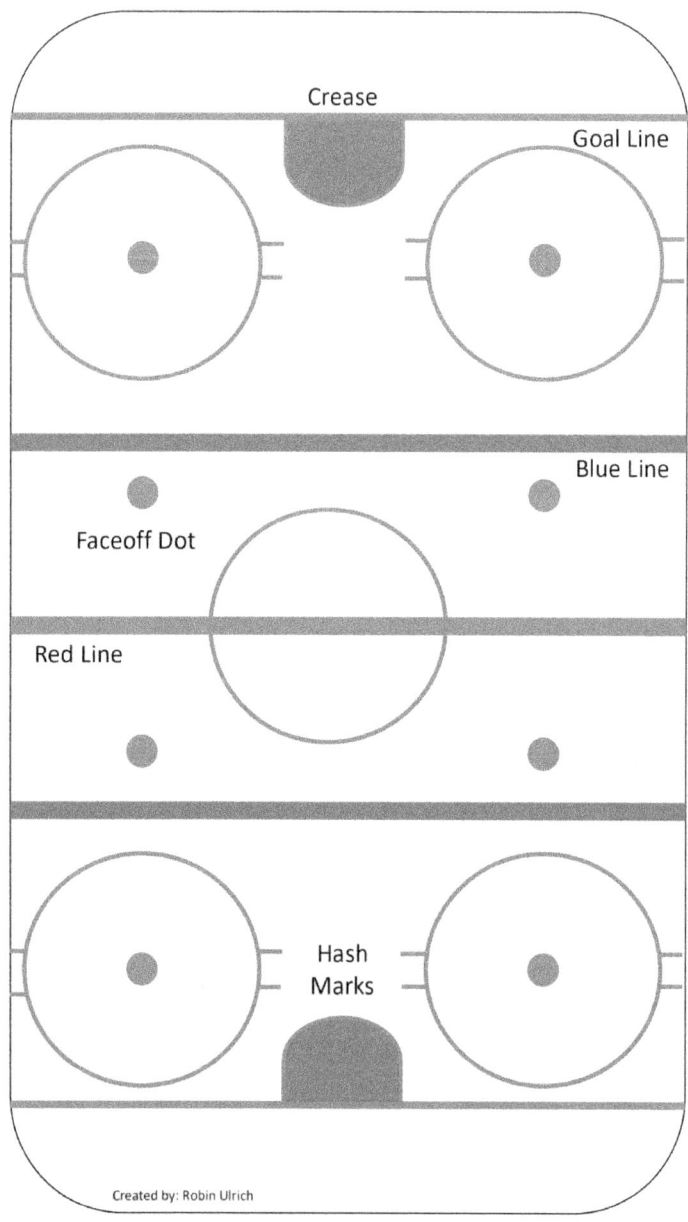

Don't forget to check out the glossary of hockey terms at the back!

1

I SQUAT BEHIND HOME PLATE. "Two away, ladies! Any bag!"

A cool breeze finds the damp spot between my shoulder blades. My knees and right shoulder ache. I think I tweaked something when I tried to throw Kathy Parker out at second. Sure as shooting, she slid under the tag and came up grinning. Thanks to a passed ball on her third strike, Miranda Omalu stands on first. Kim Scott, who already has two strikes on her, is batting. If we strike Kim out, we'll beat JL's Bike and Skate and move one step closer to the A-side league championship.

Since hockey season ended, Kim and I get along okay. She's nice enough to me at school, but I wouldn't describe us as friends. I don't think that's ever going to happen.

"Make sure you swing for the fence," I tell Kim. "Or did you hurt yourself on that last one?"

She laughs and steps into the batter's box, digging her left foot in and cocking her elbow to bring the butt of the bat in line with her chest.

Jodi Palmer's on the mound, foot on the rubber, softball resting on her hip, partially hidden by her glove. She's a beautiful pitcher—a perfect combination of technique and power. She rolls into her windup. All the momentum comes from her core as she brings her elbow towards her ear and whips her arm around, collapsing her hip and barely grazing it with the ball as she releases it.

At the wrong time.

The ball flies high and wild, smashing into the backstop behind me. I wrench off my mask, track down the ball, and whirl around, but Kathy has already rounded third, daring me to pick her off. I'm smarter than that. Miranda now occupies second. First base is open, taking away our force.

Great.

I toss the ball back to Jodi, who gives me a sheepish grin. I scoop up my mask and curse under my breath.

"Well, that makes the game more interesting," Mark says behind me.

I ignore him.

Jodi's dad is already on his way to the mound. He wears flip-flops and khaki shorts. Mr. Palmer's tall and lean, and even though I'm not supposed to notice, he's got a great set of legs. We definitely have the hottest coach in the league.

"Kim's one of their best hitters. We should walk her," Mr. Palmer's saying when I reach the mound. "It's the right thing to do."

"But I've got two strikes on her already," Jodi says. "I can finish her, Dad."

"You're sure?" Mr. Palmer asks.

"Sure I'm sure." Jodi gives her dad a wink.

Mr. Palmer turns his body to include me. "What do you think, Jessie?"

I look back at Kim, who's taking some lethal practice swings. "We can get her to chase a bad pitch. Kim wants a home run so bad she can taste it."

"Pitch around her," Mr. Palmer says. "Don't throw her any strikes. If we walk her and load the bases, we get the force back. No harm done." He turns to me. "Don't forget about asking Mark to ump again tomorrow."

"I won't." I tug my mask on as I return to home plate.

Jodi grooves one low and inside, but Kim's no sucker.

Ball two.

The next pitch is high and outside. Right where Kim likes them. But Kim watches it go by.

Ball three. Full count.

Jodi leaves her next pitch hanging over the plate, and Kim connects, drilling the ball over Kendra's head. When the ball touches the grass, it sizzles for the fence, and Kendra runs after it.

I pick up Kim's bat and toss it out of the way while my teammates scream for Kendra to throw the ball home.

Kathy jumps on home plate then turns to welcome Miranda, the tying run.

Mr. Scott, JL's third base coach, waves his arms like a maniac and screams at his daughter to go home. When she crosses home plate, JL's Bike and Skate explodes off the bench. It's like they won the World Series, instead of the first game of our league tournament.

Jodi walks over to Mark, who's shedding his chest protector and mask. "Next time, remember your girlfriend's team's supposed to win. That's why you're umping."

Mark smiles. "And here I thought your perfect season was because of your great pitching. My mistake." He drapes an arm around my shoulders. "As for umping, I calls 'em as I sees 'em."

Jodi walks away, chuckling.

As I gather up my gear, Mark tugs my ponytail. "Better luck next time, Babe."

"That'll be next season. We're on the B-side now." I watch as the winning team celebrates with their fans. "We beat them twice this year. Losing to them now really sucks."

"Yes, but losing also builds character." Mark reaches into the pocket of his shorts and puts the gold stud back in his left ear. His blue T-shirt and collar-length, dark blonde hair are sweat-soaked, but he's still the best looking guy at this ballpark—by a long shot.

My mom waves to me from the stands behind the backstop. "Do you need a ride home?"

I point at Mark, and the smile on Mom's face vanishes. She doesn't argue the point though.

Kathy struts over. "Sucks to lose on an inside-the-park home run, doesn't it?" she crows.

"Yep." I'm trying hard not to let my gritted teeth show.

"Coming over to Shauna's later? Jodi says she is." Kathy pulls off her cap and threads her fingers through her damp blonde hair. "I hope you can forget we're in the A pool and you're in the B. We could make friendship bracelets, group hug, and sing Kumbaya around the campfire."

I laugh. "Sounds good."

I haven't seen a lot of Kathy since hockey season ended. I've hung out with Jodi mostly. We've been pretty tight since the night of Jodi's fifteenth birthday party.

Jodi flops down in the backseat of Mark's truck and pitches her ball glove on the floor. "Nothing worked tonight. I couldn't hit the plate if my life depended on it."

"Don't be so hard on yourself." I turn and smile at her. "Our bats were cursed."

Jodi moans and tilts her head way back. "Don't remind me. I'm freakin' zero for four today. I need a drink."

Mark looks in the rearview mirror. "Are you girls going to Shauna's tonight?"

"Yep." Jodi digs in her bag and pulls out her water bottle. She's been carrying it with her everywhere lately. She takes a swig and hands it over the console to me.

"No thanks," I say, avoiding Mark's grey eyes. I know what he thinks about Jodi's bottle—which is laced with vodka. "Is Jordan coming?"

"Probably not. Jordan's got a baseball game in Weyburn. He and Greg won't get back till later." Jodi takes another swig and nudges me with the toe of her sandal. "Where was your dad tonight?"

"He has to ump Courtney's game."

"Too bad," Jodi says. "He's got an ass that doesn't quit. I love watching him get your equipment out of the car."

"Your dad's ass is ten times nicer," I reply. The "hot dad" thing is second nature to us. I look over at Mark to see if he's lightened up, but his jaw is rigid. He's sure not impressed with Jodi. "Hey, Mark, can you ump for us tomorrow?"

He raises an eyebrow. "Wouldn't you rather have one of my kidneys?"

"Come on. You already said you aren't doing anything."

"If the weather's decent, I'll be golfing."

I know he's yanking my chain. Mark never misses my softball games. I'm the only girl on the team whose boyfriend will ump.

Mark and I have been dating for four months, and it's perfect. Mark's perfect.

"I missed too many of your hockey games last winter," he always says. "Maybe if I'd been at more of them, we wouldn't have taken so long to get together."

"Hey, Mark, are you golfing in the Woodlawn tournament next weekend?" Jodi asks.

Mark adjusts the rear view mirror. "I haven't decided."

Mark's a two-sport athlete. He golfs on the Estevan Comprehensive School team—the ECS Elecs. He also plays elite hockey, though his previous season ended on a crappy note. Some of his U18 teammates "lacked focus"—a nice way of saying they chose partying over playing. Things came to a head when Mark's coach sent everybody home from a big tournament after five players broke curfew and got drunk. The parents hit the roof, and the coach quit. The two dads who took over to finish the season were way over their heads. Mark's AA team, favoured to a win a provincial title, got knocked out in the first round of playoffs.

While Mark and Jodi talk about the golf tournament, I wonder where Mark will play hockey next fall. He could play AAA some place, but his family and his education are important to him. I'm hoping Mark will sign with the Bruins, Estevan's SJHL team and keep going to ECS—AKA the Comp—which is where I'm headed for Grade Ten. But with Mark's dad living in Calgary, you just never know.

Mark drops Jodi and me off at my place. The garage door is wide open, and my dad's Prius is nowhere in sight. Dad must have taken Courtney for ice cream after her game. Mom, who's beaten us home, kneels next to a flowerbed, pulling weeds.

"I'm going to fill with gas and run over to Canadian Tire," Mark says. "I'll come back in an hour to pick you up." I start to climb out of the truck, but he grabs my hand and pulls me back. At first I think he's going to kiss me, but he says, "We need to talk."

He looks so serious my heart kicks into high gear. "What about?"

"I'll tell you later, when Jodi's not around." He stares at Jodi, who's talking to my mom.

"See you." I slide off the seat and get my ball bag out of the truck box before Mark takes off.

"So, you're going over to Shauna's?" Mom asks when I get there.

"Is that okay with you?"

Mom's smile is tight. "Don't stay out too late." She looks at Jodi. "Jodi, I want to talk to Jessie for a minute. Why don't you go shower? You know where the clean towels are."

"Sure do, Mrs. Mac." Jodi picks up her bag and pulls the strap over her shoulder. She uses the garage entrance to go into the house.

"I smelled booze on her," Mom says. "Have you been drinking too?"

"No, Mom." Trust Mom to pick up on the vodka, which is supposedly odorless. She has a nose like a bloodhound.

"Do I need to smell your breath?"

"No, you don't."

"Because if I have to do that to know when you're telling the truth, and I find out you're lying—"

"Mom, I have not been drinking."

"That girl is headed for trouble, and she's not even at the Comp yet. Her parents are too permissive."

Mom's not telling me anything I don't already know. Jodi's got three older brothers—all hockey players—and I think the Palmers got tired of enforcing the rules by the time Jodi came along.

Jodi sleeps over at my place nearly every weekend. I stayed at her place a few times, but Mom and Dad quit trusting her after I brought her home drunk from a party at Jordan's and she threw up on my bed. I don't drink when I'm with Jodi. One of us needs to stay in control, because Jodi's pretty impulsive when she's plastered.

"Your father and I think you should spend more time with Shauna and Tara. Like you used to," Mom says.

"I do spend time with them! I'm going to Shauna's tonight, remember?"

"You should also spend less time with Mark. You're getting too serious."

"How can we get serious?" I protest. "I'm only allowed to stay out after midnight once a week, and even then I have to be home by 1:30, or Dad will come looking for me." I don't add that he's usually sporting bed head and sweats, so I'm always home on time.

"You're just fifteen, and Mark's going to graduate next year."

"Mom, he's only two years older than me!"

"Things are moving too fast."

Too fast? I'd like to throw a few details in her face. If she only knew how considerate Mark is of me—how careful he is not to push me into anything.

"So does this mean I can't go to Shauna's?"

Mom puts her hand on my forearm and squeezes. "You're a smart girl, Jessie. You had a tough start when we moved here, but you've turned things around. We trust your ability to make good decisions."

My defensiveness drains away. "Thanks, Mom."

We head inside.

She's right about turning things around. My life is now the total opposite of what it was last September—when we moved here from Saskatoon. The first two weeks were okay. Then I stuck my big foot in my mouth and dissed Kim in front of her best friend Natalie. I hardly knew Kim before that. But I soon found how vindictive she can be.

Within a few days, Kim rallied every girl in our class against me. They started wrecking my stuff, sending me nasty notes and gossiping about me. Kim even told Marsha Schwartz, one of the tough girls at the Comp, that I called her a "fat pig," so Marsha would want to beat me up.

But when I started playing U15 girls hockey with the Xtreme, everything changed. I got to be friends with Shauna Langley, Tara Brewer, and the rest of the girls. Steve, the Xtreme coach, helped me to learn to love hockey even more than I love ringette, which is saying a lot because I love ringette.

The rest of the winter wasn't so bad—if you don't count being scared to death of Marsha and her pals. Or Kim joining the Xtreme and cutting me up every chance she got. In February, Kim and I finally called a truce, and on the bus home from provincials, I sat with Mark and caught up on a winter's worth of misunderstandings. It was the best six hours of my life. When we got back to Estevan, he pulled me behind the bus and kissed me for the first time.

Now that was definitely something worth waiting for.

As I walk into our kitchen, I glance at the calendar on the wall where I circled June 21st in red marker.

That's today—the longest day of the year. The day I've been waiting for. Because on June 22nd the nights start to get longer, and the countdown begins to my first year playing U18 girls hockey.

And as Jodi would say, it's gonna be freakin' awesome.

2

"You're overreacting," Mark says.

"You tell me you're spending the entire summer in Calgary, and you expect me not to get upset?"

"I expect you to be mature enough to understand why I'm going."

"So now I'm immature?" I sit on the bottom step of Shauna's front deck and fold my arms across my stomach.

Mark pulls off his ball cap and runs his hand through his hair. "Don't put words in my mouth."

I take a deep breath and try to calm down. He's right—as usual. I should be able to listen to everything he has to say before I fly off the handle. I have this bad habit of sticking my foot in my mouth and doing all sorts of stupid things before my brain kicks in.

"My dad wants me to work for him this summer," Mark explains. "He's going to get me a membership at his golf course and have the pro work with me. His apartment complex has a fitness centre, so I can get in shape for hockey. I'm even going to try some boxing at a local gym. These are great opportunities, Jessie. Plus I want to spend more time with my dad. I don't get to see him much."

I stand up and move away from him, walking to the end of Shauna's driveway.

One thing I love about Mark is how devoted he is to his family, and that means I've got to suck it up when he chooses them over me. I look down at the asphalt, picturing a long, lonely summer without him.

"Who am I going to talk to?"

Mark comes up behind me and slips his arms around my waist. "You can call me every day."

I try to ignore his warm breath on the back of my neck. "I'm not going to see you all summer."

"But I'll be back in late August for hockey," he says. "I signed with Estevan."

"The Bruins?" I turn around in his arms so I face him. "But I thought you said their practices will interfere with school?"

"I'm not taking calculus until second semester. I can make it work. Babe, do you want me to play here?"

Relieved, I nod.

He bends his head and kisses me.

While he's kissing me, my little voice says, two months is a long, long time, and I wrap my arms around his neck to draw him closer, but he pulls away—as he always does.

A white Mustang barrels around the curve and screeches to a halt across the street, and Mark swivels his head to look at it. Music booms from the subwoofers, spilling out the windows.

"Shauna's neighbours are going to love this," I observe. So far Shauna's managed to keep everybody in her backyard and hold the party noise down to a reasonable level.

But there's nothing quiet or reasonable about the driver of that car.

Greg Kolenick kills the engine, opens the door and disconnects himself from the leather interior. He's gained weight since hockey season. Right now he's wearing board shorts, a toque, and a white T-shirt. While Greg grabs a case of beer from the trunk, Jodi's boyfriend Jordan Decker climbs out on the passenger side, still wearing his ball uniform. Jordan's phone starts playing a heavy metal tune, and he leans against the Mustang, texting.

"Markie, how's it hangin'?" Greg shouts.

Mark doesn't say a word. He doesn't have much use for Greg, who was the goaltender—correction, the starting goaltender—for the AA team last season.

Greg swaggers across the street. He spits a stream of brown juice on the lawn then gives Mark a one-arm hug and back slap. He reaches for me next. I duck under Mark's arm, but Greg grabs my hand and drags his big, thick tongue across my palm. I can smell the plug of tobacco tucked in his lower lip. I jerk my hand behind my back, rubbing his spit on the pocket of my jean shorts.

"Lay off, Nicker," Mark says.

I know some girls would think it's cool to have a neanderthal like Greg hanging around, maybe even use him to make their boyfriends jealous. But Greg's a creep, and he comes by his creepiness honestly. His dad is one of the parents who forced Mark's AA coach to quit. But when Mr. Kolenick took over the team, he soon discovered drawing up practices and getting teenage boys to take them seriously wasn't as easy as he thought.

I hear a gate open, and Kim sprints down Shauna's driveway. She got back together with Greg two months ago, and she'll be his escort at Comp grad in a few weeks. It amazes me Kim's parents let her go out with such a slimeball. He's going to university in Regina next fall, so maybe they think he'll be out of the picture before long. It can't happen soon enough.

"You want me to fill you in on the details?" Kim asks Greg, throwing a devilish grin at me.

I gather she's referring to our softball game.

Greg checks his phone. "Details about what?"

Kim's brows knot together. "Our game! I Snapchatted you hours ago!"

"Oh yeah. That." Greg looks over his shoulder. "Let's go, Decker! Do I look like a camel?!" He spits again, this time on the driveway. "Hey, Markie, I hear your Uncle Stevie's taking a transfer up north. Is that right?"

I gape at Mark.

Besides being an RCMP officer, Steve Brewer is my coach. The man who's putting together a U18 girls team for us to play on. The man who's going to help us bring home a provincial banner. The man who's so much more than a hockey coach.

From Mark's expression, I can tell it's true. Steve's going far away, and he's taking Tara, my friend and teammate, with him.

"Steve's been transferred?" I murmur.

Mark nods.

It's like the pavement has cracked open, and I'm staring into an abyss.

"How long have you known?" I ask Mark.

He looks uncomfortable. "A few weeks. I wasn't supposed to tell anybody."

Greg grins from ear to ear. It isn't hard to guess his dad, who's a lawyer with an inside track, told him about the transfer.

Kim looks thoughtful. "I wonder who's gonna coach us."

The abyss gets blacker. Who will coach us?

"Maybe my dad would," Kim says. "He's always talking about how he'd whip us into shape if he had the chance."

Fantastic. Mr. Scott—the screamer. If he coaches, the girls will quit after the first practice. As Kathy says, Mr. Scott puts the "dick" in dictator.

Greg slips an arm around Kim and drags her towards the house, his box of beer clinking. "Enough talk. I need a cold one."

Heartsick, I follow them up the driveway. In one half hour, my whole life has sprung in a new direction—like a ping-pong ball attached to a paddle by an elastic string. Only the string's broken.

Mark hurries after me. "Jessie, we should talk about this."

"What's the point? It won't change anything."

"Look, I'm sorry I didn't tell you about Uncle Steve."

"That's okay. I'm used to it."

Mark's voice has an edge. "What do you mean—'used to it?'"

"Nothing." I move towards the gate Jordan left wide open, but Mark grabs my arm and pulls me back.

"I don't believe that for a minute. What's bothering you, Jessie?"

"You don't tell me anything. Guys tell their girlfriends important stuff, and they don't decide to move away for whole two months."

"Not that again."

Did he roll his eyes at me? There are so many things I'd like to tell him right now, but I know I'll say something stupid. Maybe it's better if I keep my mouth shut.

"Look, I'm sorry too," I say, even though I don't mean it. "I'm just tired. Let's go in and pretend nothing's wrong." I plant a big, phony smile on my face.

"Are you sure?"

I don't answer him. I wish Tara were here, so I could ask about her dad's transfer, but her family is at a wedding in B.C.

"Hey, Jessie Mac," Jodi says as I walk into Shauna's backyard. She hugs me, spilling her OJ and vodka on my T-shirt. "Why were you gone so long? We were just talking about you." She beckons to Greg and Jordan. "Greg wants to ask you something."

Yuck.

Greg ambles over and slides an arm around my waist. Double yuck. He breathes in my ear. "Jordan and me gotta know, Jessie. What kind of panties do you wear?"

Disgusted, I shove him away.

Jodi offers me her cup. "How about a sip of the water of life?"

"I'll have a coke," I say.

"Come on, Jessie Mac. Freakin' summer is right around the corner."

Mark scowls at me. What right does he have to approve or disapprove of everything I do?

On impulse, I grab Jodi's drink and guzzle it. Every last drop. It leaves a warm glow all the way down.

"All right, Jessie!" Jordan holds up his palm for a high-five.

"What do you say?!" Greg holds up his as well.

I smack both their hands, ignoring the sensation of Mark's eyes scorching the back of my neck.

"Got any more?" I ask.

3

I'M BREAKING WIDE DOWN THE ICE, and Shauna's pass lands right on the tape. I hold on to the puck and blow between the two D backing up—backing up too late because I've caught them flat-footed. The monster goaltender charges out of her crease and tries to poke-check. I deke and slide the puck to my backhand before roofing it, snapping her water bottle from the top of the net. It explodes and orange juice rains on the ice. A white glow surrounds me, and I think I must have died and ascended to Hockey Heaven, where I hear Don Cherry say, "Well done, Jessie. Well done."

Don Cherry?

Wait a minute. He's not dead. And nobody in his right mind would let that suit and tie—much as I love them—into heaven.

Claps of thunder reverberate inside my head. I cover my ears with my pillow to shut out the noise.

"Get up, Jessie," Don says.

Brightness scalds my eyelids. Mercifully a dark figure steps in front of the light and blocks it.

"Jessie, it's time."

Time for what? I sit up and my head explodes, just like the water bottle. My throat is parched, and the inside of my mouth tastes like a litter box.

"You've got twenty minutes."

Twenty minutes before what? I try to focus on the figure, but it's moving away, heading across the room, which starts to look familiar. My bedroom. I look at my phone. It's 8:00, and I'm hung over.

Jodi stirs beside me. I forgot she came home with me last night. I vaguely remember Mark bringing us here.

"You know the rule, Jessie," Mom says from the doorway. "You wake us up when you come home, or we'll assume there's a reason you didn't. We'll talk about this later. For now, get dressed. You've got a softball game."

Softball. Right. I give Jodi's shoulder a shake. She moans and rolls over. Something bothers me about Jodi being here, but I can't place it. Something to do with Greg and Jordan.

I sit up, and my body protests. My arm is connected to my shoulder by a pulsing thread of agony. My knees are stiff, and my left hand is spongy and swollen from catching last night's game. I ignore my aches and pains and pounding head and queasy stomach and start extracting my ball uniform from the tangle of clothes surrounding my bed. The clothes I wore last night are wet, but I don't remember why.

"Come on, Jodi," I croak. "You gotta pitch right away."

Jodi doesn't even budge, so I reach over and tug on the hand hanging over the edge of the bed. She groans.

"Wake up!"

She rolls over and winces at the ceiling. "Oh, my freakin' head. Whose idea was it to drink a bucket of Screwdrivers last night?"

"Yours. Now get dressed." I ball up a T-shirt and pitch it at her. "My mom's already pissed at me."

Jodi rubs her temples with her fingertips. "Is she gonna ground you?"

"Hell yes!"

Jodi slides out of bed. She's still wearing the shorts and tank top she was wearing last night at Shauna's party. Something about that bothers me too, but I can't remember what.

We don't have time to shower or eat breakfast. We spill into Mom's SUV while Mom mutters comments under her breath—some of which I'm sure are threats—and drive to the ballpark. We're the last ones there, but Mr. Palmer isn't concerned. He doesn't even make a comment about Jodi's lousy warm-up.

"Feeling a little sluggish today?" is the only comment Mr. Palmer makes.

Sluggish? I've already drunk two bottles of water, and it still feels like there are two little men banging my temples with bright copper hammers.

Mr. Palmer glances at his phone. "Jessie, did you remember to ask Mark to ump this morning?"

I nod then pause to reconsider. Did I ask Mark? Check yes. But did he actually say he'd be here for 9:00? Was he kidding about his golf game? I also have a vague recollection of him lecturing me all the way home from Shauna's last night. I can't remember what he said, but I know it wasn't pleasant.

"If he's not here in five minutes, I'll need to find someone else," Mr. Palmer says. "Any chance your dad can ump?"

"I'm pretty sure he's doing Courtney's game this morning."

Crap. Why can't I remember what Mark said to me last night?

Mr. Palmer scrambles to find another ump while Bienfait gets an extra long warm-up. Not that it would bother Jodi or me if the game was cancelled because we don't have any officials. I'd give my right arm to stretch out in the shade behind the dugout and sleep. It's flipping hot, and it's getting hotter. The thought of squatting behind home plate for two hours makes my stomach roll.

When Mr. Kowalski, Amber's dad, drives up, Mr. Palmer is on him like a terrier on a rat, begging him to ump. Mr. Kowalski puts on the chest protector and mask, and our game is on.

We suck against Bienfait, a team we've had no trouble beating all year. Jodi walks damn near every batter, and I can't throw a ball to any base. The rest of the girls don't say anything, but I can tell they're ticked. They stare and murmur while I'm on deck.

When I strike out for the third time, I hand Kendra the bat. "Too bad you picked this day to not give a rip," she says.

Amber is the only player who will talk to me. It'd take a miracle for Amber to be mean because she's the sweetest person I know. Her big blue eyes are earnest when she says, "You'll do better next time."

But pretty soon I run out of next times.

Bienfait beats us on the run limit in five innings, and because the playoff format is double knockout, our softball season is over by 10:30 am. Jodi and I line up at the concession with coupons for our free hot dogs. I don't know if I'm starving or ready to throw up.

While we're eating our hot dogs in the shade beside the booth, Kathy comes over.

"Heard you guys had some bad luck this morning," she says. "You should have left the party early like I did."

"Oh, really," Jodi drawls, "and what else did you hear?"

Kathy blushes, and that's something Kathy never does, because she's rarely at a loss for words.

"Maybe you guys shouldn't be hanging out together."

Jodi yawns. "What're you talking about?"

Kathy gives us a funny look.

What does that mean?

She peers at the diamond across the road. "Gotta go. It's time to warm-up. Good luck in your next game." She smiles her wicked Kathy smile. "Oh, right. You don't have another one. Well, enjoy your hot dogs. They're going to be the best part of your day."

She leaves.

Jodi balls up the foil from her hot dog then pulls her phone out of her bag.

"Texting Jordan?" I ask.

"Yeah, he said we might go boating today."

It bothers me that after going undefeated all season, being the first team out of the tournament doesn't bother her. "I have to pee." I stand up and pull my ball shorts away from my butt, which is damp and itchy from the grass.

I head to the bathroom on the other side of the concession. When I come out, I notice Mark's black truck parked at the outfield fence of Diamond #3, where Kathy's team is warming up.

That's great. He got here in time for her game, but not mine. I cross the road and head for the truck, never taking my eyes off the arm draped against the driver's door.

Mark's not alone. His mother sits in the passenger seat. Sunlight dapples her blonde hair, so like Mark's.

"Hot day, huh?" I ask.

Mark doesn't look at me but stares straight ahead. Colour rises in his cheeks. He's pissed about something. But what?

"Morning, Jessie." Mrs. Taylor beams at me. "How'd your game go this morning?"

"Not good," I say. "We lost."

"That's too bad. So, when do you play again?"

"That's the problem. We don't. We're done."

"That doesn't seem fair. Course it's a beautiful day. Losing out leaves you free to do other things."

Mark turns his head and stares at his mother. I can't tell what his expression is, but it's enough to make her ask, "What? Did I say something wrong?" She tries to paste on a smile then opens the passenger door. "Well, I'll leave you two to talk. I'm going to find some shade."

When she's gone, I place a hand on his smooth, tanned forearm, but Mark jerks it inside the truck. His jaw is clenched. In the four months we've been going out, he's never acted like this.

"Mark, why are you mad at me?"

He takes a handful of sunflower seeds from the bag beside him and shovels them into his mouth. He cracks a few before answering. "What makes you think I'm mad?"

He sounds like Mom when she's upset with Dad for forgetting Mother's Day.

"Isn't it obvious?"

"Where's Jodi?" He spits some shells out the window, and I jump aside so he doesn't nail me in the chest.

"I don't know. She said something about going boating with Jordan."

"Jessie, what's wrong with you?"

"What's wrong with me? What's wrong with you? You're the one refusing to talk!"

"I was ready to talk to you last night, but you decided to go get wasted and make a fool of yourself. Have you spoken to Shauna today?"

Suddenly my sore head, rolling stomach and aching shoulder are the least of my worries. "No, I haven't. Do I need to talk to her?"

"I'd be surprised if she ever wants to see you or Jodi or those two losers again." Mark uses some words—words I've never heard coming from him—to describe Greg and Jordan.

Images pour into my head. I remember making out with someone—and for a second, I'm afraid it was Greg, because if it was, I'm going to need antibiotics. That's when I remember that it wasn't Greg I made out with.

It was Jodi.

4

Sunday and Monday are the worst days of my life. And that's saying a lot because I've had my share of crappy days. For instance, there's the day Dad told me we were moving to Estevan. Then there's the day I did community service in Bienfait for something that wasn't my fault. The day I spent on in-school suspension with Kim. Definitely no friendship bracelet or *Kumbaya* that day.

Crappy days, indeed. But none of them are even close to Sunday and Monday. Nope, they definitely take the crap cake.

I don't even want to think about Sunday right now.

Monday starts with me trying to convince my mother I'm too sick to write my French exam in the afternoon. Normally, I really like French, but today I hate it. Fortunately, I already wrote my math final, or I'd hate math too, which would be a shame because I'm a pretty good at it.

Imagine how simple life would be if it was like working out algebra problems on the white board for Mrs. Graham. Whenever I screw up, I could rub out the mistake with a dry erase marker, and no one would remember it.

I spend the morning at the law office where my mom works because Mom has this bright idea I can't be trusted. I can't go anywhere by myself or stay home alone while Courtney's at school. I sit in a spare office and study for my French exam and answer Mom's coworkers' annoying questions about what I'm doing for summer holidays. Freakin' zero, since Mark won't be around, and I won't be hanging out with Jodi anymore. But that's not the worst of it.

Apparently Greg and Jordan took pictures of Jodi and me and uploaded them onto a half dozen social media platforms, so now everybody in the free world knows what we did. How could I have been so stupid?

My stomach churns, but I manage to choke down a tuna fish sandwich when Mom and I go home for lunch. I use the bathroom twice while Mom nags at me to hurry up and get in our SUV. I tell Courtney she can sit in the front, and she nearly passes out from shock. I never let her ride shotgun, but right now I don't feel like making small talk with Mom—not since she took away my iPhone again, re-issuing Dad's old flip phone—which I detest—and grounded me for the first month of summer holidays. It's a gorgeous day—perfect for hanging out beside Tara's swimming pool, not sweating in a gym without any air conditioning, trying to remember French verbs, sitting behind some kid who's allergic to deodorant.

The EJH parking lot crawls with students. The Grade Eights are writing Health, and the Sevens are writing Arts Ed. I can tell because they're all lined up with their packages of pencil crayons like it's the first day of kindergarten. Mom pulls up to the entrance, and I start to climb out. The sprinklers on the front lawn wick-wick-wick.

"Call me when you're done your exam," Mom says.

I try not to make eye contact with the girls on the sidewalk, who eyeball me like I'm wearing a pink spandex jumpsuit. I step away from the vehicle and run straight into Natalie. Natalie used to be Kim's sidekick, but apparently they've had a falling out. Not sure over what.

As soon as Mom drives away, Natalie leans in. "You're quite the little movie star. That was some show."

Oh great. They shot video too.

"Heard you and Mark had a fight at the ball diamond on Saturday. What'd he say to you?"

You got me, Babe. That's what he said.

"That's none of your business."

"If you ask me, Mark's got a broom up his ass." Natalie looks at her posse for confirmation. "It's not like you were cheating on him. Just experimenting, right?"

Seriously, what does this girl want from me?

"So what was it like? Was it a big turn-on?"

"No, it wasn't. And I don't want to talk about it." Meanwhile I'm trying to remember some of those "I" messages we learned in Health class. Ah, yes. Here's one. "You know, Natalie, it makes me feel like punching your lights out when you act like a pathetic little parasite." But I don't say anything.

"Hey, Jessie," a voice says behind me.

When I turn around, I'm face to face with some guys who played AA hockey with Jodi last season.

"We saw Greg's pictures," one of them says. "They were hot."

"Think you'd put on a show like that for us?" another asks.

Rage and shame swell in my throat, choking me. How could I have been so stupid? If Greg were here, I'd strangle him.

"There's a party at Nicker's place on Friday. Wanna come? I'll make sure Jodi's there," one says.

They laugh.

I walk away from them, but I have nowhere to go. I stare at the ground, hoping the tears blinding me won't spill over and run down my face. My nose streams, and I don't have a tissue or sleeve, so I use the back of my hand.

The gym doors open, and everyone moves towards the school. Is it my imagination or do I hear kissing noises? I walk slow, so I end up at the back of the pack.

Madame greets me at the door. "Last exam, Jessie?"

I nod, not trusting my voice.

I manage to find my desk while Madame passes out the French exams and wishes everyone good luck. She also hands out red jelly beans.

"They make you smarter," she says to someone sitting behind me.

Too bad I didn't eat a bag of them before going to Shauna's last Friday.

Madame sets my exam on my desk. The first page is covered with cute little graphics. Should be a breeze for someone as good at French as I am.

Then again, what difference does it make if I do well? When I walk out of here, my life will be just as screwed up. I've messed things up with Mark for good, just like I always knew I would. Shauna won't respond to my texts. Why did I let Jodi and Greg mix my drinks?

Why did I drink them?

I should have bailed when Greg started talking about how hot Jodi and I looked, sitting beside each other on the swing with Jodi's arm slung over my shoulders.

"Jessie Mac's my best friend ever," Jodi said. "I've had friends before, but not like Jessie Mac."

That's when she kissed me on the mouth. It felt peculiar, but I was so drunk it didn't seem like it was happening to me.

Jordan said, "Do that again. I wanna take a picture."

She did. Then Greg wanted a picture too—only with a slightly different pose. Before I knew it I was pinned under Jodi and the world was spinning, and Greg and Jordan pretended they were directing some sleazy movie.

A wave of ice-cold water hit us, and Jodi rolled off, gasping and squealing. When I crawled to my feet, Mark stood there holding an empty beer cooler. He drove Jodi and me back to my place, lecturing us the whole way about the stupidity of binge drinking. All I could think about was getting in the house before I threw up.

Then on Sunday afternoon, Mark picked me up at my house, parked a few blocks away, and in a calm and premeditated way, surgically removed me from his life.

"I thought you were different," he said.

I didn't say a word. I figured if I let him do the talking, I could ride it out.

"You know who I'm talking about, don't you? The ones who step all over each another to climb the popularity ladder? The ones who ignore their best friends from elementary school because they don't want to be seen with them? It makes me sick. Imagine my surprise when I discovered you're as shallow as the rest of them."

"Mark, I don't care about being popular," I defended myself.

"The hell you don't. You're not the girl I started going out with last February."

"I am too! The girl who made a fool of herself on Friday night is not me!" When he didn't say anything, I persisted. "Can't we go back to the way it was?"

"Look, Jessie, if you're gay—"

"I'm not gay!"

"I shouldn't have driven both of you back to your place."

"That's an awful thing to say! Jodi passed out as soon as we got back. Nothing else happened!"

"You had no business acting like that in front of everybody. It's not fair." And then he said it. "We should stop seeing each other for a while."

I pleaded with him—crying, apologizing, swearing I'd never drink again. But his mind was already made up.

"It's just for a while, right? When you come back from Calgary in August, everything will be back to the way it was?"

"Oh yeah. You got me, Babe."

I'm hoping he meant it. But now I wonder. Was he being sarcastic? Or trying to avoid a scene by telling me what I wanted to hear so I would get out of his truck?

"Jessie, you haven't written a word yet. You haven't even put your name on your paper," Madame says, jolting me back to the present.

I look up at the clock. It's already 1:30. Where did the last half hour go?

"Are you okay?" She studies me with warm brown eyes. "Do you feel ill?"

Everyone else's eyes are on me too. I can hear their thoughts: "She's pretending to be sick so she can get out of writing her French test. She isn't sick. She's scared to face us."

"I'm okay."

I am okay, I tell myself as Madame turns and walks up the aisle. I blink back tears, wipe my nose with the back of my hand, and rub my hand on my shorts. I stare at the exam in front of me, but the words swim.

Come on, Jessie, my little voice says, you know this stuff.

I don't write a thing. I keep staring at the first question. It asks me to write a short paragraph "en français" about myself.

Where should I begin? What is the French translation for "screwed up"?

Mark left for Calgary at noon today, right after his last Grade Eleven exam. His truck will be close to Regina by now.

The pit of my stomach tells me it's over. Not just for the summer, but forever. Yeah, Sunday was crappy too.

I glance up at the clock. 1:45.

The students around me are restless. Some have finished and had a teacher check their papers, and now they're waiting on the clock. At 1:55, some of them will try to hand in their exams, but Madame and the other staff will tell them to stay seated and wait with hand raised until a staff member gives the okay.

I'm flanked by Grade Sevens scratching their pencil crayons and drawing lines with their rulers like the pathetic little keeners they are. Their squeaking erasers are irritating as hell.

My little voice tries to get my attention. You've studied for this exam all week. No reason why you won't ace it. Why are you throwing it all away?

There's no way I want to walk out of here at the same time as Natalie and her posse and hear more of her clever remarks. Those girls need lives of their own.

True to form, at 1:50, Natalie starts sighing and humming and tapping her pen. Three times she leaves her desk to hand in her test, but each time Madame makes her answer more questions before she gives Natalie the nod. As Natalie walks by me the last time, she drops a folded paper on my desk.

I have no intention of opening the note. It won't be anything I want to see.

But Mr. Bottrell wants to see it. He's destined to be a principal one day because he already has that CSI instinct. He sweeps up the note with a flourish and holds it over his head, as if I'm going to hop like a toy poodle and try to snatch it back.

"What's this? Were you passing a note?" he accuses.

"I don't know what it is," I say. "You can have it."

He scowls at me in his best imitation of "the teacher look" and opens the note, staring at me the entire time. I check the gym entrance. Natalie lurks there, watching our little drama unfold.

"What's the meaning of this?" Mr. Bottrell waves the paper under my nose.

The two stick figures are labeled Jodi and Jessie. Their long serpentine tongues are intertwined.

The title? French Kiss. Bonus points for creativity, Natalie.

Madame arrives on the scene. "Is there something wrong?" She glances at my exam, which still doesn't have a pencil mark on it.

"Is this what you've been teaching your students, Madame?" Mr. Bottrell thrusts the note at her.

Madame studies the artwork, wrinkling her brow, then tucks the note in her hip pocket. "I'll deal with it. Jessie, take your exam to the office. I'll speak to you there after I dismiss the others."

I pick up my papers and move towards the gym entrance where Natalie and her minions whisper and gawk.

Natalie's eyes snap. "What did Bottrell say?"

I swear at her, hurl my exam paper in a garbage can, and exit the gym through the door beside the pop machine. Instead of turning left at the top of the stairs and going to the office, I walk out the main entrance.

Who says French doesn't open doors?

5

I TROT DOWN THE CONCRETE front steps, avoiding a sheet of water thrown by the sprinklers. At the end of the walk, I turn left. Going right would take me past the parking lot, where Natalie and her pals will be waiting.

I walk west. It's a hot, beautiful afternoon. A little breeze cools the back of my neck. The only person I know in this neighbourhood is Shauna. And since I'm going up the river once Mom and Dad find out about the French exam, this is as good a time as any to make things right with her.

Shauna's house has a front deck, which her mom decorates according to the season. Stained glass ladybugs and butterflies dangle from the roof and sway in the breeze. An old wicker rocking chair sits near the front door. I'm tempted to flop down in that chair and watch the hummingbirds zip around the feeding stations.

The front door's open, so I can't use the brass knocker, shaped like a lion's head. I don't think it's polite to yell through the screen door, so I use the doorbell.

Shauna comes to the door. She wears red shorts and a tank top, and her phone's in her hand. Her blonde brows knit themselves into a knot when she sees me. "Hey, Jessie."

"Hey. I thought we should talk."

She nods and opens the screen door. "You want a pop or iced tea or something?"

I step inside. "I'll have whatever you have."

"You want to sit inside or outside?"

"Outside."

I picture us sitting on that shady deck, sipping lemonade and listening to the birds and sprinklers, but Shauna grabs two glasses of ice tea from the kitchen and leads me out back.

Where it happened.

I sit on the swing where Jodi and I made out. Was it only three days ago? I can tell Shauna's thinking the same thing, so I jump in feet first. "About Friday. It was stupid—what me and Jodi—what I did."

Shauna slouches in her chair and closes her eyes. "You think so?"

"Yes. I'm really sorry, Shauna."

Without opening her eyes, she says, "Don't let people like Greg run your show. The guy's a loser." She looks at me then. "Greg isn't welcome here anymore. And I told Jodi the same thing about Jordan."

"Does that apply to me too?"

"Of course not."

Shauna's eyes flit away, and I know things have changed between us. I stepped over a line on Friday, and she won't forget it.

"Mark and I are taking a break for the summer," I tell her.

It's not exactly the truth. Then again I don't know what the truth is.

Shauna doesn't look surprised. "Have you talked to Jodi much lately?"

"Yeah."

I'm trying to make sense of that phone call. I thought Jodi would be upset, but she laughed when I told her how angry Mark was. "She told me Mark was making a big deal out of nothing. That he'll come around. Then she started talking about what happened at the bonfire at her place on Saturday night, like nothing was wrong."

Shauna leans forward and idly strokes the arched back and tail of her cat, Stella, who twines around her calves. "She's pulled stunts like this before, you know."

"You're kidding!"

"I'm not kidding. Maybe you think I'm a prude, but I don't agree with PDAs."

Public displays of affection. Is that what she thinks it was?

"I'm not gay," I assure her. "I was drunk."

"It has nothing to do with ... your preferences." Shauna sips her drink then places the glass against her temple. "I'd feel the same way if you and Mark made out in front of everyone."

I'm blushing—big time. Thank goodness I'm not having this conversation with my parents.

"I was relieved when Mark put a stop to it." She picks Stella up and scratches her under the chin. "Don't ask me why Kim didn't. I'd lose it if Brian encouraged two girls to act like that. For his. . . entertainment. It was sleazy, Jessie. I don't know how Kim stood for it."

I put my head in my hands and press my fingertips to my temples. Shauna's boyfriend Brian would never act like that. And neither would Mark. As for Kim, I've hardly given her a thought in the last few days. Have I just made her my enemy again?

"Here's another thing," Shauna continues. "I think Greg and Jordan egged the two of you on to make Mark mad. They enjoyed putting him through it."

"I can't believe I was so stupid. I can't believe I let them do that to us." I clasp my hands behind my neck. "Who am I kidding? I'm the one who let it happen."

"So—how was your exam today?" Shauna asks.

"I blew it." I quickly fill Shauna in on the boys' comments in the parking lot and Natalie's note.

She listens and nods, and I begin to think maybe everything might be okay between us.

"I'm glad you stopped by. There's something I've been meaning to tell you too." Shauna pushes the cat off her lap and brushes away the grey fluff sticking to her shorts.

That's when I notice the initials ND on the bottom. Before she opens her mouth to tell me, I know. She's going to Wilcox in the fall—to play with the Notre Dame Hounds. She won't be playing with the Xtreme, and she won't be living in Estevan. In the space of a few days, I've lost Mark and my three best friends—Tara, Jodi, and now Shauna.

Sometimes life sucks and it's nobody's fault. Sometimes it sucks, and it's my fault.

The gate creaks.

Mom stares at me with that frightened/angry/confused expression I've come to know so well.

"I thought I'd find you here," she says. "We're going back to the school."

So begins the worst summer of my life.

6

"JESSIE, LET'S GO TO THE PLAY PARK," Breanne says.

I stare at her across our kitchen table. "Don't talk with your mouth full."

She chews and swallows. "But can we?"

"Sure—after you finish your sandwich."

Breanne sighs and takes another bite.

Almost done.

Making lunch for Breanne, whose mother works at the same law office as Mom, is the biggest challenge of this summer babysitting gig. The kid eats like a bird. In fact, she looks like a bird—a little sparrow with cute blonde pigtails. It takes an hour for her to finish half a ham sandwich and a handful of cut-up vegetables or fruit. If I don't sit with her, she dreams and sings the hour away without eating anything. If I do sit with her, she asks a billion questions. She's five, and she wants to know everything.

"Did you know Evan's coming home today?" she asks.

Evan is Breanne's older brother, and he's as big as Breanne is small. He's going into Grade Twelve at the Comp, and he's been away at basketball camp for the last two weeks.

"So your mom told me. Three more bites, and you'll be done your sandwich.

Then we'll go to the playground. We can take the fruit as a snack."

My flip phone vibrates on the table. It's Mom.

"Hi, Jessie. I've got some errands to run after work. Can you start supper again?" she asks.

"You mean make supper," I point out.

"Right. There're pork chops in the freezer, and can you throw together a salad or something?"

"Sure."

"Thanks," she says. "I know it's been a boring summer for you, but I appreciate the help around the house. Have I told you lately you're a great kid?"

"Every day, Mom."

Well, not quite every day. She didn't tell me that the day of my French exam. She sat on the living room sofa and sobbed, which was way worse than a lecture, and reminded me that I promised last February to tell her everything. But what could I tell her? The truth about what happened between Jodi and me? No way.

"Does your sister still have her nose in a book?" Mom asks.

"Yep."

"Well, make sure she gets some fresh air," she says. "And say hi to Breanne for me."

"I will."

She hangs up.

"Mom says, 'Say hi to Short Stuff,'" I tell Breanne.

"She did not! You call me Short Stuff!" Breanne protests.

That's when I notice my July cell phone bill sitting on the counter—with all those calls to Calgary highlighted.

"You're chasing him," Mom said to me last night, holding the bill under my nose. " Don't you have any pride?"

Not where Mark is concerned.

It's not easy to chase a guy who clearly didn't mean it when he said, "You've got me, Babe." But I deserve an "A" for effort.

I know his dad's home number by heart—his work number too. Not that it helps. Sometimes when I call the home number, I get Mr. Taylor, who's always nice. He asks me how my summer's going and all that chit-chatty kind of stuff. He says he'll get Mark to call me back. Sometimes this other guy answers. I have no idea who he is, but he says the same thing about giving Mark my messages. But Mark's never phoned me. Not once.

"Jessie, I'm done!" Breanne points at her plate. "Can we go?"

I move back to the table and start clearing it. "Pack your fruit and vegetables."

Breanne skips over to the counter and gets a container out of the top drawer. Courtney comes in the kitchen, holding her own plate and glass. She's wearing a T-shirt and pajama shorts, and her long blonde hair is scraggly. Has she even brushed her teeth today?

"We're going to the playground. Go change please," I tell her.

"Can't I stay home and read?" Courtney whines.

I shake my head, and she sighs loudly and droops her shoulders. You'd think she was the one who was trying to fly under the social radar. Then again— maybe she is. She grew a couple of inches this summer, and she's feeling super awkward about it. What can I say? She's going into Grade Five in the fall. "Bring your book," I tell her. "I'll take the first shift on the teeter-tooter."

She stomps out of the kitchen and all the way up the stairs to her bedroom.

"She's got an attitude," Breanne observes.

My phone vibrates again as we're headed for the door. When I see the caller is Jodi, I let my voice mail pick up.

"Why aren't you answering?" Courtney asks.

"Never mind. Let's go."

Breanne rides her pink two-wheeler with the training wheels and flag while I carry the Dora backpack stuffed with her snacks, water, sunscreen, baseball cap, hoodie, Nerf softball, and plastic bat. After a block, we stop so I can loosen the strap on her bicycle helmet because she says it's choking her. Otherwise, we arrive at the playground beside Courtney's elementary school without incident. My sister shuffles along, her nose still stuck in her book, occasionally stumbling over a crack in the sidewalk.

Courtney finds some shade under the slide. While Breanne plays on the monkey bars, I stare at the red brick façade of the junior high across the street. The last time I was inside the school was the day after my French exam. Mrs. Wright, the principal, didn't buy my story of having a headache or being tired from playing softball on the weekend. She tried to get me to nark on Natalie and her pals, but I wouldn't. That would mean telling her the truth about Jodi and me, and there was no way I was doing that. Not even after she laid Natalie's note in front of me.

Thank goodness she never showed it to my mom. It was a hell of a bargain. A completed French test in exchange for that cartoon going through a shredder.

I aced the test, but I still wasn't allowed to attend the Grade Nine Farewell dance. My parents thought it would be punishment, but under the circumstances, it was a relief to miss out.

"I'm hot," Breanne says, plopping beside me.

I unzip her backpack and hand her the water bottle. She slurps and wipes her mouth. "Evan likes you," she announces.

This is news to me. Not exactly welcome news. I like Evan too—as a friend.

"He spends an hour in the bathroom putting goop in his hair before he drops me off at your house," she says. "He doesn't even do that when he gets ready for church."

Mr. Gedak is a pastor, so the family spends a lot of time in church. Not my church, mind you. "Are you going to be Evan's girlfriend?" she asks.

A white Mustang drives by.

Greg.

I duck beside the bench and dig in the backpack, pulling out the container of fruit. "Want a snack?"

Out of the corner of my eye, I see the Mustang turn right at the corner and keep going. Good.

I pop a piece of pineapple in my mouth. "Want to go on the swings? I'll push."

"You're talking with your mouth full," Breanne says.

I roll my eyes and keep chewing.

"Who's Mark?" she asks.

I nearly choke on the pineapple. Acidy juice burns my throat. "Who told you about him?" I say when I'm done coughing.

"Courtney."

I stare at my sister's bare feet sticking out from underneath the slide. "Courtney and I are going to talk later about minding her own business. As for Mark—"

I never finish my sentence because the Mustang turns the corner and pulls up next to the chain-link fence. Nuts.

Greg climbs out and waves to me over the roof. "Hey, Jessie!"

"Who's that?" Breanne wrinkles her nose.

"No one you should meet. Go tell Courtney it's time to go home."

"But we just got here!" Breanne protests.

"When we get home, we'll play kickball in the backyard."

"Courtney too?" Breanne asks.

"Yes."

Breanne races to the slide and ducks underneath.

I cross the playground and stare at Greg through the fence. "What do you want?"

"Lookin' good, Jessie." He walks around the front of his vehicle and leans against the passenger door. "Always looking good."

"I repeat —what do you want?"

Greg heaves a sigh. "Are you coming to Jodi's party this weekend?"

There's nothing he and Jordan would like better than to get me and Jodi and a bucket of Screwdrivers together again.

"No." I grasp the chain-link with my fingers and hold it so tight it cuts into the creases.

"Aw, come on. You gotta be bored to death hanging out here." He shakes his head. "Aren't you ready to cut loose?"

"Just because I'm not putting on a show for you and your friends doesn't mean I'm not having a fabulous summer."

He puts a hand on his chest. "You're breaking my heart, Jessie Mac. You really are."

"Don't call me that." I bite off the words. "Don't you ever call me that."

"Hey, don't get your panties in a knot." He leers. "Or whatever you're wearing."

Courtney and Breanne show up then. Breanne already has her bike helmet on.

"We're ready!" She tugs on my shorts.

"You ladies need a ride?" Greg points a large forefinger at Breanne. "I bet you like riding shotgun."

"I'm not supposed to get in a car with strangers," Breanne replies.

"That's right." I step back from the fence, dropping my arms. Breanne's hand slides into mine.

Greg says, "I'll get Jodi to call you."

I walk away.

"See you this weekend!" he shouts at my back.

I keep walking.

Breanne's hand squeezes mine. "Jessie, are you scared?"

"No."

"Was that Greg?" Courtney asks, hurrying to keep up.

"How do you know who Greg is?" I demand.

Courtney shrugs. "I heard you talking to Tara on the phone."

"I do not appreciate you eavesdropping on my conversations." I hold Breanne's bike steady while she climbs onto it.

Courtney hangs her head. "Sorry, Jessie."

"Is Greg your boyfriend?" Breanne asks.

"Not a chance."

"That's good," Breanne says. "He looks like a loser."

"You got that right, Short Stuff."

7

I SAW A HANDFUL OF SJHL games last year. Because of my hockey schedule and my parents' medieval ideas about curfew, I didn't have much time for the Estevan Bruins—the biggest show in town. But I'll be the Bruins' biggest fan if Mark makes the squad.

The Black and Gold intrasquad game is the grand finale of the Bruins' training camp at the end of August. If a player makes it this far, it's his last opportunity to stand head and shoulders above the other rookies. According to Kathy, the game is an arena where guys literally fight their way onto the roster.

I've never seen Mark fight. With his smarts, speed and sick hands, he doesn't need to. Of course, I could be biased.

I open the program and scan the roster. I don't have far to look. Team Black. Taylor. 4. That's Mark's number. I hope it'll be lucky for him.

As the Zamboni makes an orbit of the big B at centre ice, I think about my own hockey season—only six weeks away. My outlook has changed a lot since June, when I could hardly wait. Now I dread it. What'll our U18 team be like without Steve? Amber's dad has offered to step up as head coach. Mr. Kowalski's a great guy, but I don't know if he's got the backbone to handle Brittni Wade and Cory Coates, two of the older players. I've heard they're skilled, but they go through coaches like underwear. Without Tara—our top scorer—will we have much offence? Even worse, we've lost our best defensive players since Shauna's gone to Notre Dame and Carla Stonechild decided to play with the Oxbow boys team again. Carla jumped ship because she knows we're going to suck.

A hand taps me on the shoulder. I turn around to find myself looking into Mrs. Taylor's grey eyes.

"Have a nice summer, Jessie?" Mark's mom asks.

"Sure." If only she knew how brutal it was.

"Go any place interesting?"

We discuss my babysitting job, golf lessons and a camping trip, but I only want to ask her about Mark. Instead we stick to safe subjects—like her pottery studio. Mrs. Taylor's an amazing artist who sells frescos to churches all over the province.

"Actually, I have some exciting news. I've got a six-month artist-in-residency in Muenster," she tells me.

"That's great." Inside I'm thinking, Muenster is a long ways from here. What will this mean for Mark?

"Did you come by yourself?" she asks.

"The other girls will be here soon," I tell her.

"Well, enjoy the game." She walks away.

Mrs. Taylor is so unflappable. At least, she is compared to all the dads lined up at the rail, looking like they're dying a thousand deaths, wondering if their sons are going to make the final cut.

You've got me, Babe.

I've hung on those words for two months. Hung on them even when Mark didn't return my calls from the dark side of the moon. He was cold. Remote. Unreachable. My little voice started telling me, you've lost him for good. You royally screwed things this time.

I go downstairs to use the washroom before the game, and while I'm there, I run into Amber Kowalski and Larissa Bilku. I haven't seen either of them for weeks. Amber got her hair cut short, and it suits her. It makes her big blue eyes even bigger. She asks me if I'm excited about going to the Comp. I give her the usual "yeah, sure" I give everyone. But the truth is I'm terrified. I don't even have the guts to attend the New Student Orientation.

Larissa's parents were both born in India, but her dad grew up in Nairobi. "You've been a hermit all summer." Larissa stares at me with thoughtful, dark eyes, like she's making a diagnosis. Not surprising—since her dad's a doctor.

"I was babysitting for the Gedaks," I tell her. "I didn't get out much. How was the safari?"

"I uploaded tons of pictures. If you ever went on Instagram, you'd have seen them," Larissa says.

"Not possible." I dig my flip phone out of my skinny jeans and show her. "No data."

"Not again?" she says. She doesn't ask why, so I figure if she must already know I'm grounded.

We hear the buzzer signaling the start of the Black and Gold game, and we head for the stairs. When we walk into the arena, I spot Tara and her boyfriend Nathan. Tara spent most of the summer in Yellowknife settling in, but her parents let her come back to Estevan for a few days before her classes start up north. Supposedly, she came home for the farewell party we're having for her at Teneil's tomorrow night, but most of us figure she's lonely for Nathan.

Believe me, Tara, I know the feeling.

Tara's let her black hair grow out, and it frames her tanned face in long, rippling waves. I like how she never messes with the colour. With her, what you see is what you get. She hugs Larissa, Amber, and me, and I line up at the rail, shoulder to shoulder with her, while Nathan stands on her right. Amber and Larissa snuggle in beside me on the left. We talk about Yellowknife and Tara's hopes for a girls hockey team there. Then we cover Nathan's week at Bruin training camp. Tara gives us the details as Nathan's too shy to tell us himself.

"He got cut Thursday," she explains. "Looks like it's AA for him again this year."

"How do you feel about that, Nathan?" I ask him.

He smiles and shrugs.

"Mark's sure to make the Bruins," Amber says.

"Coming to Teneil's tomorrow night?" Tara asks me.

"Plan to." I keep an eye on the ice, watching for Mark.

Tara leans over and whispers in my ear. "I'm sorry about you and Mark."

The words cut like a knife. Does she know something I don't? Am I stupid for not admitting to myself it's over?

Then Mark steps on the ice, and everything else disappears. He looks focused and confident as he lines up for a faceoff in his end. I don't recognize the name of his D-partner, but that doesn't mean he's not local. I've only been in Estevan for a year, and I don't know many guys Mark's age. I'm not counting Greg and Jordan, of course. Losers.

The linesman snaps the puck, and the game is underway.

Mark makes the game look easy, the way he banks passes behind the net, so the puck pops out to his D-partner. Gets body position along the boards. Uses the glass to hurl the puck over the blue line. He's patient at both ends of the ice, keeping the trash away from the front of his own net and creating scoring opportunities in the Gold zone.

"He definitely won that shift," I tell Tara. With Tara, I don't need to pretend. As Mark's cousin, she knows him pretty well.

"I haven't talked to him much this summer," Tara says. "I don't know where his head is anymore."

That gets me wondering. What has Mark been up to in Calgary? He doesn't interact much with his teammates on the bench. He leans on the boards, moving closer to the gate as each defensive pairing takes their turn. On one shift, he lays out the Gold centreman with a perfect check then steps off the ice like he's embarrassed.

"Highlight reel hit," Nathan murmurs.

The four of us go outside during the intermission between first and second period. Some people I don't know approach Tara, inquiring about her parents' new jobs up North.

"Are you going to talk to Mark after the game?" Amber asks as we climb the stairs for the start of the second period.

"I hope so," I tell her.

"It'd be awesome if he stayed in Estevan to play hockey, wouldn't it?" she asks.

Only if he still cares about me. If he doesn't, I don't know if I can stand it.

During the second period, most of the play is in the neutral zone with only a handful of scoring chances. Ten minutes in, both squads switch out goaltenders. I'm too busy talking to Tara to pay much attention to who they are.

Mark steps on the ice for a faceoff in his end. The Black centreman wins the draw back to Mark, who takes the puck behind his net, eludes the winger, and accelerates out of the zone. He finds the Black left winger with a long saucer pass.

"Chuckin' sauce," Nathan says.

There's a give-and-go between the winger and centreman, and a blistering shot on the Gold goalie, who makes a theatrical glove save. Mark and his D-partner return to the bench.

There's something familiar about that goaltender. I take a quick look at the program to see who he is. Greg Kolenick.

"No way. I thought Greg was going to university in Regina." I'm hoping someone will tell me there's another Greg Kolenick on our planet. A kinder, gentler, more civilized Greg Kolenick.

"Guess he isn't." Tara gives Nathan an elbow. "What's going on with him anyway?"

Nathan shrugs.

"Dad says he heard Greg's marks weren't high enough," Amber volunteers. "He's going back to high school to retake calculus and English."

"Lucky us," Larissa says.

"You don't go to the Comp yet," I point out. "You won't have to put up with him."

"This town isn't big enough for Greg." Larissa puts a hand to her throat and pretends to have difficulty breathing. "He's using up my air."

Two minutes later, Mark is back out, and I push all other thoughts aside. The Black centreman has the puck deep in the Gold zone and he feeds Mark, who's open on the point. Mark one-times a slapshot at Greg's head. It rings off Greg's cage and deflects into the stands.

"I think Mark did that on purpose," Tara says, straightening.

Greg shouts something at Mark, but Mark doesn't respond. He lines up for the faceoff, and seconds later, when he takes another shot from the point, he repeats the performance. This time the puck whistles past Greg's ear and smacks the Plexiglass behind his head.

Greg barrels out of his crease and flings his stick aside. His pads don't hamper him in the slightest as he launches himself at Mark. Every fan leans in their direction. The linesmen jump in and wrestle the two of them apart. Mark skates to the bench while Greg picks up his stick and points it at Mark threateningly. The ref doesn't issue any penalties.

"What in the hell was that?" Larissa asks.

"I know Mark doesn't like Greg much, but I've never seen him take a head shot before. Have you, Nathan?" Tara says.

Nathan shakes his head.

The teams play the rest of the second period without further incident, not counting the scoring. Mark has an assist on two Black goals. Black dominates the play, with the exception of Greg, who makes save after save.

The score is tied 2-2 when we step into the bright sunshine outside the arena. Kim's talking to Mr. and Mrs. Kolenick, who puff their cigarettes like a pair of dragons.

"Kim's going to be happy Greg's hanging around for another year," Amber observes.

"I'm amazed she's still going out with Greg after the stuff he pulled this summer," Larissa says.

"What stuff?" I ask.

I don't have a chance to find out because Kim comes over. "How're you, Tara?" she asks, ignoring me.

Tara and Kim do some catching up, and since Kim's mostly talking about Greg, I shut my ears and look around for familiar faces. I see Jodi sitting on one of the cement benches, talking to two tall girls wearing high-waisted short shorts that reveal their long, tanned legs.

"Is that Brittni and Cori?" Amber asks.

"It's Brittni for sure," I say. "I met her at the Estevan Fair—when Jodi was competing in Junior Idol. She and Jodi are friends."

"Jodi's got a great voice, huh?" Amber reflects. "She's good at everything. Must be nice to be so popular."

"Get real," Larissa says. "We're popular."

"I don't think Dad's looking forward to coaching Brittni and Cory," Amber says. "Their team folded by Christmas last year. I hope that doesn't happen to us."

"Hope what doesn't happen?" Kim asks.

All of us start a little. I wonder how much of our conversation she's overheard. Hopefully, nothing.

"We were just saying we hoped you're still planning to play U18 girls," I say.

"Thinking about it," Kim replies. "Too bad about you and Mark."

"We took a break for the summer," I say, "because of him going to Calgary."

"Sure, I'd tell myself that too if it helped me sleep at night." She crosses her arms over her chest. "Guess now you know what it feels like to get dumped."

She doesn't say it in a mean way, but it hurts. The sidewalk blurs as she walks away. I smear the tears from my eyes.

Tara slips an arm around me. "Don't take it too hard."

"She shouldn't be so smug," Larissa says. "Greg cheated on her this summer with a girl from Weyburn."

"No way!" Amber says.

"I'm serious," Larissa says.

"You don't know that for sure," Tara says, "so you shouldn't be repeating it."

"It's true." Nathan breaks his code of silence. He smiles then catches Tara's eye and clears his throat. "Anybody want to come get popcorn with me?"

Amber and Larissa volunteer.

"Spill the beans, Nathan," Larissa urges as they walk away.

"Jessie, you look upset. Do you want to go home?" Tara asks.

I shake my head. "I don't want to miss any of the game."

She keeps her arm around me as we head up the stairs. She doesn't say anything else until we're at the rail again, and the Zamboni does its last circuit of the ice. "You know about Mark's dad, right?'

Mr. Taylor. Tall. Silver-haired. Super nice. "Know what?"

"He's gay, Jessie."

8

THE GEARS TURN, AND THE COGS slide into place. A series of still frames plays in my brain.

Me asking Mark, "Your parents seem like such nice people. Why did they split up?" and Mark not answering. Mark telling me, "It's not fair" when he gave me such a hard time about making out with Jodi. Mark being so distant and shutting me out. That guy. What was his name again? Gary. Yes. Gary answering the phone at Mr. Taylor's place.

"You didn't know?" Tara puts a hand on my shoulder. "Mark thought you did."

"I didn't," I tell her. "But knowing that sure explains a few things."

No wonder, my little voice says. No wonder.

"No wonder is right," I murmur under my breath, watching Mark make a lap around his net.

The horn sounds, signaling the end of intermission. Mark lines up for the opening faceoff. Team Black is starting the third period with a power play, thanks to a Gold hooking penalty with fifteen seconds left in the second. The Black centreman wins the draw back to Mark's D-partner, who goes wide and takes the puck as far as the hash marks. Team Black sets up in the Gold zone, cycling the puck, Mark and his partner on the move. Mark sneaks down low and one-times a slapshot top left corner. The ref points at the net, and the red light flashes. Mark and his teammates sweep past Team Black in a bench run.

Greg comes out of his crease. He doesn't drop his stick this time. Instead, he takes a two-handed baseball swing at Mark's head. Mark ducks. Greg's thrown off balance and goes down, but Mark gives him all the time he needs to get back up and shed his blocker and glove. Mark's fists are already bare, and he's circling Greg. He looks like someone who knows exactly what he wants to do.

I feel sick.

The crowd eggs on the two combatants. The other players and linesmen back away. No one will pull them apart this time. Mark takes a few punches. It's like he wants to get hit. He gets close enough to grab the front of Greg's jersey, and throws Greg off balance, yanking on the collar with one hand and feeding him punches with his right. Greg outweighs Mark, but his goalie pads are too much of a hindrance.

When Greg starts to go down, Mark eases his descent, holding the front of his jersey with both hands. He says something in Greg's ear before releasing him and skating away. No arms raised in victory. No acknowledgment of the cheering from the stands. He keeps his head down as he steps off the ice. One of the linesmen helps Greg, his nose leaking blood, to the exit.

Nathan arrives, holding a box of popcorn, flanked by Amber and Larissa. He recognizes the situation immediately. "I missed a fight." He nearly drops his popcorn as he pushes between us. "Who was it?"

While Tara fills him in, he shovels handfuls into his mouth, his eyes huge. "Wow," he keeps saying.

"I'm sure Greg had it coming," Larissa says.

"Mark would only fight for a really good reason, right, Jessie?" Amber asks.

"I guess."

"Aunt Maggie won't be impressed," Tara says. "She hates fighting."

"That'll be quite the dressing room if both Mark and Greg make the team," Larissa observes.

How true.

My next thought is—Greg found out about Mark's dad, and he's been baiting Mark. I'd like to get Tara alone again and ask for more information, but I don't get the chance because she's focused on Nathan, and I don't want to interrupt.

After a while Mark comes up from the dressing room. He's showered and wears a dark grey suit, black shirt, and wine-coloured tie. There's a big bruise on his left cheek that matches his tie, and his lip is cut. Still, he's the best-looking thing I've seen in a long time.

He stops to hug Tara and talk to her and Nathan. He and Nathan do that thing guys do—where they could be talking about anything—weather, hockey, politics, the price of oil—and you can't tell. But it's a safe bet it's hockey.

Then Mark sees me. He pauses in mid-sentence, sort of winces, and goes on talking. What does that mean? I keep staring at him, not wanting to miss the moment when he looks at me again. Come on, Mark, I say to myself. Look at me. But when he finally does, his face has no expression. He's a store mannequin.

"I'll talk to you later," he says to Nathan and Tara. He starts to walk away.

I've been waiting two months for this. He's not getting off that easy. I start after him, and I can feel a hand grabbing at my arm. I know it's Tara, trying to do what's best. But I can't stand it any longer. I need to know.

"Hey, Mark. Wait up."

He keeps walking.

"Mark! It's me!"

People stare, but I don't care. I didn't win that coveted 100 m final on Track and Field Day for nothing. I sprint after him then slow down when I'm beside him.

"Hey, Mark, how was Calgary?" I ask. "How's your dad?"

He stops and stares at me for a few seconds before saying, "Who wants to know? You—or Greg?"

"I don't know what you mean," I tell him.

"I don't have time for this." He keeps going.

I follow him to the other end of the rink where he hugs his mother, who's standing at the rail. Mrs. Taylor is with a girl I don't recognize. She's slightly built with wispy brown hair, streaked with blonde and red highlights. Mark hugs her too and drapes an arm around her neck as he talks to his mom. I feel like I've been kicked in the stomach.

Tara slips her hand around mine and squeezes my fingers. "I'm sorry, Jessie."

"Who is she?" I whisper.

"Holly Chamberlain—from Calgary. She's Gary's niece. I guess she's Mark's girlfriend now."

9

Tara's farewell is at Teneil's house on Poplar Bay. Tara will spend part of the evening with us, but Nathan will come pick her up at 10:00.

I'm not even sure I want to go to Teneil's. The only reason I *do* go is because it's my last chance to see Tara for a long time. Shauna's already left for Notre Dame, so she won't be there. Carla texts Tara to tell her she can't find a ride in from Oxbow, but most of us figure she's already cutting her ties to our hockey team.

Kim makes an appearance. She says she's going to another party with Greg, so she can't stay long. Apparently Greg didn't make the Bruin squad and needs consoling.

Kathy whispers in my ear, "To Whom It May Concern, Mr. Kolenick is way too pushy, and Greg's attitude sucks. He's a great goalie, but he's uncoachable. Signed, Bruin Head Coach. True story."

"But Mark made the team, right?"

"Sure did," Kathy says, "and not as any lame seventh D-man either. That boy has Dub written all over him."

After Kim leaves, I get Tara alone and try to pump her for information on Mark and Holly.

"Jessie, you've got to get over him," Tara says.

"I *am* over him," I lie.

Tara says Holly's in her first year of university in Saskatoon. Mark met her this summer, and they've been dating a few weeks. That's the extent of what Tara knows about Holly, except that she wants to get into pharmacy.

"Saskatoon's a long ways from Estevan," I say.

"You're not over him, no matter what you say," Tara says.

I feel like Mark's on a crude wooden raft drifting further and further out to sea. No. It's more like *I'm* on the raft, while Mark and Holly wave from the rail of a cruise ship.

The rest of the girls act like there's nothing wrong. They crank up the tunes and dance. While I'm contemplating my bleak and Mark-less future, Miranda Omalu, our goalie, sits beside me on the couch. She holds a plateful of snacks.

"Want some?" Miranda has to lean close because the music's so loud.

"No thanks."

She pops a potato chip in her mouth and crunches it in my ear. "Wanna hear what happened in Team Gold's dressing room before the game? I heard it from Kim."

Apparently Greg made some crude remarks about Mark's dad, and Mark caught wind of it during the game. Miranda doesn't think it's true—the part about Mr. Taylor being gay. She's assuming Greg's just being Greg.

"Greg's such a tool!" Miranda shouts.

"You got that right." Jodi flops beside Miranda. "But not as much of a tool as Jordan."

I cock an eyebrow at Miranda, and she cocks one back. This is definitely news.

"Do tell," Miranda says.

Jodi starts listing the reasons for her recent break-up with Jordan. She slurs her words. Her water bottle must be full of vodka again. Between that and the loud music, I don't catch much of her story. Teneil's mom made it clear there's no alcohol allowed, but Jodi doesn't care about rules. She comes by it honestly. I've heard Jodi's mom say that since Jodi's going to party anyway, she might as well do it in someone's home where she can't get hurt.

"Enough boy talk!" Jodi grabs Miranda's hand. "Let's party!"

Miranda hands me her plate as Jodi yanks her off the couch. Jodi's one hell of a dancer, but so is Miranda—and Miranda isn't wasted. She shows Jodi some moves and then catches her before she falls back against a bookshelf. Jodi laughs and staggers towards me, pointing.

"You're next, Jessie Mac!" she calls.

I've seen the looks the girls have been giving Jodi and me. Plainly they know about Shauna's party, and they're weirded out by it. To avoid a scene, I pull Jennifer McQueen out of the recliner and start dancing with her instead. Jennifer's from Bienfait, and she's the only girl on the team with virtually no sense of humour. She doesn't pluck her eyebrows or wear makeup, but she should think about it because she's so pale.

Jennifer manages to move her hips in time to the music. Maybe she's starting to loosen up. She crooks her finger at me, and I lean closer. "Think Jodi's plastered again?"

I try to think of a way to change the subject. I don't want Jennifer going on a crusade to get Jodi sent home.

"Well, don't you think she's headed for trouble?" Funny that Jennifer should use Mom's exact words.

"I don't know."

"How she is going to get through three years of high school?" Jennifer asks.

"I have to go to the bathroom," I tell her. "I'll talk to you later."

We spend most of the next two hours dancing and eating and laughing. At one point Jodi stands on the couch and does her "hockey is religion" routine. Then she does a handstand, cartwheel, and back walkover across the living room. She took gymnastics up until a few years ago, and it's amazing how flexible she is. But when she tries to do a backflip off the coffee table, Teneil recruits Jonathon, her gawky older brother, to drive Jodi home even though Jodi doesn't want to leave. Miranda has to promise to go along before Jodi will get in the car.

After they leave, Nathan comes to pick up Tara. He's taking her to Mark's place to hang out for a while. There was a time when I'd be part of that group, but not anymore. I am sick with regret. Then Mark's new girlfriend comes to the door, and I feel even sicker.

"Hey, everybody, this is Holly," Tara says. "She's going out with Mark."

"Hello!" Holly waves at us. "I wanted to meet the girls who play hockey with Tara."

Played hockey, Holly. Tara's moving out of my world, just like Mark did. I can feel everyone's eyes on me. It's all I can do to stand there and paste on a polite smile.

Now that I see her up close, I realize how built Holly is. She's barely five feet tall, but the muscles ripple in her slender calves and biceps. And damn it, she's pretty.

"What sport do *you* do?" Kathy asks Holly point blank.

"Wrestling," she says. "I'm trying out for the U of S team."

The girls heave a collective sigh.

"That is so cool," Teneil says. "Think you'll make it?"

"I hope so, or I'll have wasted most of my summer lifting weights with Mark," Holly says.

"Do you wrestle with him too?" Amber asks.

Now everyone stares at her.

"I didn't mean that like it sounded," Amber says.

Tara introduces Holly to everyone. When Tara gets to me, Holly smiles and nods, like she did for everyone else. My name means nothing to her. It's bad enough being the ex-girlfriend, without being the ex-girlfriend Mark doesn't even mention.

"I want to watch some Bruin games this winter," Holly says. "Maybe I'll be able to catch one of yours."

The girls all look at me, to see how I'm taking it. I keep on smiling. I must look ridiculous.

After Holly leaves, everyone teases Amber about the wrestling remark. She blinks her big blue Bambi eyes and says, "What's wrong with that?"

Life's so strange. Things would be easier if Holly was a bag, but she isn't. It's perfectly obvious why Mark likes her more than me. I'm a train wreck, while Holly's mature, focused, and smart.

Kathy leans on my shoulder. "Jessie, if you ever need someone to talk to, Auntie Kathy's here for ya."

"Thanks, Parker."

She continues, "Sometimes you win, and sometimes you lose. When you do, you gotta tighten your laces and make the best of it because that's all you can do."

Yeah, life is strange. And right now I don't like it much.

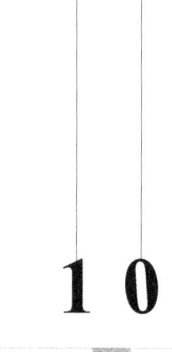

1 0

MARSHA SCHULTZ, THE GIRL WHO terrorized me last winter, is the first person I see when I get to the Comp for my first day of Grade Ten. The way things have been going, should that surprise me?

She's smoking with some other tough looking kids across the road from the school when Dad and I drive by.

"Look at those kids," Dad says, slowing down. "Shouldn't somebody report them?"

How can he be that socially unaware? "Keep going, Dad," I urge.

My eyes are glued to the side mirror as we drive up the gravel road to the north parking lot. Sure enough Marsha and her friends are watching us. And here I thought using the rear entrance would be the best way to avoid attracting attention. Before that business with Jodi, I always pictured myself pulling up to the Comp in Mark's truck. Plan A. Only thing is I had no Plan B.

When Dad stops the Prius, I jump out and grab my backpack.

"Hey, you have a great day." Dad smiles at me. "High school will be the best years of your life."

"Right." I close the door and watch him drive away.

Dad's not speaking from experience. He was bullied all through high school because he was a math geek and not a jock or tough guy. To this day I don't know if Dad loves hockey by choice or simply because a boy growing up in rural Saskatchewan had no alternative but to play the sport. He never played competitively, and I'm sure he was relieved when he was finally old enough to play rec, where there's no hitting. People say adolescence is easier on guys, but I don't know. At least it's all right for a girl not to be athletic, as long as she's pretty.

"Hey, Jessie! How're ya doing?" A voice calls to me when I reach the main foyer. It's Riley Henderson, a boy I went out with last September and for a few weeks last winter. But that's another story.

There're some other guys with him.

"I'm great." I stop for a minute and shift my backpack, which is cutting into my shoulders. "How was your summer?"

While Riley's telling me about it, I take note of his friends. Two of them are the jerks who bugged me on the day of my French exam.

"Hey, when're you going to post some new pictures?" one of them asks.

Does he honestly believe I posted them? "Greg did that—not me."

"That's right!" another one says. "Good ol' Nicker."

I hope Riley will intervene—shut these boys down. But he doesn't. Maybe he feels lucky to be hanging out with them.

"See you, Riley." As I walk away, I ignore the whistles and catcalls behind me. Losers.

I walk past the office. To my left is a row of lockers, and above them, another causeway. Kids lean against the rail, looking down at me. In another time and place, this wouldn't be frightening. But to me, it's a gauntlet. I stare straight ahead, trying to shut my ears to the buzz. Half of me hopes I'll see Mark. Half prays I won't. I don't need the world watching when he shuts me down.

I'm about two-thirds of the way down the hall when voices shriek my name. Miranda and Teneil laugh and wave at me from above. Reinforcements at last.

"Hold on, Mac!" Miranda shouts. "We're comin' down!"

Soon we're hugging in the middle of the hall like we haven't seen each other in two years—instead of two days. I'm choked up, but I get a grip on myself.

"Isn't it awesome?" Teneil says. "We're finally here!"

I wish I could be as excited as they are.

"We were waiting for you," Miranda says in a mock angry tone. "What took you so long to get here?"

"Let's go to the courtyard!" Teneil tugs on my hand like an impatient four-year-old.

The buzz swells to a roar—a fluctuating column of male bass intertwined with female soprano—as we turn down yet another hallway. We enter the courtyard, which rises three stories to a skylight. Kids line the two levels overlooking the open space. A brightly painted banner advertising the special events planned for the first week hangs from the highest level. Trees and tables make this the perfect meeting place. Even though I'm new to the Comp, I know this courtyard is its heart. The space might be smaller than EJH's playground, but the social dynamics are similar—and also more sophisticated.

I scan the sea of faces. No Mark.

No one notices us. Everyone's too busy getting caught up on the summer's events. An announcement interrupts the piped-in music, but no one pays any attention.

Teneil pulls me towards the table where Kathy sits with two older girls.

"Hey, chicks!" Kathy stands up and waves us over. At least I think she said that. It's so loud I can't hear myself think.

The two girls grin and make room for us to squeeze in.

"This is Erica and Brooklyn," Kathy says, dispensing with last names. "They play with the U18 team. They're in Grade Twelve."

Erica is heavyset with broad shoulders and a plain but wholesome face. I can't tell the true colour of her hair because she's got it tucked under a woolen toque. Even Kathy doesn't wear her toque in the summer. There's a stud below Erica's lower lip and a ring through her eyebrow.

Brooklyn's hair is dyed black, and her eyes are big, brown pools. She'd be pretty if her teeth weren't so crooked. I can't tell how tall she is because she's sitting down, but I'm betting she'll be the tallest player on our team.

"What position do you play?" I ask Brooklyn.

"We're D-partners." Brooklyn points at Erica. "Nothing gets by us, except the puck."

They know they're bad? So much for hoping we'll have a sniff at stopping teams from peppering us with shots if our two oldest D say stuff like that.

"Do you think Kim's dad's gonna help coach us?" Teneil asks.

I shrug.

"Please—not Mr. Scott," Kathy says. "Softball season was the longest two months of my life."

"At least he likes you," Miranda says. "He always said to me, 'I thought you people were supposed to be fast?'"

Teneil looks at Brooklyn and Erica. "Could your dads help coach?"

Brooklyn makes the gesture to ward off evil. "My dad tried coaching three years ago. He quit."

"My dad quit halfway through last year," Erica says.

"Never mind," Kathy says, "I've got big news. And I want you all to hear it." We all huddle close.

"Dad got us a bus!"

"A bus!" Miranda's eyes nearly pop out of her head. "Seriously! A bus!"

Teneil folds her hands and raises her eyes to the skylight. "If Jodi were here, she would say, 'Freakin' hallelujah and amen.'"

"Hallelujah!" Erica shouts.

"Amen!" We say in unison.

"So what kind of bus is it?" Erica asks.

"Has it got TVs?" Brooklyn asks.

"Has it got a bathroom?" Teneil asks.

"Ah, white, no and no," Kathy says.

We all look at her in confusion.

"You'll see," she says.

The buzzer for Period One scares the crap out of me. There's a collective groan, and everyone starts moving. My first class is ELA, and I have no trouble finding it because it's in the lecture theatre on the first floor, right across from the courtyard. I sit next to Michelle Purdy, who was in my homeroom last year. She's the only person I know, and I don't know her well.

"Did you have a good summer, Michelle?" I ask.

Her skin's so white I'm pretty sure she didn't spend any of it outside. She immediately starts telling me about prepping for her Grade Eight piano exam. Some boys snicker behind me, but Michelle's chatter prevents me from hearing everything. I pick out Jodi's name. Greg's. I try to tune them out. Ms. Peters, our ELA teacher, enters and—to my relief—shuts down the boys at the back. She hands out our course outline. Our first unit is going to be all about—wait for it—us.

And us—or rather, me—isn't something I want to examine close up.

After class, Michelle and I make plans to meet for lunch in the cafeteria, and I head down to the band room for attendance. I used to think it's cool that homerooms at the Comp are made up of students in all three grades. Today I wish there was just one female hockey player in mine.

I've been warned about the good side/bad side of having homeroom with Mr. G, the band teacher. The bad side is the band room is a long way from most of my classes. That means I'll go through the gauntlet to the band room after first period every day. But the good side is—Mr. G himself. As I walk down the ramp to his domain, Mr. G stands in the doorway, wearing a big smile. He's a big man.

"Good morning," he says. "Jessie McIntyre, right?"

"Right." How come he knows my name already? Does he know what Greg and Jordan posted last June?

"Hockey player. Runner-up for the EJH math award."

Whew. "Yes."

He takes my hand and shakes it once. "I do my homework on new students. Welcome to ECS."

"Thanks." I start to pull away, but he keeps a firm grip.

"Ever think about taking up an instrument?"

"No." I'm feeling the jaws of a trap. I try to avoid his eyes. I'm also trying to extract my hand, but he won't let go.

"Math students are notoriously good musicians. My marching band could use a few recruits."

"I'm trying out for volleyball," I tell him.

He arches an eyebrow.

"Um. I'll think about marching band," I lie. The grip on my fingers loosens.

"Beautiful!" Appeased, Mr. G beams and steps aside, ushering me into the band room.

Students lounge on the carpeted lower level. Everyone looks comfortable. I look for a familiar face, but I can't find one.

"Hey, Jessie," a male voice behind me says. "How's it going so far?"

I turn around and stare at the sternum of Evan Gedak, Breanne's older brother.

"Good, Evan. How's Breanne?"

"Good." He nods his giant head.

"She all excited about her first day of Kindergarten?"

"Uh huh."

I find myself nodding along with him. "I didn't know you were in Mr. G's homeroom."

He folds his long arms and keeps bobbing.

"How's the Comp basketball team look this year?" I ask.

Evan shrugs his broad shoulders and sways his head back and forth. "We should be all right."

"That's good."

It's brilliant conversation. Pure poetry.

I'm relieved when Mr. G. starts attendance and reads us the announcements. The only one he shows any interest in is what's for dessert.

"For those of you who don't know, Mondays are special," he informs us. "It's the day the cafeteria staff bakes cookies. Don't gorge on Dino Buddies."

"Dino Buddies?" I whisper to Evan.

"Chicken nuggets in the shape of dinosaurs," he says. "They're epic."

After homeroom, I have math with Mr. Politis, who's a whiz with a slide rule—not that I've ever seen one before today. He challenges us to try to beat it with our calculators, but we lose every time. After math I have Mr. Kemp for Social Studies. He looks like a dinosaur, but he grabs my attention when he tells us he's crossed the Sahara Desert eight times. He's seen most of the stuff we'll be learning about.

As I head to the cafeteria for lunch, my stomach is queasy again. I know Teneil, Miranda and Kathy will meet me there, but I have no idea where they'll be sitting. When I walk through the doors, rock music blares and wide-screen televisions replay school news and sports highlights. Many of the tables are occupied. I don't see anyone from the Xtreme. No sign of Michelle either, but then again she has band right after third class. Should I look for Mark?

And what would you do if you found him, my little voice wonders.

Not a clue.

The food lineup isn't long. I pick up a tray and shuffle along, trying to decide whether or not to eat healthy. It's my first day of high school after all. Would it be a crime to celebrate with Dino Buddies and fries?

Finally it's my turn to place an order for a hot meal. The stocky girl behind the counter has her back to me. When she turns around, I'm eyeball to eyeball with Marsha.

11

"Hey, rich girl, I thought I saw you this morning," Marsha says. She no longer has any piercings. Well, the holes are still there, but the metal has vanished. She wears a white paper hat, white pants, a white shirt, and a white apron with grease stains. Whoever said good guys wear white has never met Marsha.

"So you're going to be here for three years," Marsha drawls. "Isn't that special?"

An icy finger tickles my spine. "You work here?"

"No, I'm shooting an ad for Chef Boyardee."

"Guess you must be taking commercial cooking, huh?"

She tilts her head against her shoulder and yawns loudly. I notice there's no piercing in her tongue anymore either.

"What are you staring at?" she demands.

"Nothing." I drop my eyes.

She leans towards me. "Whadda you want? I haven't got all frickin' day."

"I changed my mind. I'm having a salad." I pick up my tray.

Marsha delivers a scornful snort at my back. "All you skinny-ass rich girls are the same. You eat like frickin' rabbits; then you go home, scarf down a box of pizza pops and jam your frickin' fingers down your throats."

I wheel around and set my tray in front of her again. "On second thought, I'll have the Dino Buddies and fries. And don't skimp on the gravy."

She hands me a plate of deep-fried cholesterol without even a second glance. "Next!"

I'm relieved Marsha never threatened to kick my ass. Maybe she really is going to leave me alone.

I pay for my lunch at the till and make my way into the dining area, which is nearly as big as the ECS gym. Long tables crammed with students are arranged on wide tiers that lead down to the stage. I've been in this room a few times for special assemblies and the ECS musical production of Grease, but I've never eaten a meal here.

I scan the room for my friends. Do I look like an idiot? Why does it feel like everyone's staring at me?

"Hey, Jessie! Over here!" Someone waves at me.

It's Brittni Wade. She sits at a table with a bunch of girls I don't know.

I hesitate. I've already made up my mind to steer clear of Brittni. The Brittnis of this world serve up girls like me as appetizers for their friends. She makes Kim look like a rank amateur. On the other hand I can't ignore her and go sit at a table by myself. That would label me "stuck up." And Brittni's going to be a teammate this year. I take a firm grip on my tray and start towards her.

On the way, I see a few options, including some kids from my homeroom last year. But guys from Mark's old hockey team, including Greg, are seated at the next table. As I get closer, I notice Kim, who sits beside Greg—nearly on top of Greg to tell the truth. Greg sees me, and his eyes light up. No way. I give both groups a wide berth and make my way to Brittni's table. Too late I realize that the dark-haired girl with her back to me is Jodi.

Oh no.

"How was your morning?" Brittni asks in a way that seems genuine.

Nothing about Brittni is genuine. She's got gel nails and a fake-and-bake tan and hair dyed so blonde it's nearly white. Today she's wearing a short pink skirt and white cotton sweater. Her long brown legs are crossed at the knee, bobbing a silver sandal at the end of her perfectly pedicured toes. A long stemmed rose is tattooed above her ankle. She clears a space for me next to her and directly across from Jodi.

"It was good." I sit down and give everyone a breezy smile. The rest of the girls look at me like I'm a rare insect who might require squashing. "Hey, Jodi. How's your first day so far?"

Jodi looks at me, but I can't read her expression at all. "I got lost on my way to my IP class, but Mitchell helped me." Funny how Jodi's a lot less animated when she's not drinking.

"Who's Mitchell?" Brittni picks a fry off my plate and pops it in her mouth.

Jodi yawns. "You know. Mitchell-with-the-long-red-hair-Mitchell? I don't know his last name." She sets her head on her arms. "Don't bug me. I just wanna sleep."

"Jodi stayed up too late last night," Brittni tells me. "Got a little wasted. I keep telling her she's gotta lay off the vodka, but she won't listen."

"Shut up." Jodi turns her head away from us.

The girls laugh.

"So—Jessie." Brittni steals another fry and nibbles it. "What're your thoughts about the U18 team this year? Think we'll have too many players?"

"No." I munch on one of my Dino Buddies. Delicious.

Brittni casts a glance sideways at Greg and his friends. "I heard Kim was a pain in the ass last year."

No way. Not going down that road again. Not ever. "Kim had a rough start, but she turned out all right. Wouldn't you say, Jodi?"

Jodi stands up. She looks awful. "I'm gonna get some fresh air. I don't feel so good."

Her departure is a relief.

Brittni watches her walk away. "What do you mean 'rough start?'" She pounces on another fry. "I thought Kim was good enough to play with the guys."

I decide not to expand on the comment. "I've never seen her play with the guys, but she's good with the puck."

"And Kowalski's going to coach," Brittni says. "I hear he's a wimp."

What's Jodi been saying about him?

"So all you girls got equal ice time last year?" Brittni asks.

"Wasn't hard. There weren't many of us."

"You all got to do PK and the power play?"

"Pretty much."

"Is that fair to girls who've been on the team longer—say two or three years?"

I see where this conversation's headed. I also see why both Erica's and Brooklyn's dads quit coaching.

"If there's one thing I can't stand," Brittni says, "it's a rookie who figures she deserves as much ice time as a vet."

I smile at Brittni in a more courageous way than I'm feeling. "I heard we're getting a bus."

"Who told you that?" Brittni reaches for one of my Dino Buddies.

"You're pushing it!" I say in a mock menacing tone, tapping the back of her hand.

Silence. Brittni and the others stare at me with raised, perfectly plucked eyebrows.

Now what?

Brittni's eyes narrow. "Jessie, why don't you tell us what happened with Jodi at that *party* back in June? We're dying for some details."

It's frightening—this whole Girl World thing, and I am in serious need of a GPS. I whisk my tray away, and the Buddies skitter off my plate. "Love to, but I gotta go. See you later."

Heart pounding, I head towards the table of EJH kids I know. At the next table, Greg notices me and grins, watching my approach. I ignore the snickers and comments around me. Damn, this is hard.

"Jessie!"

Teneil waves at me from a table on the third tier. She's with Miranda and Kathy. Awesome.

When I set my tray down, Miranda folds her arms across her chest and thrusts out her lower lip. "You were planning to ditch us, weren't you, Mac?"

A bubble of laughter verging on hysteria rises in my throat. "Oh no, I wasn't." For the first time in hours, I take a deep breath and let it out. Slowly.

I feel a tap on my shoulder. Michelle stands in the aisle, looking at me with uncertain brown eyes.

"Can I sit with you?" she asks.

"Sure. Girls, this is Michelle. She's in my ELA class. Remember her from EJH? Move your skinny butt over, Miranda."

Miranda obliges, but Teneil screws up her freckled nose.

Whatever, Teneil. What does it cost us to let someone who's not a hockey player—or popular—sit with us? Besides, I think I know how Michelle feels.

Michelle sits down and smiles at me. It's easy to make a difference to somebody, and it sure feels good when you do.

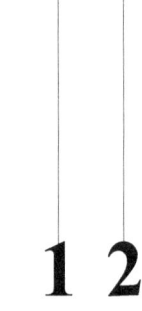

12

"ANYONE GET LOST ON THEIR FIRST DAY?" Erica asks, as she holds the door open for Teneil, Miranda, and me.

All three of us raise our hands, and Erica laughs.

"I love you rooks." She tucks a stray strand under her toque. "You're going to be worth the price of admission every damn day."

We descend the steps and turn onto the wide walkway in front of the Comp. Students congregate in little groups on the sidewalk and bask in the sun on the bright green lawn.

"Hey, Erica, can you drop me off a few blocks from my house?" I ask. "I don't want my parents to see how I got home."

"Get a life, Mac," Erica says.

"Do you think it'll be pleasant when my mom interrogates you?" I ask her. "Because that's what's going to happen if she finds out I got a ride with a stranger."

"Hey Jessie, there's Mark," Teneil says.

He's standing at the bottom of the walkway, next to the Comp's access road. He's deep in conversation with Evan. It's my first glimpse of Mark all day.

I don't know what to wish for. Should I hope he'll finish the conversation and leave before I get there? Or hang around long enough to snub me when I say "hi"?

My little voice says, Look, Jessie, you've had a decent first day. Are you going to let him spoil it?

"Are you going to talk to him?" Miranda asks.

I shrug.

"You might as well," Teneil says. "It's not like you can avoid him forever."

"Whoa, whoa." Erica pulses her hands in a perfect imitation of Mr. G. conducting. "Will someone tell me what's going on?"

Erica is obviously one of the few students at ECS who doesn't know about my stupidity last June, and I don't want to get into it with her now. These girls will still be dissecting my life when the sun comes up tomorrow, and I'll have missed the opportunity to talk to Mark.

I start walking, and they fall in behind me. Miranda mutters that all girls make mistakes— that friends should stand up for each other. I hope she can keep her mouth shut long enough for me to say my piece to Mark.

What exactly do you plan to say, my little voice wonders.

No idea. I'll have to wing it.

I've almost reached Mark, and I don't think he's seen me yet. He's wearing plaid shorts, sandals, and a blue short-sleeved cotton shirt. The last few buttons are undone and his shirt-tails flutter in the breeze. His signature ball cap is jammed backwards on his head and his blonde hair, which curls around his collar, is sun-bleached. A tiny stud glints in his left earlobe. Mark's tall, but even so, Evan towers over him.

I march right up to them. "Mark, we need to talk."

He digs out his phone and examines it. "Team meeting. Gotta go. I'll call you later. We'll shoot a few baskets."

There's no way he means me. He hasn't looked at me.

"Please, Mark." To my ears, I sound calmer. More mature. More Holly-ish.

Mark hesitates.

"Evan, I need to talk to Mark. Alone."

"Sure." Evan backs away. He towers over Miranda, Teneil, and Erica.

I cut to the heart of the matter. "Mark, I didn't tell Greg about your dad."

Mark looks startled.

"I didn't know anything about your dad until Tara told me at the Black and Gold game."

"That's good to know." He turns away from me. "Later, Evan!" He crosses the road and hurries down the stairs leading to the lower parking lot.

Paralyzed by despair, I watch him go.

Someone behind me gives me a little push.

"Don't let Holly win!" Miranda says. "Fight for him!"

She's right. So what if I'm stupid and immature? So what if his girlfriend's three years older than me and cute as a button?

Good thing I know which truck is his. I run down the steps and charge ahead of him, plastering my back against the driver's door, spreading my arms wide. "Will you please listen to me?"

You managed to get through the whole day without making a spectacle of yourself. What in the hell are you doing, my little voice says.

I eyeball Mark as he approaches. He's looking over my head, still ignoring me.

You've lost him, Jessie. Don't lose your dignity too, my voice pleads.

Some things are more important than dignity. "Mark, we need to talk." I hold my head high. I'm Cleopatra confronting Julius Caesar.

Only Julius Caesar never had a key fob for his half-ton. Mark engages the alarm function, and I jump away. He climbs into his truck, locks the door, and starts the engine.

I pound on the window with my palms while he pulls ahead, barely missing my toes.

As he drives away, I think, that's it, Jessie. You did all you could, and you've lost him.

Evan walks up behind me. "I'm sorry, Jessie."

"What're you sorry for?" I retort. "You're not the one who screwed things up!"

Miranda's arms slip around me, and she tells me the only thing I need to hear. "Let's go get a Slurpee. My treat."

1 3

"KIM LOOKED PRETTY UPSET WHEN Ms. Wilms subbed you in, Jessie," Mom says.

It's October. Kathy and I are in the back of our SUV while Mom and Courtney are up front. We're headed home after our volleyball game and a quick detour through the Dairy Queen drive-through.

"Kim's ticked because she didn't make the senior team," Kathy volunteers. "You should hear her excuses for being cut. Her mother made a *huge* scene."

"That must have been embarrassing for Kim," Mom says.

"Well, the rest of us sucked it up." I take a mouthful of my cookie dough Blizzard. "Playing on the junior team isn't so bad."

"Why doesn't Jodi play volleyball?" Courtney asks.

"She didn't try out," I tell her.

"She could have made the senior squad easy." Kathy takes a long, rattling pull on her straw. "Teneil made it. Then again, Teneil's a figure skater, so she's got that extra pop in her vertical. Listen to Auntie Kathy, Little Mac. If you stick with figure skating, you're gonna make the senior volleyball team one day."

"Okay," Courtney says.

"If Auntie Kathy keeps drinking chocolate shakes after every game, she's never gonna have a vertical," I say.

"Ouch," Kathy says.

"Jessie, who were those boys who kept chanting your name?" Mom asks out of the blue.

"Nobody," I say, hoping she'll drop the subject.

Greg and Jordan show up for most of our home games. They cheer so loud whenever I touch the ball, I could crawl under a rock and die.

"Jerks," Kathy says.

"Will Kim play hockey with you girls?" Mom asks.

I swallow a spoonful of ice cream. "*That* is the million-dollar question."

"Miranda thinks Kim's embarrassed to play girls hockey," Kathy says. "That's why she ignores us at school."

"It's sad her parents put her under so much pressure," Mom observes, then adds, "I talked to your friend Michelle, Jessie. She seems like a nice girl. And smart. Kind of lonely though. You should invite her over sometime."

"Sure," I say. I probably won't. I don't mind hanging out with Michelle at school, but I don't think I'll have time to hang out with her beyond that. Hockey season is around the corner, and my schedule will be full of games and practices.

"Jessie hangs out with Michelle lots at school." Kathy rolls her eyes at me.

It bothers me that Kathy and some of the others have adopted this attitude towards a non-hockey player. Non athlete. If they only knew how crappy I feel every time Michelle talks about EJH. She says whole days went by when not one kid talked to her. She was like a ghost. I had no idea her life was like that.

"Do you know who's being extra nice to me?" I ask Kathy, attempting to change the subject.

"Who?"

"Marsha." I mouth the name. Marsha Schultz is a swear word in our house.

"No way," Kathy mouths back.

"Way. She gave me an extra Dino Buddy yesterday," I whisper.

"Shut up!" Kathy hisses.

"I know. I nearly fainted. She tried to make it look like an accident, but I know she meant to do it."

"The stories I hear about Jodi aren't good," Mom interjects. "Is it true she's dating a nineteen-year-old?"

Trust the figure skating moms to be on top of all the Estevan gossip. Now it makes sense why Mom wants me to have Michelle over. She doesn't want me hanging out with Jodi again. Ever.

"Yes, she is," Kathy says. "The Bruin captain."

"What's her mother thinking?" Mom says. "Jessie, you won't be dating anybody that old any time soon."

"Fine with me," I tell her.

"What about Evan Gedak? Is he okay for Jessie?" Kathy asks.

I elbow her in the ribs.

Mom adjusts the mirror so she's making eye contact with Kathy. "Jessie could definitely do worse, don't you think?"

"Definitely," Kathy agrees, turning sideways so my next jab hits her square in the back instead of the ribs. "Oooof!"

I like Evan, but he's not boyfriend material. Not for me at least.

"Isn't there a Sadie Hawkins Dance next week? Maybe you should ask Evan," Mom suggests.

"I'd rather watch hockey with Dad," I reply. "As a matter of fact, I'd even watch the Leafs."

Kathy, who's a big Leafs' fan, gives me a smack.

We pull into Kathy's driveway.

"It's my birthday tomorrow," Courtney says, looking at us between the seats.

"That's great, Little Mac," Kathy says. "Is Auntie Kathy invited to the party?"

"We're going bowling," Courtney says. "Do you like bowling?"

"I love bowling," Kathy says. "My specialty is the gutter ball. Are you inviting all your friends from school?"

Courtney turns away from us. "Just my skating friends."

That strikes me as peculiar.

"Why aren't you inviting the girls from your class?" I ask.

Mom's phone chimes inside her purse, and Courtney answers it.

"It's Daddy," Courtney says after a brief conversation. "He says Breanne's mom called, and she wants Jessie to babysit tomorrow night."

"Tell him I'll call Mrs. Gedak when I get home," I say. I'd rather not babysit— especially if Evan comes home early to hang out with me.

"Have a nice Thanksgiving," Mom says to Kathy as she climbs out of the vehicle. "Have you got any plans?"

"Turkey, pumpkin pie, and a nap," Kathy says. "What about you, Mrs. McIntyre?"

"We're headed to Regina on Saturday. Somebody wants a new hockey stick."

"I need a new stick." I open my door and get out.

"Bobby Orr never used a composite stick!" Courtney calls.

"You've been listening to Dad again!" I call back.

I'm hoping I'll score more goals with the new stick. I worked all summer on my shooting, and the garage wall has the scars to prove it. My wrist shot is decent, but my slapshot still needs work.

I toss Kathy her gym bag. "See ya." I reach up to pull down the hatch on the SUV.

"Hey, wait a sec. Did you hear Mark got traded to Humboldt?" Kathy asks.

I pause with my arm in the air then lower it. "No, I didn't."

"Makes sense." Kathy puts the strap over her shoulder. "His mom is only a few miles away."

And Holly—at the University of Saskatchewan—is only an hour away.

"Still, it's a tough place to play. All that history," Kathy says. She's referring to the tragic bus accident that took the lives of sixteen people, including ten Humboldt players, a few years ago. "I hope Mark can handle it."

"He's got a good head on his shoulders," I say.

"Does it bother you that he's leaving?" Kathy asks.

I take a deep breath and let it out. "Maybe it's better if I don't see him around. I hate it when he passes me in the hallway and refuses to look at me."

"Well, at least he won't have to listen to ignorant comments about his dad." Kathy gives me a quick hug—uncharacteristic for her. It feels nice. "See you tomorrow, Mac."

Courtney and Mom chat it up the rest of the way home, making plans for the birthday party, so I'm left to my thoughts. I push Mark out of them and focus on hockey. Part of me longs for our first practice. Part of me is worried sick.

What if Mr. Scott helps Mr. Kowalski coach? The only player he likes on the team, besides Kim, is Kathy. He has three categories for everybody else:

1) puck hog,

2) lazy-assed, and

3) weak-assed.

Last year, I was Category 2. Not sure where he'll place me this year. Hopefully I've improved enough to move up to Category 1.

I remember what it felt like going to my first practice last year—how determined I was not to enjoy the experience, how afraid I was of making a fool of myself. Now I'm afraid it won't be any fun. It's basic math. What do you get when you take away Tara and Shauna and Carla and Steve? And add Brittni and Cory and two D who can't skate and a coach who's too nice?

Disaster, that's what.

14

"YOU WANT ME TO STICK around for practice?" Dad opens the rear hatch on our SUV and manhandles my hockey bag and shiny new stick out of the back.

"I'll be okay." I sling the bag over my shoulder and stagger under the weight.

"Work hard." Dad closes the hatch. "Try to break a sweat."

"Right, Dad."

He's teasing. I've heard him talk about our team when he doesn't think I'm listening. He loves the way we play—when we're playing well, that is. Not when we're running all over the ice or letting the opposition beat us to the puck.

"I'm glad hockey season is here," he says, as if to make up for his previous remark. "You seem kind of down, lately. Hockey will pick you up."

"Sure, Dad."

"You know who I saw the other day?" Dad asks.

Here we go.

"Riley Henderson. Do you ever see him at school?"

My dad misses his conversations with Riley. They're both huge Boston Bruin fans. Too bad Dad can't date Riley.

I shift my hockey bag to my other shoulder. "This is getting heavy. Mind if I go now?"

"Sure thing. I'll be back at 8:30."

The parents gathered in the lobby of the Blue Goose wear those bright smiles that say, "Isn't it great to be back?"

I check the white board by the office. U18 Girls—Dressing Room #1.

A man hurries to open the door for me and gives me a big grin as I maneuver my hockey bag past him. "A chick with a stick," he says. "You go, girl."

Yeah, that's what I'm talking about.

"Thanks."

I breathe in the ice's fresh, cool scent. A younger boys team, probably U11, has practice. I drop my equipment and watch a few drills. What would it be like to coach my own son or daughter someday?

"Ready for the season?" It's Mr. Kowalski. His hairline has receded even further, and he looks nervous.

"I'm ready." I can't help smiling. "Is Amber here?"

Mr. Kowalski nods. "She's in the dressing room already. She wanted to be the first one." He smacks his soft brown leather gloves together, as if trying to keep his hands warm. "Will you do me a favour?"

"Sure, Coach."

"Keep an eye on Amber. If anybody says anything mean to her, please let me know."

"Sure." By "anybody," I gather he means Brittni. "How's the team looking so far? Did lots of girls sign up?"

"Enough," Mr. Kowalski says. "Should be an interesting year."

A dozen scenarios have already played out in my head. What happens if the other teams in our new league walk all over us? What if all the girls quit by Christmas?

"I've asked Blaine Scott to help coach."

Oh yeah, they'll quit.

I know Mr. Scott badgered Mr. Kowalski into asking him. Kathy says Mr. Scott is ticked because Estevan Minor Hockey wouldn't let him coach his son's team. He had a showdown with the rest of the parents—said he wouldn't have anything to do with the team. I'll bet they shot off fireworks after he stormed out.

Mr. Scott yells all the time. I had a teacher once who yelled too, but he said funny stuff when he did it, and we knew he liked us. But that's not how it is with Mr. Scott. Mr. Scott doesn't get hockey—or kids—at all. Furthermore, I don't think he likes the female game. Or us.

As I open the dressing room door, Amber's jam pours out. She's dancing by herself, and she's shaking her bootie because she thinks nobody's watching. Then she sees me, and she blushes beet red. I drop my hockey bag and bust a move. Soon we're both up on the bench, dancing.

The others start to straggle in—Jennifer, Kathy, Miranda, Teneil, Erica, Brooklyn, Kim, and Larissa—who's usually the last to arrive. And pretty soon there's a team dance party going on. Not Kim, mind you. She's on her phone.

Crystal Jordan from Torquay brings her equipment so she can play out. She's decided she'll only play net if Miranda can't.

At 6:40, twenty minutes before our ice time is scheduled to start, there's no sign of Brittni, Cory, or Jodi. I'm impatient to get on the ice. Although I skated a few times in September, I haven't put on my equipment since last season. Amber says we're supposed to stay in the dressing room until after the coaches talk to us.

Brittni and Cory breeze in at 6:55.

"Sorry we're late!" Brittni shouts over the music.

Cory is a brunette clone of Brittni—tall, tinted, tanned, and tattooed. "What in the hell are you guys listening to?" she demands.

Amber blushes. "The Bee Gees."

It's a bad habit, I know. Is it *our* fault all the fun music was written long before any of us were born?

"Time for some *real* music." Cory connects her phone to her own speaker and raunchy, X-rated rap pours out.

While Brittni and Cory undress and unpack their equipment, they check their phones every thirty seconds.

"They don't look like they're in any hurry to get on the ice," I whisper to Kathy.

"I'd love to smack their heads together," she mutters back.

Miranda's mom comes in to see if we're ready. Mrs. Omalu will be our team trainer and manager. Besides being an LPN, Mrs. Omalu drives a school bus part-time, so she'll come in handy on road trips. She's as round as Miranda is skinny.

She stomps right over and shuts off the smart speaker. "Why aren't you girls dressed?"

Brittni and Cory—stripped down to lacy bras and thongs—glare at her.

"Get your equipment on! Are you hockey players or *what?*" Mrs. Omalu marches out.

Cory turns to Miranda. "That's *your* mom?"

Miranda nods.

"What a witch," Cory says.

Miranda looks furious, but she doesn't say a word.

The *other* older girls—Erica, and Brooklyn—stare at their feet and make last minute adjustments to their equipment. Pretty good indication they're not going to be team leaders.

"That was ignorant," Kathy says.

Cory locks eyes with Kathy from across the room. "Are you talking to me?

"You're gonna apologize to Miranda right now."

We haven't even hit the ice yet. The way things are going we won't make it out of the dressing room.

"I am?" Cory advances on Kathy in a menacing way.

Kathy stands up. In full equipment she's intimidating. "Take one step closer, and that slingshot you're wearing is going into orbit."

I smother a snort of laughter.

Brittni tugs on Cory's arm. "Let's get dressed."

Score one for Kathy. But Cory never apologizes to Miranda. Instead she puts on her gear in slow motion while Brittni scrolls on her phone. It's 7:20 before Cory's decent enough for the coaches to come in.

Mr. Scott is right behind Mr. Kowalski. Super duper.

"Welcome back, ladies," Amber's dad says. "I hope you're ready for a great season."

"We're ready to kick Weyburn *ass*," Kathy says.

Mr. Scott eyes shoot lasers. "Let's get this straight right here and now. You girls need to get here and get dressed so we can hit the ice on time. Also, there'll be *no* blurting out remarks when we're addressing the team. Is that clear?"

I can't believe he said that to Kathy. She's one of the players he likes.

Kathy folds her arms across her chest.

"Is everybody here?" Mr. Kowalski asks. His gaze roves over us.

"Jodi went to Weyburn to watch Jordan's game," Brittni says.

Jodi's back together with Jordan? This is news to me.

"She's watching her *boyfriend* play hockey? When she has *practice*?" Mr. Scott demands.

Yes, Mr. Scott. We don't like it any more than you do, but since your own daughter might skip practice one day for a lame-ass reason, you better not make a scene.

"Your first game is Sunday night against Notre Dame. Here. All of you better show up ready to play hockey."

"And exactly what else would we be doing?" Brittni asks, still scrolling.

"Well, I can tell you one thing we're *not* doing." Mr. Scott crosses the room and stands over Brittni. "You're not going to sit there and play on your *device* while your coaches are talking!"

Brittni blinks at him. "You don't like my device?"

How's this for irony? Next to Cory and Brittni, the person who's spent the most time on her phone is Kim.

While Mr. Scott fumes, Mr. Kowalski looks as if he's hoping the floor will swallow him. "We'll hand out the schedules after practice. I know some of you have part-time jobs and other commitments. All Blaine and I ask is that you let us know ahead of time when you can't make it. We've decided to teach you girls some new systems—"

"Are Cory and I playing together?" Brittni asks.

The big vein in Mr. Scott's forehead pulses. "Did you hear me say players will *not* interrupt the coach when he's talking?"

"Yeah, I heard you," Brittni says calmly. "But are we?"

"Put that phone away!" Mr. Scott screams.

Brittni smiles and sets her phone on the bench.

Mr. Scott puffs out his chest, like he's won. "You girls developed some bad habits under your previous coaches. Things are *different* now."

"Whatever," Cory says under her breath.

Mr. Scott whirls and faces her. "What did you say?"

"She said, 'I can't wait to play on a line with Brittni and Jodi.'" Brittni turns up the wattage of her dangerous smile.

Mouth open, Mr. Scott glares at her while I contemplate how Steve would handle these two players. Would he have his hands full?

"I'm got some great news," Mr. Kowalski says, rubbing his palms. I have a feeling he's trying to change the subject. "H & B Electric is sponsoring new uniforms— thanks to Teneil's dad."

Teneil grins. "Surprise, surprise."

The girls—except for Brittni and Cory—cheer and high-five.

The U18 team last year wore blue and green Canuck jerseys, but there aren't enough for our team.

"What a sweetheart Mr. Howard is—besides being the world's sexiest electrician," Kathy says.

The Hot Dad jibes are already on the table.

"Shut up!" Teneil says.

"What'll the new uniforms be like?" Cory asks.

"We'll talk about it later. Let's hit the ice," Mr. Kowalski says.

"Sure thing, Coach." Brittni moves towards the door. "Got any ideas about team captain?"

"Later," Mr. Kowalski repeats.

Brittni beams an angelic smile and leaves.

And here's the post-dressing room summary. Brittni and Cory: one; Kathy: one; coaches: no score.

I fall in with Amber. "Your dad has his work cut out for him," I whisper.

"I know."

Brittni and Cory don't dress or act like *real* players. Their hockey pants are far too short and tight, like something U11 boys would wear. They complain about every power-skating drill. They whine for the pucks until Mr. Kowalski finally tosses them out. Then they grumble about the puck-handling and shooting drills, which are either too easy or too hard. In short, everything sucks. The sad thing is—they're decent skaters, passers, and shooters—not in Jodi's league obviously, but still pretty good. Cory has a wicked wrist shot, but when Mr. Kowalski tries to break down the stages of a slapshot for her, Cory skates away.

"As if I don't know how rip a *slapper*," she says to Brittni, loud enough for Mr. Kowalski to hear. "Who does he think he is?"

Meanwhile Mr. Scott, for all his tough talk, stays clear of all the older girls. He hides at other end of the ice with Jennifer and Kim, even though Erica and Brooklyn could use some pointers. Erica's transitions from forwards to backwards skating are brutal. She stumbles every time.

"I feel sorry for Erica," I say to Kathy as we await our turn in an offensive passing drill. "Do you think she got relegated to playing defence because she's so *slow*?"

Kathy looks over at Brittni and Cory, who lean on the boards, backs turned to the drill. "Maybe someone wanted to protect her from *those* two."

Miranda went to a goalie camp this summer, and she now flops all over the place. Sure, she can do the splits—both ways—but if I can shoot over her in practice, what will Notre Dame do in a game?

Our practice concludes with a short scrimmage, where the coaches change up the offensive lines and defensive pairings. At least, they try to change them up. Somehow, Brittni and Cory *always* end up together. As I head for our dressing room, I have no clue who I'll be playing with on Friday.

Before we get undressed, Mrs. Omalu hands out our schedules. We tear into them as soon as she leaves. It's awesome to have the next four months of my life mapped out.

"We go to Swift Current for a doubleheader in two weeks," Kathy says. "Now that's what I call a road trip!"

"Where's TBA?" Amber asks.

"Huh?" We all look at our schedules.

"It says TBA right here," Amber says, pointing to her paper. "Where's that?"

'TBA means To Be Announced. Stupidity must run in your family," Cory says.

"That's done it!" Kathy leaps to her feet. "You take that back!"

"Sit down, Rookie," Cory says.

"Hey! You *stepped* on me!" Teneil's white under her freckles and there's blood on her foot.

"Shit!" Kathy says.

"Anybody got a clean towel?" Brittni demands.

"Teneil, I'm sorry," Kathy says, kneeling.

"I have one!" Jennifer pulls a folded hand towel out of a large Ziploc baggie.

"Good thing you're a germophobe, McQueen," Kathy says.

"You're kidding me, right?" Cory says to Jennifer.

Jennifer ignores her. "You need latex gloves?" she asks Brittni, pointing to the pair in the baggie.

"No. That's okay," Brittni wraps the towel around Teneil's foot, elevates it, and applies pressure.

"I'll get my dad," Larissa says. "He'll be out there waiting for me." When Brittni gives her a blank look, she adds, "You know he's a doctor, right?" She leaves.

"I hate the sight of blood," Kathy says.

"Tell me about it," Teneil moans.

"Somebody wrap a coat around her," Brittni says. "She could go into shock."

I think Brittni might be showing off, but it doesn't hurt to be cautious. I grab my zip-up hoodie and pull it around Teneil's shoulders.

"You're pretty good at this," I say to Brittni.

"I'm a lifeguard," she says.

If Brittni showed this side more often, I might like her a little.

Kathy looks as pale as Teneil. "Does it hurt very bad?"

Teneil shakes her head, but she's biting her lip.

Dr. Bilku, Teneil's mom, Mrs. Omalu, and the coaches arrive. Dr. Bilku, calm and professional, takes over from Brittni. Soon Teneil is hurried off to the hospital for stitches. Kathy mops the blood off the dressing room floor with an old T-shirt, and then she tosses it in the garbage can.

"What went on in here?" Mr. Scott demands.

"It was an accident," Larissa says.

"Sorry guys. This was all my fault," Kathy says.

I notice Cory doesn't say a word. She picks up her stuff and leaves with Brittni.

A custodian comes in with a mop and pail and finishes Kathy's cleanup. The team files out. There's just Amber, Jennifer, and me left.

Amber says, "Kind of like riding a roller coaster, isn't it?"

Jennifer's up to her shoulders in her hockey bag. "Has anybody seen my surgical tape and gauze?"

"Better stock up on field dressings," I tell her. "Looks like we're in for a few casualties."

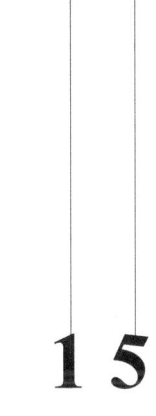

15

"APPLY THE BRAKES SOONER, JESSIE," Dad instructs, adding, "Slow down!"

The SUV's tires squeal as I turn onto Souris Avenue, but I avoid hitting the curb. That's progress.

"What's the hurry?" Mom asks from the back seat. "The game doesn't start for ninety minutes."

"I want to get there in time to talk to Shauna." When I press the gas pedal, my heel slips, and we jerk forward.

"I want Daddy to drive on the way home," Courtney says.

"Ditto," Mom says.

"I just need more practice. Dad, can we go driving this week?" I ask.

"I'll check my life insurance policy," he says.

"Stop sign!" Mom shouts.

"How's Teneil doing?" Dad asks.

"She's out for a few weeks because of the stitches in her foot," I explain. "She's not impressed about missing hockey *and* volleyball."

When I turn into the parking lot, a cheese wagon is parked near the entrance of the Blue Goose. Young women in red jackets and dress pants unload equipment bags.

I stop the SUV behind the bus and reach for my door handle. "Dad, if I pull up here, will you—"

"Don't forget to shift to Park," he interrupts.

"Right."

Once I'm out of the vehicle, I search for Shauna's blonde hair amongst the Hounds. I don't see her. Is she not playing tonight? Her teammates, who wear the ND crest on their jackets, look confident. They should be. They've been on the ice for several weeks and have played some exhibition games. We haven't.

Shauna steps down from the bus. She sees me and comes right over to give me a hug. "How're you doing, Jessie?"

"I'd be a lot better if you were playing with *us*. Are you disappointed about not making the AAA team?"

Shauna laughs. "Yeah, but I'm getting lots of ice time. There's always next year."

I start to fill her in on our dressing room drama then realize her eyes are directed over my right shoulder. I turn and see her parents are approaching.

"I'll talk to you after the game," I say, taking a step back.

"For sure," Shauna says.

I watch her greet her family while the rest of the Hounds file into the Blue Goose, under the supervision of a formidable woman in a red jacket. Must be Shauna's coach.

I feel like another chapter has ended. Maybe if I hadn't acted like an idiot back in June—

"You'll never believe it, but we somehow managed to park the vehicle without you," Dad says.

He shoulders my bag while Courtney attempts a practice swing with my new stick, which is way too long for her.

"I'll take both of those," I say.

As we head towards the rink, Mom walks beside me. "Think *you'd* like to go to Notre Dame?"

"Where'd that come from?"

"Just wondering," she says. "We'd let you go—if that's what you wanted."

"You're not getting rid of me that easy," I tell her.

I know she loves watching me play as much as I love playing. Also, I'm not ready to move two hours from home.

I take a deep breath as I enter our dressing room. Before Thursday practice, Mr. Kowalski said he'd rotate the letters for the first few games, and then let us vote on who gets to wear them for the rest of the season. Brittni was extra sweet to us rookies, and Cory sucked up to Mrs. Omalu.

"I hope the music's appropriate," Cory said.

"Right," Mrs. Omalu said, one eyebrow raised.

We managed to get through Thursday practice without anyone being sent to the hospital, but the atmosphere in the dressing room was strained. Teneil wasn't there obviously, and Jodi didn't make it either, although nobody knows why. From what I hear, Jodi isn't taking school seriously. She's been cutting classes, so it's not just us.

Our pre-game routine parallels our first two practices. We're having a high old time until Brittni and Cory arrive.

Brittni wears a C on her jersey. Are Mr. Kowalski and Mr. Scott trying the appeasement strategy? Well, if didn't stop Hitler, I doubt it's going to stop Brittni.

"Mr. Kowalski's afraid to say 'no' to her," Jennifer whispers in my ear while I tighten the straps on my elbow pad. "He's leaving the dirty work to us."

"Brittni's not captain material," Kim says under her breath.

I have a feeling Kim wants to wear the C herself. Right now she's got an A taped on her chest. The other assistant captains are Kathy and Cory.

"Anyone know if Jodi's coming?" Kathy asks.

"Good question," Kim says. "It'd be nice if she'd show up for our home opener."

"We can win without Jodi," Kathy says, then punches her fist against her palm. "Are we gonna let Notre Dame come into our house and push us around?"

"No way!" Miranda shouts though she looks as nervous as the rest of us.

Ten minutes later, Jodi sails in with a big grin on her face. Everyone looks relieved. In fact, we're so relieved nobody says anything to her about ditching practice.

If Jodi's concerned about not wearing an A, she doesn't show it. She looks great in warm-up, although she's not as sharp as last year. She's so skilled that even on a bad day, she's still the best player on our team.

Mr. Kowalski and Mr. Scott told us what to expect from the Hounds, who like to test the limits of the rulebook. They're aggressive and physical.

Mr. Kowalski tells me to play right wing—with Larissa on left. The other combinations are Cory and Brittni—naturally—and Crystal and Amber. Kathy and Jodi will rotate as our centres. We have four defence—Jennifer, Kim, Erica, and Brooklyn.

Considering it's only our first home game, we've got a good-sized crowd. However, there are two fans I can do without. Greg and Jordan stand on the north end of the rink, pounding on the Plexiglass whenever I come near them during warm-up.

"I'll break your arm if you look at Greg again," Kim mutters under her breath when she lines up behind me during a shooting drill.

I don't say anything. What could I say—except "Your creepy boyfriend won't leave me alone"?

During "O Canada," I spot Michelle. I don't think she's been to a hockey game in her life, so it's pretty cool she came. Evan and Breanne stand with my family. I hope I give all of them something to cheer about.

Shauna starts on defence for the Hounds. It's strange to see her decked out in red and white. Meanwhile, until we get our new uniforms, we're suited up in our old black and gold Xtreme jerseys. I'm wearing 13 again. Kathy and Teneil had to give up 10 and 14 because Brittni and Erica wanted those numbers, and veterans take precedence over rookies. Kathy and Teneil aren't happy about it.

The anthem ends, and the rock music begins. My heart pounds in my chest. Last October I was so afraid of making a fool of myself I didn't *want* to play. Now I can't wait to hit the ice.

Brittni, Jodi, and Cory get tied up in our end when Erica and Brooklyn can't clear the puck. The Hounds fail to score on four shots, and Jodi can't work any magic because of all the hooking and holding. Brooklyn takes an interference penalty, and I find myself—along with Kathy, Jennifer, and Kim—on penalty kill.

On the draw, Kathy wins the puck back to Jennifer, who passes to me. I get tied up on the boards—two Hounds trying to hack the puck away from my feet. One of them hooks my skate out from under me, and I go down, which doesn't faze the Hounds in the slightest. They just keep hacking.

"Blow the whistle!" someone screams. I think it's Mom.

The ref puts an end to the scrum, and we reposition ourselves at the faceoff dot.

There's still 1:32 left in Brooklyn's penalty.

This is going to be a long game.

The Hounds' centre wins the draw back to Shauna at the point, and she one-times a slapshot on net. Miranda knocks the puck down, but before she can cover it, one of the Notre Dame wingers fires it in—top shelf.

The referee points at the net, and the Hounds' bench crows. Notch one for the Visitors. Brooklyn leaves the penalty box.

"I couldn't move that winger out of the slot," Jennifer tells our goalie. "Sorry, Miranda."

Miranda swears under her breath.

As we return to the bench, Mr. Scott screams. "If that's the best you can do, you can set your pathetic, lazy asses on the bench!"

I made myself a promise I wasn't going to let him suck all the joy out of hockey, but it's going to be hard to keep that promise. Really hard.

I lean towards Larissa. "If we blow this game, do you think he'll quit?"

Larissa watches while Mr. Scott rails at Jennifer at the other end of the bench. "I think he's going to self-destruct."

"He'd better lay off her," I say.

Then Jennifer starts giving it back to Mr. Scott.

"Too late," Larissa says.

I watch my teammates chase the Hounds around in our end until Jodi intercepts a pass and rockets down the ice on a breakaway. Before she can shoot, she gets hauled down by a Hound winger, but the ref doesn't raise his arm. The Hounds score twice more while Kathy and Brittni take turns in the penalty box. Brittni gets two minors—one for roughing after the whistle and a second one for a dirty slew foot on Shauna. Kathy takes a penalty for body contact and another for holding. She also takes them in the offensive zone when we're finally able to sustain some pressure. Still, I can't blame Kathy for being frustrated. We all are. Steve would lose it if he saw how we're playing.

It's tough to tell which end of the bench is worse. At one end, Mr. Scott yells at our defence. Jennifer argues and pouts when Mr. Scott makes her sit out a shift. Even Kim looks uncomfortable. At our end, Cory harps at Crystal for not coming off soon enough, and Brittni stays out as long as she wants, which is often way longer than two minutes. Sometimes *my* shift is only ten or fifteen seconds. Amber hardly sees the ice.

As we shuffle off the ice at the end of the first period, Mr. Parker, who's manning the sound booth, announces the shots—thirteen for the Hounds, and three for the Xtreme.

"The Zamboni only has to flood half the ice," Kathy observes.

Mr. Kowalski starts to draw up a play on his tablet while Mr. Scott struts to the middle of the dressing room, booting aside Cory's equipment bag. Steve always made us stuff our bags under the bench so we wouldn't trip, but the older girls don't seem concerned about tidiness.

"What the hell's *wrong* with all of you?" Mr. Scott yells.

Here we go.

His rant is long and accusing. Apparently we're terrible skaters and passers. Lazy. Stupid. Weak. He's so busy yelling he doesn't notice Cory and Brittni are on their phones. Jodi's pulled a second water bottle out of her hockey bag. I can imagine what's in *that*. Then Jennifer yanks off her jersey and flings it on the floor.

"What are you *doing*, McQueen?" Mr. Scott snaps.

Jennifer rips open the straps on her shoulder pads. She's wearing a sports bra underneath.

Mr. Kowalski starts to panic. He looks everywhere *but* at Jennifer. "Jennifer, do you want to talk about this?" He darts a desperate glance at Mrs. Omalu.

"Jennifer," Mrs. Omalu says, "you must keep your equipment on when your coaches are in here."

Jennifer fires her shoulder pads into her hockey bag and starts unlacing her skates.

"Go ahead and run, McQueen," Mr. Scott challenges her. "That's what Bienfait girls do when the going gets tough."

We stare at him. Even Brittni's jaw drops.

"Shut up, Dad," Kim says, "or I'm gonna start taking off my equipment too."

"Is that a fact?" her dad says.

"Yes, it is," Kim says.

Father and daughter glare at one other. Jennifer has one skate untied, but she's not working on the other one. She looks back and forth between Mr. Scott and Kim like she's watching a table tennis match. Mr. Kowalski looks like he's going to throw up.

"You two must leave. At least until this girl gets her jersey back on." Mrs. Omalu takes charge, steering Mr. Kowalski and Mr. Scott out the door. Then she faces Jennifer, who's slumped against the brick wall, staring at the ceiling. "What do you want us to do?"

Tears slide down Jennifer's cheeks. She opens her mouth and closes it.

Brittni moves across the dressing room, stepping carefully in her skates over open hockey bags and Jennifer's discarded equipment. She sits next to Jennifer and puts a hand on her knee. "Talk to us."

Jennifer wipes the corners of her eyes and sniffs. "I can't play like this. My U11 coach yelled all the time. He hated me."

"You think that's bad," Kathy says, "I had a coach once that—"

"Never mind," Brittni says gently. "Go on, Jennifer."

Nice Brittni has shown up once again. It amazes me how she can be so self-centered and cruel one minute and so nice the next.

Jennifer rubs her nose with the back of her hand. "Does anybody else feel like quitting?"

"Hell no," Kathy says. "Even bad hockey is better than no hockey at all."

Jodi takes a glug of her water bottle and shrugs.

Brittni says to Jennifer, "Do you want to keep playing?"

"I don't know," Jennifer says.

"Should I go get your parents?" Mrs. Omalu asks.

Cory squawks like a chicken.

I'm really starting to dislike her.

"No," Jennifer says, reaching for her jersey. "I'll play."

"Good girl," Mrs. Omalu approves.

A fist bangs the door, and Mr. Scott shouts, "Let's go!"

"Time to go back on the ice," Miranda says.

"Are we ready to kick Notre Dame ass?" Kathy yells, strapping on her helmet.

The girls respond with half-hearted cheers, but I'm relieved we've got some team energy back.

"Let's go then!" Kathy marches across the dressing room, as if leading a charge. She hooks her skate blade and craters, landing inside Miranda's hockey bag. We all laugh, even Jennifer.

"And that's how we roll," Erica says.

16

THE SECOND PERIOD STARTS OUT BETTER. Miranda makes a beautiful glove save to stop the Hounds' captain from scoring on a breakaway, and our fans go nuts. We skate and forecheck aggressively, pinning the Hounds in their end. We even get two shots on net. When Shauna takes a hooking penalty in front of her net, we get our first power play. Mr. Kowalski sends out Kathy, Larissa, Crystal, Jennifer and Kim.

Why isn't he sending Jodi, I wonder. She should be out there.

"Nice." There's no mistaking Brittni's sarcasm. "I love watching rookies when the vets should be playing."

Nasty Brittni is back.

Kathy loses the draw, and the Hounds manage to ice the puck. Jennifer races to get it, with a Hound riding her the whole way. Miranda comes out of her net to relay the puck up to Jennifer, but she isn't quick enough. The Hound winger knocks the puck down and shoots it in our empty net before Miranda can get back. The Hounds have just scored short-handed—the ugliest of goals. Mr. Scott swears, but he doesn't say a word to our first power play unit as they come off.

"Rookies," Brittni says, stepping on the ice with Cory right behind her. They don't even wait to see who Mr. Kowalski wants to send out next. Even though she's a winger, Brittni lines up at centre to take the draw.

"Go play right wing, Jessie," Mr. Kowalski says while Mr. Scott gestures impatiently at Erica and Brooklyn.

Brittni wins the faceoff and passes the puck back to Erica. Erica pushes it over the red line and manages to shoot it into the Hounds' end. I chase the puck, all the while wondering why we're dumping-and-chasing on a power play.

Sure enough the Hounds ice the puck *again*, and Brooklyn hurries to retrieve it. Miranda stays in her crease this time. Brooklyn waits behind our net until Brittni comes back for the puck and heads up the ice. I have no idea why the Hounds aren't pressuring her. I'm wide open on the wing, but Brittni tries to rush. She's forced wide in the Notre Dame end and gets rubbed out along the boards. She punches the Hound who took her out of the play, but the ref doesn't notice. Two quick passes, and the Hounds fire another shot on Miranda. She freezes the puck, and we find ourselves facing off in our own end with a minute left in Shauna's penalty.

"Who's got the *power* play?" Mr. Scott screams.

Jodi, Kathy, and Amber step on the ice, and I head for our bench.

"What the heck," Crystal says.

I realize Brittni and Cory never came off. They're going to stay out? Our lines are so messed up.

"Let's go!" Mr. Scott screams.

Brittni ignores him. Jodi stays out, but Kathy and Amber return to the bench. We're lucky we don't get a penalty for delay of game. Steve would call a timeout and put an end to this gong show, but Mr. Kowalski just looks flustered while Mr. Scott paces and waves his arms. We hang our heads.

"This is ridiculous," Kathy says.

When the linesman tosses Brittni out of the faceoff circle for a stick infraction, Jodi replaces her. She wins the draw back to Brooklyn, who takes the puck back behind our net. Two Hounds follow her. Jodi is wide open.

"Look up, Brooklyn," Kathy says between gritted teeth.

Erica goes behind the net to help Brooklyn, which leaves no one in front of the net. A Hound cross-checks Erica across the shoulder blades. She goes down hard, and the ref raises an arm. The Hounds quickly touch the puck before Miranda can skate to the bench.

"Throw 28 out!" I hear Kim' mom shout from the stands. "That's checking-from-behind!"

It feels weird to agree with her.

The ref calls cross-checking, and 28 joins Shauna in the penalty box. We're five on three. If we don't score now, we never will.

Mr. Kowalski doesn't pull Brittni and Cory off the ice, but Mr. Scott sends Jennifer and Kim to replace Erica and Brooklyn. Jodi loses the faceoff, and the Hounds' centre tries to ice the puck. Kim chops it down and passes to Jennifer, who banks it off the boards up to Jodi. Jodi makes a brilliant cross-ice, tape-to-tape pass to Cory, who catches the puck outside the Hounds' blue line. Cory goes wide of the defence and stops on the hash marks, playing keep away until everyone is set up in the Hounds' zone. It's the first time we've looked like a hockey team for the entire game.

Miranda pounds her stick to warn her teammates there's seconds remaining in Shauna's penalty. Cory cycles the puck to Brittni behind the net. Brittni tries to stuff it in through the side door, but the Hound goaltender jams her skate against the post. The ND defence gets her stick in there, and the puck pops out to Jodi in the high slot. There's nothing but bodies between her and the net, so she makes a hard, quick pass to Jennifer on the blue line. Jennifer fans on the shot and the puck dribbles down the ice.

Shauna barrels out of the penalty box, snaps up the loose puck, and storms into our zone on a breakaway. She comes in fast on Miranda and takes a high wrist shot, glove side. Scores.

What's worse than giving up a short-handed goal?

Giving up two of them.

Our dressing room is a morgue between the second and third periods. Mr. Kowalski and Mr. Scott only come in for a few minutes. I get the feeling they're afraid we're *all* going to quit if they say the wrong thing. Brittni and Cory keep us posted on what's going on in the SJHL—thanks to Snapchat—while Jodi chugs her water bottle.

I'm afraid for that girl.

In the third period, I don't play for the last fifteen minutes because I get kicked in the crotch during a scramble in front of the Hounds' net. I even throw up a little in my mouth as I head for the bench, doubled over as hot waves shoot through my pelvis. I sit and put my head between my knees, so I don't faint. Mrs. Omalu asks me a few questions but has to desert me when Crystal takes an elbow to the head and sees stars.

Amber pats my arm and murmurs, "That sucks when you get boxed. Will you be okay?"

I don't even try to croak an answer. I just want the game to be over. I don't care when Jodi dekes the goalie and scores with a lethal backhand. Whatever she's got in her water bottle doesn't seem to affect her ability to find the net.

The game ends in a 5-1 loss.

I hobble back to the dressing room, trying not to think about my you-know-what. I'm still throbbing. Greg and Jordan holler at me, but I have no idea what they're saying.

"That was a good game, if you overlook Notre Dame out-shooting us 35-14, and having almost all of the play in our end," Erica says.

Is she for real?

Brooklyn laughs. "Well, no place to go but up, right?"

"No place to go—but another *team*," Kathy says.

Kathy sounds serious. My worst fears are already coming true.

I can't get out of the dressing room fast enough, but I'm not as fast as Brittni and Cory. Obviously they've got places to be. I'm hoping to see Shauna in the hallway, but Michelle's the one waiting for me.

"Good game, Jessie. Even if you lost. Evan missed the end because he had to take Breanne home," she says.

I know she means well, but right now, I don't want to be here.

"So when you push the puck over your blue line, is that what you mean by 'clearing the puck?'" Michelle asks.

"Yes." I'm glad she's catching on, but I'm not in the mood for a game debriefing.

Mom and Dad and Courtney come over. The first words out of Courtney's mouth are, "Why didn't you play at the end of the game?"

Mom's eyes are concerned. "Did you get hurt, Jessie?"

"I don't want to talk about it."

"You held them scoreless in the third. So technically the last twenty minutes belongs to you girls," Dad observes. "Did your coaches point that out?"

I shrug. Truth is, they didn't say much. Sure Mr. Scott carried on for a while, but he didn't tell us how to fix ourselves. He just said we have to try harder next time—and get into shape. But how much will conditioning help if Brittni and Cory decide *when* and how *long* they're playing? For all his screaming, Mr. Scott never said a word to them about the lengths of their shifts.

"You'll do better in your next game," Mom says. "You girls need more practice."

I nod, but inside I'm thinking, last year we lost by a worse score, but Steve never let us feel defeated.

Dad starts up a conversation with Kathy's parents. Great.

"Can we just go home?" I beg.

"I have to go to the bathroom," Courtney says.

"I'll wait for you," Mom says.

"Give me the keys so I can take out my equipment," I say to Dad.

He hands them to me without even looking. He'll be the last one out of the rink at this rate.

When I open the door to the lobby, I can tell right away something's wrong. There's a sea of backs turned towards me, and a female voice is shouting, "Let's step outside then if you think you're so tough!"

It's Cory.

I push through the crowd. Cory, Brittni, and a pair of Notre Dame players—one of them is Shauna—stand near the exit. Cory's blocking the doors.

The Hound with short dark hair—pretty sure she's the captain—drops her equipment bag. "*I'll* step outside. And then I'll kick your ass."

"Both of you cool down," Shauna says.

The Notre Dame coach barges past me. "What's going on?" Before anyone replies, she says, "Get on the bus, Chantelle. You too, Shauna." She swings her head in Cory's direction. "Where's your coach?"

"Who cares?" Cory says disdainfully, but she steps to the side to let Shauna and the other girl walk past. "See you skanks in a couple of weeks."

The Hound captain lets loose a victory howl. I hate that sound, and I hate the way Shauna looks back at me—like she feels sorry for me—before she leaves. The Hound fans pour out the door behind her.

A clammy palm touches my neck, and I nearly jump out of my skin.

"Need a ride home?" Greg asks.

I push his hand away. "No. My parents are here."

"Tell them you're coming with us," Jordan says.

"What about Kim?" I ask Greg. "Are you giving *her* a ride?"

Greg winks. He is such a sleeze. "Not if you're coming."

"We'll be waiting outside," Jordan says.

They leave before I have a chance to tell them what I really think.

A shove from behind sends me sprawling against the pop machine. My sticks clatter on the cement, but my equipment bag stops me from falling.

"I told you to keep away from him!" Kim screams, green eyes blazing.

"Look Kim—"

"Wasn't it enough for you to steal *Mark*?!" she demands. "Now you have to take Greg away from me too?"

I wait till she's gone before I drop to one knee and pick up my sticks. When I straighten, my mom and dad are standing there. From their expressions, I know I have some explaining to do.

1 7

On Monday, Kim doesn't sit with Greg in the cafeteria. She parks herself at a table with Natalie and some other girls she hasn't hung around with for a long time. I wonder if this is a good move for her.

"Kim posted herself as #flyingsolo," Kathy says.

"About time," Erica says.

I look over at Greg. He sticks out his tongue at me and wiggles it. He makes my skin crawl.

"Pig," Miranda says.

"Loser," Teneil says.

"Tell us what happened after the game," Kathy says. "I hear Kim pushed you in the lobby."

"It's nothing," I lie. Just like I lied to my parents last night. I don't want my teammates to know that Kim blames me for breaking up with Greg. What will they think of me then? "She was upset about the loss. Took it out on me. No big deal."

Kathy's light blue eyes look unconvinced.

Our team chemistry is toxic when we host Caronport on Tuesday night. Kim won't talk to me except to insult me, so we're right back to the way things used to be. Jodi sucks on her water bottle, but still manages to score two goals without breaking a sweat. Brittni and Cory do whatever they want. They keep bugging Mr. Kowalski about our new uniforms—and lately, new jackets. My question is—who *wants* anyone to know what team we play for?

Brittni and Cory are unbearable on the bench. How can Mr. Kowalski let them tape letters on their jerseys? They're awarded points on both of Jodi's goals because they're in the ref's face, insisting they got assists.

The score's tied 2-2 when Caronport's 19 slams Amber's head into the glass, and the ref totally misses it. Player 19's looking back over her right shoulder, admiring her handiwork, so she doesn't see Kathy bearing down on her like a freight train. Kathy flattens her then salutes our bench before heading to the penalty box.

Mr. Kowalski groans.

"Nothing like a little hockey justice," Larissa says.

I think Kathy wanted an excuse to take out her frustration on someone else.

Caronport scores on the power play. Then we take a bench minor for too many players and climb on the merry-go-round of taking another penalty before we can kill the previous one. Caronport scores three more unanswered goals, and we end up losing 6-2.

"Let's face it. We're terrible," I say to Kathy when we're done shaking hands with the other team.

"You got that right," she says.

Marsha splats some whole wheat fettuccini Alfredo on my plate. "Heard you losers got slaughtered *again*."

"Uh huh."

"Who was it this time?"

"Weyburn."

We've actually lost to Weyburn *twice*—once in their rink and once in ours. I hate losing to them. I hate their snarky smiles when we shake hands after. And I hate the way everyone at the Comp—except Evan—chirps us about our losing skid. It's humiliating.

"Where're the Dino Buddies?" I ask Marsha—to change the subject.

Marsha flips a piece of garlic toast at me. "Cry your eyes out, rich girl. Your Dino Buddies are extinct. We don't make them anymore. They're not healthy enough for skinny-ass girls like you."

Crushed, I take my tray to our usual table and sit between Michelle and Miranda.

"Hello, Jessie," Michelle says.

I nod and stuff a forkful of fettuccini in my mouth.

"No more Dino Buddies," Miranda wails. "What's the world coming to?"

We eat in silence.

"Bet you're all excited about going to Swift Current this weekend," Michelle says.

Kathy gives her a sardonic smile. "The Cougars are the toughest team in our league. Are we *supposed* to be looking forward to an ass thrashing?"

"Not one little bit," I say.

"At least there'll be shopping," Teneil says.

"Mom and I are going to Swift on Friday after school for that very reason," I say. "We'll hit the mall on Saturday morning."

"What about Little Mac?" Kathy asks.

"She's staying home with Dad so she can go trick-or-treating." A memory from last year swims to the surface—me getting picked up by the cops in Bienfait on Halloween. Even losing to the Cougars won't be as bad as that.

"Remember I'm coming too," Michelle says.

I look at her. "You are?"

"Your mom asked me," Michelle says. "Didn't she tell you?"

Kathy raises a blonde eyebrow at me.

"Never mind," I mouth back at her. "Sounds good," I say to Michelle.

Mr. Scott tries to bag skate us at Thursday practice, but the more he yells, the slower we skate. Jennifer hasn't been to practice since before our home opener, and Jodi only comes when she feels like it, which isn't much. After practice, Brittni gives a long speech about team spirit and positivity, as if she deserves to wear the C. Brittni and Cory are anything *but* positive. Nobody has any fun in the dressing room or on the ice.

"Where's Jennifer anyway?" Cory asks, eyes glued to her phone.

"Why don't you text her and ask?" Kathy says.

"She's not *my* friend," Cory replies. "And another thing. Why aren't we taking a bus to Swift Current?" She glares at Kathy. "I thought your *dad* was getting us one."

"He's still working on it." Kathy looks uncomfortable.

"I'd rather drive myself," Brittni says.

Cory turns to Kim. "I got a question for you too. Your dad is supposed to be a good coach?"

Kim swears and storms out.

None of us—not even Kathy—stand up to Cory. It's not worth the effort. We all undress as quick as we can and get out of there. Something needs to change—and fast—or we won't have a team after Christmas.

At lunch on Friday, Brittni comes over to our table to announce she isn't coming to Swift Current. Cory neither. They have other important plans—a Bruin game and a Halloween party. What's even more interesting is Brittni doesn't want our coaches to know they're not coming. She thinks this'll be "payback" for the way Mr. Kowalski and Mr. Scott have been "screwing over" the vets.

"How are *they* getting screwed over?" I ask as I watch Brittni saunter back to her table. "The coaches give them whatever they want."

"Yep," Miranda says.

"Should I let Amber know they're not coming?" I look around at everyone. "She'll tell her dad."

"Do you *want* Mr. Kowalski to put up a fuss and make Brittni and Cory come along? Because I sure as hell don't," Kathy says.

"Good point," Teneil says.

"I'll bet we'll have more fun without them," Michelle says.

Everybody looks at her then at me. Cut her some slack, I think.

"I sure hope so," I say.

Mom and I sit in the front seat of the Explorer on the way to Swift Current while Michelle chatters away in the back. Mom holds up the other end of the conversation while I pretend to sleep. I never knew Michelle had so many opinions and ideas on so many things. She must be making up for those junior high years of having no one to talk to.

After Mom checks us into our room, we order pizza and head down to the pool to get in a quick swim.

"There's a rule about curfew on the night before a game," I tell Michelle, "but for the life of me, I can't remember what it is."

Mr. Kowalski, Amber, and Kim show up. Amber's excited about our first overnight road trip, but Kim hardly says a word. She slides into the pool, still wearing her T-shirt, and starts swimming laps while Michelle, Amber, and I lounge in the hot tub. Mr. Kowalski sits at a table and marks a stack of science tests. Sucks to be a teacher sometimes.

"Does your dad know Brittni and Cory aren't coming?" I ask Amber.

Her big blue eyes get bigger. "Are you sure?"

"Brittni told us at lunch today," Michelle affirms.

It bugs me the way Michelle inserts herself in the middle of "team business," but I let it go. "Where's Mr. Scott?" I ask Amber.

"He had to work, I guess. Last minute thing," Amber says.

"Lucky us," I breathe.

"Dad asked someone else to help coach."

My ears perk up. "Who?"

"Sue Hannah. She works at SaskPower," Amber explains.

"So does my dad. Funny he's never mentioned her," I reply. "Did she play hockey?"

"Pretty sure she did, or my dad wouldn't have asked her," Amber says.

"I'll bet she'll make a great coach then," Michelle says.

"Just because she's played hockey doesn't mean she knows how to coach," I say.

The only coach you want is Steve, my little voice says.

You got that right.

While Michelle and Amber babble away, I watch Kim swim laps in the pool. She butterflies from one end to the other, pushes off the wall, and drives back. Maybe this would be a good time to try and work things out with her—before the rest of the girls arrive. I don't want to have another year with her like the last one.

I sit cross-legged at the deep end and wait for her. She's doing a backstroke now, her legs rarely breaking the surface, her arm movements crisp and controlled. I don't move when she reaches the wall, and her hand brushes my foot. She turns onto her stomach and grabs the edge then wipes the wet hair from her face.

"Hi Kim."

She pushes away from edge and treads water.

"Look, I'm sorry about whatever happened between you and Greg."

She glares at me.

"I also want you to know I had nothing to do with it."

"You're lying." She's panting, and I don't think it has anything to do with exerting herself in the pool. "You can't keep your hands off my boyfriends, can you?"

"Kim, please listen."

"You're going out with Greg," she says.

"No, I'm not."

"He says you are."

"He's lying."

"Whatever." She swears at me under her breath.

I can't believe this is happening again. "I'll talk to you about this some other time. I'm obviously just upsetting you."

I start to stand up, and that's when I notice something strange about her left leg. Lines ripple along the top of her thigh. At first I think the fluorescent lights have created shadows, but then I notice the colours. Some are thin and dark red. Some are wide and pink. Why haven't I noticed them before?

Because Kim never showers with the team, my little voice says. She's always in a hurry to get out of the dressing room. And here I thought it was because of the cracks Cory and Brittni make about her dad.

"Kim, what happened to you?" I ask. "Did you hurt yourself?"

Kim swims for the ladder and climbs out, yanking down the hem of her T-shirt. I hurry towards her.

"Those look like cuts."

"Never mind." She pushes past me.

"Kim, what's going on?"

She turns and jams a finger in my face. "Don't you tell anyone about this," she hisses. "Not anyone—understand?" She swears at me again, grabs a towel and exits the pool area without looking back.

I walk back to the chairs where Michelle, Amber, and Mr. Kowalski are watching me.

"What happened over there?" he asks.

I shrug in what I hope is a convincing way. "Kim's just tired—and so am I. I'm going to bed."

As I head up to our room, I don't know if I'm shivering because I'm wet and cold—or because I'm scared. Scared *for* someone I used to be scared *of*.

18

I HARDLY SLEEP THAT NIGHT. Of course it doesn't help that I have to share a bed with Michelle. She snores, farts and cuddles—a deadly combination. I keep seeing those cuts and Kim's angry—or was it panicked—face. What if I'm overreacting?

The image of those thin red lines, dozens of them, makes me shudder. There's no way I'm overreacting. Kim is cutting herself. And I'm part of the reason. First Mark. Now Greg. She must hate my guts.

A girl in my old elementary school cut herself, so I know a little about it. Our teacher said the kids who do it are unhappy with themselves and need some way to deal with it. I didn't understand it then, and I still don't. But I *do* know Kim's the most insecure person I've ever met. Still there's no way I'd tell anybody without Kim's permission. Not after all the stuff that's happened between us.

I make up my mind to get her alone and convince her to talk to somebody who can help. Which brings me to the next question. Talk to who? It's a question that keeps me awake half the night.

The next thing I know Michelle's standing over me, fully dressed. "Hey, it's 8:30. Your mom's already downstairs. Do you want to grab breakfast and go shopping? Or are you sleeping in?"

I drag myself out of bed and shower. We eat breakfast at the hotel restaurant—with no sign of Amber, Kim or Mr. Kowalski.

After a morning of shopping and lunch at Boston Pizza, we hang out in the hotel room for a few hours. I sneak in a short nap, so I'm feeling better by the time we eat our pre-game meal and head to the rink. We get to play our games at the same rink where the Swift Current Broncos, the city's WHL team, play. It's the biggest and nicest arena I've ever played in.

Not that I'm in a state of mind to enjoy it. My stomach has been tying itself in knots all day at the thought of talking to Kim. I'm also nervous about taking on the Cougars, who are currently tied with Notre Dame for first place. According to their stats, the Cougars have two of the league's top three scorers.

As soon as we walk in the rink lobby, I notice a tall, athletic-looking woman with short, blonde hair. Her broad shoulders and thighs make her look like a hockey player. Mr. Kowalski goes over to her and talks to her for a bit, then gestures to us.

"This is Sue Hannah," he says.

Sue shakes hands with us while he makes the introductions.

Michelle gets right down to business. "Where did you play university hockey?"

"Minnesota," Sue says.

"Do you have any coaching experience?" Michelle asks.

I'm so embarrassed. "Michelle!"

Sue raises an eyebrow. "Is this a job interview?"

"Of course not. We're glad you came along this weekend," my mom tells Sue. "Aren't we, Jessie?"

I mumble an appropriate reply.

"I was here on business yesterday, so it was no trouble," Sue says. "And, yes, I do have experience. I was an assistant coach at Grand Forks while I was doing a Masters in Engineering. Do I meet the minimum requirement for U18 girls?" Her tone is sarcastic.

"I guess," I tell her.

Sue turns to Michelle. "Do you play hockey too?"

"No," Michelle says. "I just hang out with Jessie."

"Good for you," Sue says. "Hockey wouldn't be much fun without fans."

When she leaves, Mom says, "She seems nice."

"We are really lucky she agreed to help out this weekend," Mr. Kowalski says.

I think I can read his thoughts. Maybe she can help him get this train wreck of a team under control. I'm not sure anyone can do that.

"Nice isn't the word I would use to describe her," I tell her. "She never smiled once. Did you notice that?"

"Maybe she's not a smiley person," Michelle says.

Yeah, and she isn't Steve either.

♥

The pre-game atmosphere in the dressing room is more relaxed without Brittni and Cory. Miranda throws on some music. Teneil dances on the bench because she doesn't trust us around her bare feet. Not that I blame her. If I had to miss a month's worth of games, I'd feel the same way.

Jodi does a cartwheel in full gear. We don't encourage her to do any more tricks because she's chugging on her water bottle.

"You need to talk to her," Jennifer whispers in my ear. "She shouldn't play if she's been drinking."

"Why me?" I whisper back. "We're not exactly friends anymore."

"Well, talk to Mr. Kowalski then," Jennifer says.

"Not my problem." I'd like to tell her I've got enough issues with girls on this team without adding Jodi to the list.

Kim says nothing. She's always been moody, so no one but me seems to pay any attention to her. I'm pretty sure she's pissed because of what I saw last night. She's been avoiding me ever since. I try not to stare at her as she puts on her gear. She wears long nylon shorts and a long-sleeved shirt.

She meets my gaze and snaps, "Are you creeping on me or what?"

I clear my throat. "I was wondering if that shirt is designed for heat or cold."

Kim narrows her eyes.

My question sparks a discussion on the desirability of wicking away moisture and retaining warmth to increase muscle efficiency.

Kim eventually adds a few comments of her own, and I pretend to look interested. But inside I'm wondering—Kim, how am I going to help you?

I've been pondering my course of action all day. I can't go behind her back. I've got to get her alone sometime and convince her to talk to somebody she trusts. But who will that person be?

Her mom or dad? Hell no. They're part of the problem.

Mr. Kowalski? Not likely. Kim doesn't respect him.

Sue Hannah? No. Didn't know Sue existed until yesterday.

Mrs. Omalu? Maybe.

I need someone to come with me when I talk to Kim—someone Kim doesn't hate. Maybe if there's two of us, she won't punch me out.

After careful consideration, I choose Larissa, who is caring and level-headed. Also, since her dad's a doctor, maybe we can convince Kim to talk to *him* about her cutting. Everybody loves Dr. Bilku. He's so funny, especially when he says stuff like, "Don't be afraid to get in their kitchen, girls. Turn up the heat!" This means I need to talk to Larissa first. There's got to be a minute when I can get her alone.

Mr. Kowalski, Sue, and Mrs. Omalu walk into the dressing room. Teneil fades out the music, and we slap on our game faces. Sue doesn't say a word while Mr. Kowalski gives his pre-game talk, but I feel her eyes measuring us. Does she think we're worthy of her precious time? If not, I could care less. We don't need a coach with a superiority complex.

Mr. Kowalski says Kim's going to play with Erica, and Jennifer's going to play with Brooklyn. The older girls are stricken by the news of their divorce.

"But Coach," Erica protests, "I've played with Brooklyn my whole life. I don't know if I can play with anybody else."

Mr. Kowalski says, "We're up against one of the best teams in the league, Erica. We need to capitalize on your experience, so we're going to share it with the younger girls. What do you say?"

I can tell Erica doesn't buy his excuse. "Aw, Coach," she says, "we both know that's not true."

"I'm okay with Jennifer," Brooklyn says. "Somebody's gotta compensate for her speed."

"Kathy, tape on a C," Mr. Kowalski says. "Kim, Jennifer, and Jodi are wearing A's."

I catch Larissa on the way out of the dressing room. "We need to talk."

"What about?" she asks.

"Later," I tell her.

Shuffling the defence seems to help. Because they're slow skaters, Brooklyn and Erica are better suited as stay-at-home D. This allows Jennifer and Kim to generate some offence. Sometimes too *much* offence.

Early in the game, Jodi's wide open, but Kim puts her head down and tries to stickhandle between the Cougar D. One of them poke-checks the puck up to her centre, who blows by Erica like she's duct-taped to the ice and rips a slapshot over Miranda's glove. Sue, who's running the defence, doesn't say anything to Kim. Instead she gives Kim a pat on the helmet when she comes off.

We get through the first period with only one penalty, and we kill it without giving up a power play goal. Kim and Jennifer stay out the entire time while Larissa, Jodi, Kathy, Crystal, and I rotate on the front end. The Cougars only get three shots on net.

I'm pumped when I come off the ice, but I can tell Teneil isn't pleased about missing her shift. Mr. Kowalski sends Amber and Teneil out right away, which is a good thing because Larissa and I are gasping for air. Jodi looks even worse. Maybe the partying has caught up to her.

One of the Cougars takes a cross-checking penalty against Amber in the neutral zone, and Mr. Kowalski throws Jodi, Larissa, and me out with Kim and Jennifer for the power play.

When Jodi won't put her stick on the ice, the lineman tosses her out of the faceoff circle, and I replace her. I've taken a handful of draws in my short hockey career, and though I lose this one too, I manage to tie up the Cougar centre. As Jodi pokes the puck free and makes a rush, I follow her up the ice. Then she flicks the biscuit between her skates—as slick a back-pass as I've ever seen. Since she's screening the goalie, I move across, turn, and fire the puck, low blocker.

It's in!

"Way to go, Jessie Mac!" Jodi screams through her mouth guard, pounding me on the shoulders.

It's the first time we've touched each other since June, and I think, maybe I've finally put that night behind me. As I soar past the Xtreme bench, slapping outstretched gloves, I feel like I've conquered the world.

Mr. Kowalski sends Amber, Crystal, and Teneil for the remaining thirty seconds. Erica conveniently falls in the path of the Cougar captain and takes her out of the play. We head to the dressing room tied up 1-1.

Sue doesn't say a word while Mr. Kowalski gives us positive feedback. I wish she would say something—especially to our defence who could use some constructive criticism. Right now a wrong decision could cost us the game.

Then Mr. Kowalski says, "Sue, do you have anything to add?"

Sue clears her throat. "I know you girls are learning certain systems, and I don't want to interfere. But keep your heads up and look for somebody to be open. Jessie, for instance, is playing conservatively. But good job on that goal. See what happens when you finally decide to get off the boards and jump into the play?"

I'm dumbfounded. I scored an important power play goal. Was she criticizing me?

"Don't trip on that bottom lip," Kathy says, as we head out for the second period.

"I'm not pouting," I reply.

"Right," she says.

The Cougars hit the ice hard and set us on our heels. We see only their top lines for the first few minutes, but Mr. Kowalski keeps rolling all of ours. It's a battle to move the play out of our end. Finally Teneil chips the puck past a Cougar D, and Jodi jumps on it, exploding to top speed in a few strides. She drives for the net, and the Cougar goalie leaves her crease to cut down the angles. Jodi fakes right, and the goalie goes with her, opening her legs. Jodi pulls the trigger and scores, five-hole.

We are now one goal up on a team we don't deserve to be beating. The momentum of Jodi's goal carries us through the next ten minutes. We forecheck and backcheck like crazy. Maybe *too* crazy because we end up defending a five-on-three after Kathy takes a roughing penalty, and Kim gets called for hooking one minute into the PK.

Mr. Kowalski calls the referee over and questions him about Kim's penalty. It gives us a few more seconds to rest. Sue walks to our end of the bench and leans over my shoulder. "You're going out there on D, Jessie. Keep them outside the hashmarks and you'll be okay."

Is she *nuts*?

That's how I find myself playing defence for the first time in my life with a minute left in a two-man disadvantage. It's just me, Jodi, Jennifer and Miranda out there to defend our flimsy lead. My stomach flips over, and my heart hammers in my ears as I line up in front of Miranda. She taps the back of my legs with her stick in support. I *have* to do this.

Jodi loses the faceoff. The Cougar centre rips one at our net, but Miranda's blocker deflects the puck into the corner. Jennifer dives in and battles with two Cougars, pinning the puck against the boards. The ref finally blows down the play, and we line up. Mr. Kowalski calls Jodi off, and Crystal takes her place.

The puck drops, and we're defending again.

With forty seconds left in Kathy's penalty, we keep battling. Crystal jumps into the passing lane between two Cougars and tips the puck out over our blue line, forcing the Cougars to leave our zone. One of the Cougar defence carries the puck back in, but I force her wide and her wrist shot bounces off the glass.

Jennifer beats the Cougar centre to the puck and rings it around the boards to me. I manage to ice the puck. The Cougars hurry back to set up again, and all three of us bail, with fresh horses coming in the form of Larissa, Brooklyn, and Erica.

I wonder about the wisdom of this combination, but Mr. Kowalski and Sue have no choice. The three Xtreme clash along the boards—lifting sticks, fighting for body position, grinding it out. Erica, who normally can't shoot the puck from one end of the ice to the other, catches a lucky break when she steps on 12's stick and goes down, drawing a tripping penalty.

While 12 argues with the linesperson all the way to the penalty box, Mr. Kowalski sends Jodi, Jennifer, and me back out. We are now three defending against four, but the faceoff is outside our zone with seconds left in Kathy's penalty.

Jodi wins the puck back to Jennifer, who ices it on a high, hard wrist shot. Miranda pounds the ice with her stick while Kathy leaves the box with rested legs, and we are four-on-four. Kathy forechecks hard behind the Cougar net, intercepting a pass between the two defence and slinging the puck to Jodi who's moved down low. Jodi fakes a shot and passes back to me at the Cougar blue line. Trying to shake off the left winger, I move to the middle and shoot the puck to the right of the net. Kathy picks it up and fires it back to Jodi, whose quick shot hits the goalie right in the chest. The goalie falls on the puck, freezing it. Jodi is right on her but takes a punishing cross-check from one of the Cougar D.

The whistle blows. Kathy skates over to the ref and angles for a Cougar penalty, but he backs away, shaking his head. Go figure.

There's only fifteen seconds left in Kim's penalty and with any luck we'll hold off the Cougars long enough to enjoy a one-player advantage for the last minute of the period.

The doors of our player box open, and Teneil, Amber, Erica, and Brooklyn take our spots at the faceoff dot. At this point I don't know whether it's better to be on the bench watching or on the ice.

The Xtreme dukes it out in the neutral zone until Kim's penalty elapses. Kim skates to our bench, and Jodi jumps on the ice. She picks up the puck on the Cougar side of the red line and fires it in deep, giving Erica and Brooklyn time to come off. Kim and Jennifer take up the defensive positions.

Teneil arrives at the puck right on the heels of 16. She flails at it while 16 shuffles it along the boards with her feet. Another Cougar jumps in to help her teammate. Teneil fishes the puck to Amber, who takes a shot. The goalie makes a stick save, and the puck rebounds to Jodi. She fires it in, blocker side, and our bench and fans erupt with cheers. Soon we head to the dressing room with a two-goal lead.

"We've got them on the ropes now." Larissa gives me a nudge. "What did you want to talk to me about?"

Before I can answer, Jennifer jumps us from behind, wrapping her sweaty arms around our sweaty necks. "Sue's a *huge* improvement over Mr. Scott, huh? What can we do to get her on the bench full-time?"

"I like her too." Larissa cranes her head towards me. "So what's up, Mac?"

"Nothing." Nothing I'm going to discuss in front of Jennifer.

"So what were you doing on D?" Kim says behind me.

I stop and pull away from Larissa and Jennifer.

"It was Sue's call," I tell her.

Kim snorts. "Doesn't she know better than to put you back there when we're short-handed?"

"I don't know *what* she knows," I say to Kim. "It worked out okay, didn't it?"

I want to tell her I loved playing back there. I want to tell her how good it felt to make things happen, instead of waiting or hoping they would. But there's no point.

"Maybe next time we won't be so lucky when you screw up."

"Me screw up?" I say. "*You're* one to talk! *You're* the one who's screwed up!"

Kim grabs me by the collar, throwing me off balance. She's still wearing her gloves, so her grip isn't great. "You don't know anything about me! For the last time, leave me alone!"

Her shove sends me reeling. Larissa and Jennifer grab for me, but I hit the rubber mat hard. Kim walks away without a backward glance. As the girls help me up, I wonder how I could be so stupid.

"What's going on between you and Kim?" Larissa asks.

"Yeah, what's *with* her?" Jennifer says, straightening my jersey.

By this time, Mr. Kowalski, Mrs. Omalu, and Sue show up, and I'm too busy covering up for Kim to explain anything to the girls.

One thing's for sure.

Kim needs someone to help her, and I'm obviously not the person for the job.

19

WE BEAT THE COUGARS 3-2, which makes our dressing room a happier place than it's been in weeks. That is, if you don't count the fact Kim won't talk to me or look at me. I opt to go back to our hotel room after we eat, instead of hanging out with the other girls before curfew.

I can tell Larissa and Jennifer are dying to get me alone and find out what's going on, but I don't dare make things any worse than I already have. No use now to try to get Kim help through Larissa. I'm over my head.

Mom tells me to call Dad and share the good news about the Xtreme's first win of the season—and my first goal.

Dad's pumped. "I wish I'd been there. Tell me exactly how it happened."

I do, but my heart isn't in it. I keep picturing those cuts on Kim's thigh and wondering what the hell I'm going to do about them.

After I hang up, I say, "I think I'm coming down with something. I'm going to bed early tonight."

"Good idea," Mom says. "Do you mind if I don't stay with you? Some of the parents are getting together for a few drinks to celebrate."

I know what that means. Hours and hours of discussion about the future of our team. One win and we're on our way to winning the league championship.

Hockey parents.

Michelle opts to stay with me in the room.

"You can hang out with the girls," I tell her. "They won't mind."

"I'd rather not," Michelle says.

I fall asleep listening to her talk about an upcoming piano recital.

Our Sunday afternoon game against Swift Current is nothing to call Dad about. Miranda lets in a weak shot in the first minute of play. Another goes in off Jennifer's skate, and a third on 17's breakaway. It's a tough job to dig ourselves out of that deficit, and predictably, we don't. We score two goals late in the second, but it's not enough to counteract the Cougar offensive juggernaut. They win 7-2.

Kim glares at me in the dressing room, but at least she doesn't say anything.

Mr. Kowalski and Sue tell us we played well, we never gave up trying, and all that jazz. I have a feeling Sue would like to tell us a great deal more, but she doesn't.

We give Crystal and her mom a ride back to Estevan. At least Michelle can talk to Crystal for five hours, so I don't have to say anything. The two of them maintain a steady stream of chatter as soon as they climb in our SUV. Crystal's happier after our loss than she was after our win. Is it because she got a point in Game Two? It's funny what makes some people happy.

All I want is to crawl into my own bed. Two nights of sleeping with Michelle is enough to drive anybody crazy.

"Do you think Sue'll coach us again sometime?" Crystal asks me.

"I have no idea." I close my eyes and rest my head on the pillow tucked against the window.

"I hope so. I think you girls played better for her. What do you think?" Mom asks Mrs. Jordan.

Crystal's mom should get a medal for tact. "I think the girls finally got it together. I hope they skate like that when we play Davidson next weekend."

Crystal says, "I hope Jodi comes."

"Maybe Jodi's turning over a new leaf," Mom says.

I seriously doubt it.

"Kim was quiet today," Crystal says.

I bite the insides of my cheeks and keep my big mouth shut.

2 0

"SO, YOU FINALLY WON A GAME." Marsha slops mac and cheese on my plate. "That's precious, rich girl."

I take the plate from her, ignoring the cheese sauce dripping over the edge. "Wow, Marsha, you're really following the team. I scored a goal too. Do you want my autograph?"

"I want your skinny ass outta here. Next!"

The girls at our table get a big kick out of my daily tussle with Marsha.

"She's trying to bond with you," Kathy teases.

"She's trying to remind me we'll never move in the same social circles," I counter. "Not that I mind."

"Anybody hear how Brittni and Cory took the news?" Teneil asks. "They gotta be ticked they weren't there for the win."

We look at Brittni's table where she's in deep conversation with Jodi. I wonder what kind of spin Jodi's put on the weekend. Kim walks past us, heading straight for the table where Natalie and her gang sit.

"Do you think Kim has any real friends?" Teneil asks.

"Nope," Miranda says.

"Has anybody else noticed those cuts on Kim's legs?" Kathy asks.

I drop my fork.

"Yeah." Miranda pinches her chin between thumb and forefinger." How long do you think she's been doing *that*?"

Just like that, everybody's looking at me.

"What?" I put on what I hope is an innocent expression. This is not playing out the way I'd pictured. "Why are you looking at *me*?"

Erica raises the eyebrow that's pierced. "Why'd she shove you after Game One in Swift Current?"

"She shoves me once a week," I tell her. "I'm starting to look forward to it."

"Oh no, you don't." Brooklyn shakes a long finger at me. "There's something you're not telling us."

Why should it surprise me Kathy and Miranda noticed the cuts? The girls notice *everything*. If one of us gets a new highlight or top, or glances sideways at a guy sitting at the next table, they always see it. However, the school cafeteria is not the place I'm getting into this. Not with Michelle joining us any minute.

I take a deep breath. "I don't know any more than you do."

"We should get together after school and talk about it," Kathy says.

"Let's meet at my place," Teneil says.

I take a quick look at Kim's table. "I don't think I can make it."

"You afraid of Kim?" Miranda asks, poking me in the arm.

"Yes!"

"Hello, gals," Brittni says behind me.

I don't turn around, but I can see the tension in everyone's faces.

"So Jodi managed to pull off a win for you," Brittni says. "Good thing she was along for the ride."

"Are you and Cory coming to Davidson on Saturday?" Kathy asks.

Brittni shrugs. "Not sure. The Bruins are playing in Melville on Saturday night, so we might go there. Jodi's thinking about coming too."

"Have fun," Kathy says.

"See you later," Brittni says.

When she's gone, Teneil folds her arms on the table and lays her head on them. "If Jodi doesn't come, Davidson's going to waste us."

"Maybe so," says Kathy, "but there's no way I'm begging anybody."

I push my tray into the center of the table. "We can't depend on them. Sooner or later, we've got to get used to playing without them."

"Jessie's right," Miranda says, "I'd rather lose without them than win *with* them."

"That's easy to say now—when you're not having your asses handed to you," Kathy points out. "If we only win one game this year, you're gonna feel differently later."

"Do you think Jodi took all the credit for us beating the Cougars?" Brooklyn asks.

"Jodi's not like that. Brittni was blowing smoke," I say.

"Who knows what Jodi's like anymore? She's sure not like she used to be." Kathy looks over our heads. "Incoming."

"Hey, what's happening?" Michelle stands next to me, holding her lunch tray.

"You can have my seat, Michelle. I'm going to the library." Miranda picks up her own tray and pushes her chair back.

"I'm coming too," Teneil says.

"Then you have to let me study," Miranda says. "If I don't get a good mark on this test, my mom will ground me."

After they leave, Michelle sits and prattles to us about jazz band. I can tell everyone's minds are elsewhere—thinking about what's going down with Kim and Jodi and the others.

Kathy picks up her tray. "See you at Teneil's later?"

I shrug.

Before long, it's just Michelle and me. The same thing's happened before, and I know it's time to talk to Michelle about listening more and talking less when she's around my teammates. But not today. I've got more on my plate than mac and cheese.

Michelle steps all over my heels when I run into Evan on my way out of the cafeteria. "I didn't see you in homeroom," I say.

"I had a basketball meeting," he replies. "Heard you girls beat Swift Current on the weekend. That's great."

"Thanks." I start to move away from him.

"When do you play at the Blue Goose again?" he asks. "I'll come watch."

I give him the details about our next home game and make a quick exit, feeling guilty but relieved.

"He likes you, Jessie," Michelle says. "Why don't you go out with him?"

"*His* mom and *my* mom work together. It's easier if we stay friends. And it bugs me that Mom thinks it's okay for me to go out with him even though he's the same age as Mark. She always said Mark was too old for me. Does that make sense to you?"

"No," Michelle says.

She follows me to my locker.

"So what's happening with Kim?" she asks. "Is she still mad at you?"

"I don't want to talk about it," I tell her.

At 3:30, I retrieve my backpack from my locker and start for the foyer where Erica and Brooklyn will be waiting for me.

"Hey, Jessie! Wait up!"

It's Greg. I'll try to lose him in the crowd surging towards the stairwell. With all the noise around me, I can pretend I don't hear him. Then his big hand's on my shoulder, pulling me back. Tough to ignore that.

"What's your hurry?"

I face him, backing towards the lockers to avoid the jostling crowd.

"I don't want to miss my ride." I pull off my backpack and hug it against my chest, trying to create some personal space.

"I'll give you a ride," he says. "Where do you need to go?"

"Never mind." I pretend to look for something in my backpack.

"Heard you girls won a game," he says. "Good for you."

"Thanks."

He inches closer. "You heard Kim and me broke up, right?"

I'm wearing my team jacket and a hoodie, and the heat is stifling. I need fresh air. "That doesn't have anything to do with me."

"Oh yes, it does," Greg says. "Let me tell you how much."

My stomach turns over. "Kim's a friend. I've already made her unhappy enough."

"Kim's pathetic." Greg leans in. "And she's no friend of yours."

"Did you know she *cuts* herself?"

He raises a thick eyebrow. "So she scratches herself with a paper clip. You're making a big deal out of nothing."

My heart wants to leap out of my chest. "How can you say that? Don't you care about her?"

"Kim's a drama queen. She just wants attention."

"Well, she's got my attention. Do her parents know what a *loser* you are?"

As I push past him and hurry away, I concentrate on my feet, so I don't trip over them. I need to talk to someone right now. And the only person I can imagine understanding is Mom.

21

ERICA AND BROOKLYN AREN'T HAPPY about dropping me off at the Civic Auditorium, where Courtney has figure skating practice, instead of taking me to Teneil's as planned.

"Text everybody and tell them I've got a family emergency," I explain, as I climb out of the backseat of Erica's green Sunfire. "That's what phones are for, right? Relaying important information?"

"Kathy's gonna lose it," Brooklyn says.

"Jessie, you need to tell us what's going on between you and Kim," Erica says.

"It'll have to wait until later." I grab my backpack and close the door. Much later, I think as I watch them drive away.

The Civic's lobby is deserted, if I don't count the little girls playing hide-and-seek under the tables. I walk straight through the doors leading to the ice surface and the dressing rooms.

Skating lessons are underway. I spot Courtney in the farthest group, working on her lutz. Her bright green sweater's a giveaway. She spots me and waves her little white mittens. I wave back. Mom sits in the stands with some of the other moms.

"Hi, Jessie." Mom looks startled but pleased. "I wasn't expecting you."

One of the moms says, "Congratulations on your goal this weekend. Your mother was just telling us about it."

I blush. I can imagine what she's been saying.

"Haven't seen you much this year," another says. "How're things going at ECS?"

I make small talk for a while. They were all so nice to me last year when I used to hang out at Courtney's figure skating practices to avoid running into Marsha.

"Mom, can I talk to you alone for a minute?" I ask when there's a lull.

"Must be a boy," one of the moms says and they all laugh.

Mom turns to one of the moms. "If Courtney comes off the ice, tell her I'll be right back." She shoulders her purse and follows me up the steps to the concourse.

Mom sets her purse on the rail and leans against it. "So, what's up?"

I explain what's going down with Kim, starting with my discovery in the hotel pool at Swift Current and concluding with my encounter with Greg. I don't tell her what went down with Jodi last June, or Greg hitting on me. Mom presses her hand over her mouth and stares, wide-eyed, the whole time.

"He never cared about her, Mom. I don't know if anybody does. She's really unhappy. I'm worried about what else she might do to herself."

"Jessie, this is terrible," she says. "And she's taking her anger out on you too." She covers one of my hands with hers. "Your dad and I didn't see what happened after that Notre Dame game, but—"

"This isn't about me, Mom," I interrupt. "What do we do about Kim?"

"We need to talk to the Scotts. Whatever we think of them, they're still her parents." Mom rubs her forefinger across her lower lip, considering. "They're not the most approachable people."

She takes out her phone and texts Mrs. Omalu to get Mrs. Scott's cell number. Her call goes straight to Mrs. Scott's voice mail.

"Kim's brother might be having hockey practice at the Blue Goose," I say.

"Why don't we check?" Mom suggests.

The other rink is a five-minute walk across the street and parking lot and through the Leisure Centre.

"What if she's not here?" I ask, quickening my pace to keep up with Mom.

"Then I'll call her again." Mom says, her breath coming faster.

When we reach the Blue Goose, there's no sign of Mrs. Scott at ice level, but her son's team is practising. I recognize their coach, who goes to our church.

"I'll check upstairs." Mom heads for the door leading to the viewing area above the north end of the rink.

I decide to wait in the lobby. Mrs. Scott doesn't have any use for me since Kim and I were suspended for fighting last year. When Mom called Mrs. Scott to find out what was going on, Kim's mom blew a gasket. She threatened to turn her lawyer on us. When Mom explained she worked for the same lawyer, Mrs. Scott hung up. To my knowledge, that's the last time Mrs. Scott has exchanged words of any kind with my family.

Mom comes back a few seconds later. "She's not up there," she says, looking frustrated. "One of the moms told me she left a while ago, but she doesn't know where she went."

It's hard to imagine Mrs. Scott not sitting up there, watching the drills and finding something to complain about.

Then Mrs. Scott walks through the entrance to the parking lot, clutching her phone to her ear. She doesn't even acknowledge us as she breezes past and heads for the washroom. She disappears inside, still talking. Mom looks at me and shrugs.

"Good luck," I say. "There's no way I should go in there."

Mom takes a deep breath and follows her. When neither one of them come out after a few minutes, I take it as a good sign. Part of me wants to peek, but I know it's better to buy a bottle of water and wait. I dig through my pockets and scrounge up enough change for the machine, which promptly eats all my money without spitting out a bottle of water or a Gatorade or anything else no matter what button I push. So much for that.

Dying of curiosity, I place my ear against the washroom door. I can't hear anything because three little boys barrel in from the Leisure Centre and start playing monkey in the middle with a toque. Just when I'm about to freak on them, the door opens, and I nearly fall into Mrs. Scott. She gives me a vacant look then heads straight for the ice surface.

"Mom?" I open the door wider and look inside the washroom.

She's leaning against a sink and staring at the mirror like she doesn't recognize her own reflection.

"What happened, Mom? What did she say?"

"Not much. It wasn't exactly the reaction I was expecting."

I let the door close behind me.

"I changed things up," Mom says. "I told her I saw the cuts myself at the pool. That way she wasn't getting the story third-hand. I explained how concerned I was about Kim. I never said anything about Greg. I asked her to talk to Kim about it, tell her how worried you and I are about her. You should have seen her,

Jessie. When I said the word 'cuts,' her face . . . collapsed. I asked her if I could call her later tonight, and she said she'd appreciate that."

"Wow." I lean against the door, then jump aside when I feel it start to open. A little hand dangling a toque appears. "I'm gonna throw it in here!" a voice taunts. "You're gonna have to go in the ladies' room!"

The toque drops on the floor, and the hand is withdrawn. A big tussle, punctuated with loud squeals, begins on the other side of the door. I lean hard against it to prevent the three rink rats from spilling into the room.

Mom doesn't say anything. She isn't looking in the mirror anymore. She's looking straight down, shaking her head.

"Mom, what's wrong?"

"Jessie, if you were *really* unhappy, you'd tell me, wouldn't you?" Her voice breaks a little, and I know she's fighting tears.

"Yes."

"Because you didn't last year. How do I know if you—"

"I'm fine, Mom."

For the first time in a long time, I believe it. I am fine. Compared to Kim, my life is damn good.

Mom glances at her phone. "We'd better go see how your sister's doing. I didn't expect to be gone this long."

"Sure." I step away from the door, and the rink rats fall into the room. They freeze—eyes and mouths wide. Then one of them scoops up the toque and, waving it over his head like a trophy, bolts through the door, his buddies in hot pursuit.

"I'll say one thing," Mom says to me as we leave the washroom. "Life was simpler when all I had to worry about was stopping you from shoving peas up your nose."

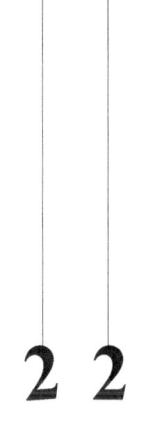

22

My mom calls Mrs. Scott on Monday night, but there's no answer. Miranda, Kathy and Teneil text me, begging for details on Kim, but I don't tell them anything, afraid I'll make things worse.

On Tuesday morning, I steer clear of the ECS courtyard. In ELA, I tell Michelle I'm not eating lunch in the cafeteria. In homeroom, Evan asks about our weekend in Swift Current. He's such a good listener, I end up telling him more than I'd planned though I don't say anything about Kim.

"Sounds like you finally got yourselves a coach," he says.

"We *had* a coach," I tell him. "Sue's never going to be as good as Steve."

"Stop living in the past, Jessie," Evan says.

Easy for him to say.

Kim isn't at practice Tuesday night. Neither is her dad.

"Kim wasn't at school today," Miranda says while she's pulling on her jersey. "Do *you* know why?"

"No." I don't consider it a lie. I really don't know.

"I've been texting her all day, but she doesn't respond," Kathy says. "She's as hard to get hold of as Jessie is." She looks at me pointedly.

"Where is Mr. Scott?" Erica extends her palms. "I ate fries and gravy today!

I *demand* to be bag skated!"

No one laughs.

Mr. Kowalski runs the practice alone. He doesn't say much when the girls ask him why Mr. Scott's missing. I have a feeling he knows more than he's saying. The whole thing makes me angry and uncomfortable.

"Do you think Mr. Kowalski at least *tried* to get Sue to help out with practice?" Crystal wonders.

"Why don't *you* ask him?" I snap back.

Without Kim, we're down to three defence.

"I know you like playing the wing," Mr. Kowalski says to me, "but we need you on D right now."

"Okay," I say, heart fluttering. What is he thinking?

Jodi doesn't show up. Brittni and Cory arrive twenty minutes late.

"They're trying to screw us over for Saturday," Kathy whispers while we're waiting our turn in a passing drill. "What's the point of practising the power play with them, when we all know none of them will show up on the weekend?"

"I think Mr. Kowalski's right to play the three of them together," Crystal says. "At least we can practice with our regular lines."

Kathy rolls a puck onto her blade and bounces it a few times. "I wish those girls would make up their minds. Are they hockey players—or *what*?"

After messing around for the entire practice, Brittni blows the lid off the whole Kim situation.

"Her parents took her to Regina," she tells us in the dressing room. "She's going to live with her aunt." She gives us a few more details about the move.

I think about Greg's words to me: "You're going to make things worse." Is that what just happened?

"How do you know?" I ask Brittni. "Did you talk to Kim?"

"I talked to Natalie," Brittni says. "She says Kim's mom took her phone away and told her she shouldn't talk to any of you. The Scotts say *you're* the problem."

"You've got to be kidding," Kathy says.

"They think *we've* been bullying Kim?" Larissa asks.

Cory says, "Have any of you said anything mean to her?"

"Who are *you* to be asking that question?" I demand.

"Do they have girls hockey at Luther?" Jennifer asks, carefully folding her practice jersey.

"I don't think so," Erica says.

"Then maybe Kim could play for one of the Regina teams," Jennifer says.

"Are you for real?" I reply. "Maybe Kim's not worried about playing hockey right now. Maybe she's got bigger things to worry about."

"But what if we play against her in the Regina tournament?" Jennifer asks.

"And what if the moon is made of freakin' cheese?!" I explode. "Will you quit worrying about where Kim's playing hockey!? Show a little empathy! The girl's been scratching the crap out of herself with a paper clip!"

Everyone stares at me.

"Jessie, it's time to come clean," Kathy says.

I explain what happened between Kim and me in Swift Current, the whole time conscious of Brittni's watchful expression.

When I'm done, Jennifer says, "So that's why Kim shoved you."

Brittni stands and wraps a towel around herself. "You're all making a big deal out of nothing."

Funny she should echo Greg's sentiments.

"Kim wasn't trying to hurt herself. She was trying to be the center of attention—*again*," Brittni says

"Now *that* sounds like Kim," Cory says.

"You're wrong," I tell them. "Kids cut themselves because they're depressed, not because they're looking for attention."

Brittni shrugs. "Whatever."

"They get a rush from it. It's addicting, and we shouldn't take it lightly." I can't tell if I'm making any headway in convincing her. "Think about all the pressure Kim's parents put on her to be the best at softball, volleyball, and hockey. She must hate herself when she doesn't live up to their expectations."

Jennifer stuffs a skate in her hockey bag. "We can't keep losing players like this. Pretty soon we're not going to have a team."

"Will you grow up and quit worrying about how this affects you?!" I shout at her.

Jennifer doesn't say a word. She jams in her other skate, zips up her bag, and leaves.

"Way to go, McIntyre," Cory says.

I roll my eyes, but I bite my tongue. She's a fine one to criticize.

"It's a good thing Kim's getting out of town for a while," Larissa says. "I agree with Jessie. She'll never get her act together living with her parents."

"She needs to get away from Greg too," I add.

"What—so you can get close to him?" Brittni asks.

"Jessie, that's gross," Amber says.

All I need is for Brittni to get the rumour mill spinning. "I had nothing to do with Kim and Greg breaking up."

"Sure thing, McIntyre," Cory says.

"I hate to sound like Jennifer, but it does suck to be short another player when we go to Davidson," Crystal says.

Brittni sighs. "Yeah, we feel bad about leaving you girls in a bind, but it can't be helped." She disappears into the shower with Cory.

We undress in silence. I can tell everyone's thinking about Kim—and the future of our hockey team.

Crystal sits beside me on the bench. "Is Brittni right about you and Greg?"

I give her what I hope is a dirty look. "What do you think?"

Larissa wiggles between Crystal and me. "We can't forget about Kim just because she's in Regina."

"We should do something for her," Crystal says.

"Like what?" I ask.

"I don't know. We could send her a Snapchat," Crystal suggests.

"We're pretty pathetic if that's the best we can do," I say.

Larissa says, "Her mom took away her cell, remember?"

We discuss the possibilities. Eventually we decide to make a card and give it to Mrs. Scott to take to Kim in Regina. We ask Amber, who's a good artist, to draw some pictures. Amber says she'll deliver the card to the Scotts. Maybe the Scotts will never give it to Kim, but we have to try.

It's lame, but it's better than nothing.

The much-awaited bus materializes for our four-hour road trip to Davidson, but it's not the glorious 40-seater we imagined. It's more like a white school bus—with no bathroom. Not a glamourous set of wheels, but it's sure nice to throw all our equipment on the shelf in the back.

"All aboard the Beastie Bus!" Mrs. Omalu calls.

My dad and Dr. Bilku come along. Dr. Bilku leads us in a rousing chorus of "The Wheels on the Bus" as we pull out of the parking lot in front of the Blue Goose. I love the way he says "wills" instead of "wheels."

I hang out with Jennifer for most of the trip, picking her brain about playing defence. I don't want to make a fool of myself in front of Sue, who's meeting us in Davidson. It's a good thing Jennifer's not upset with me for what I said to her after Thursday's practice.

"I kinda deserved it," she says after I apologize. "I *was* being selfish. Do you think there's time to stop and see Kim on the way to Davidson?"

"When Amber dropped off our card, Mrs. Scott told her that Kim doesn't want to see *us*," I tell her. "It's going to take her a while to realize who her real friends are."

"And by that you mean us?" Jennifer asks.

Maybe it's time to change the subject. "Are your feet as cold as mine are?"

"Freezing."

We buck an icy head wind all the way to Regina. The bus heater works overtime to keep us thawed out. By the time we're an hour from Davidson, most of the girls have climbed up on top of our gear, where it's definitely warmer.

"Hot air rises," Mr. Kowalski says.

"Typical science teacher," Teneil says. "Always angling for an opportunity to teach us about thermodynamics."

Before our warm-up, Mr. Kowalski reads off our forward lines and then says to Sue, "Anything you want to say to the defence?"

Sue tugs on her earlobe. "Just watch your gap and try not to get beat."

I know about gap. Shauna and Carla talked about it lots last year. Gap is the crucial distance the defence maintains between herself and a forward on the attack. Too much gap, and the forward has room to maneuver and shoot. Too little gap, and the defence gets beat—or ends up taking a hooking or tripping penalty trying not to get beat.

Sue sends Jennifer and me out for the opening faceoff. The Davidson Badgers wear white, red, and black uniforms. They're not a big team, but they mean business. A left winger wearing 17 skates right over top of me, creating a two-on-one. While I scramble to my feet, the centre catches 17's pass and hits Miranda square in the chest. There's a jumble in front of the net, and I barge in, cross-checking 17 on top of Miranda.

With only eleven seconds gone in the first period, I find myself in the penalty box, watching the Xtreme face off short-handed in our own end. The Badgers score twenty seconds into the power play, and I return to our bench, head hanging.

The only thing Sue says to me is, "That's not how to protect your goaltender."

Right.

I find out what she means the next time I line up in front of Miranda for a faceoff. I tap her pads and give her a nod, and Miranda says to me, "Don't push anybody on top of me again. That's how goalies end up in the hospital."

Which is why Miranda isn't happy with me later when I'm trying to keep my outside shoulder lined up with the Badger winger's inside shoulder, and end up backing right over top of her. It's a miracle Davidson doesn't score before I untangle myself from Miranda's pads and crawl out of the net.

She glares at me reproachfully. "You're starting to annoy me."

"I'm sorry. I'm learning a new position."

"Learn it outside my crease," she says.

I'm not the only one having problems. Brooklyn loses the puck at the Badger blue line and puts herself offside. Later Amber's on a breakaway and decides to go for a change without even attempting a shot on net. The Badger goaltender, who came way out of her crease, watches Amber skate away with the puck.

Even though we lose 7-5, we have a blast. Kathy and Teneil zip up Amber inside her hockey bag and leave her there when the coaches come into the dressing room. Mr. Kowalski can't figure out where the giggles are coming from, and by the time he does, we're cutting up. Even the corner of Sue's mouth twitches.

It's dark and freezing when we leave the rink. Mrs. Omalu can't fire up the bus, so the whole team gives it a push start across the parking lot.

When we stop to grab fast food, Brooklyn trips and dumps her chicken salad all over Erica.

Staring down at a lap full of lettuce, Erica says, "Now that's what I call a tossed salad."

Back on the bus, Miranda cranks up some tunes, and Dr. Bilku lip-synchs and dances at the front while Larissa rolls her eyes. Fortunately, my dad doesn't join in.

It's pretty much the most fun I've ever had on a road trip. I don't even mind Crystal talking my ear off all the way home.

"Are you going to the Bruin game on Wednesday afternoon?" Crystal asks when we're only a few miles from Estevan.

I draw a complete blank. "Why would the Bruins play on a Wednesday afternoon?"

"It's Remembrance Day." Crystal puts away her earbuds. "They're playing Humboldt."

I've pushed Mark to the back of my mind for the last few weeks. With all the stuff going on with Kim and the Xtreme, the winding down of volleyball season, and piles of homework, I haven't given him much thought.

"Think he'll be playing?" Crystal asks.

"Who?"

She nudges me with her elbow. "You know."

I shrug and shake my head, but my pulse is already racing. I won't be able to talk to Mark—only see him from a distance—but one thing's for certain.

There's no way I'm missing that game.

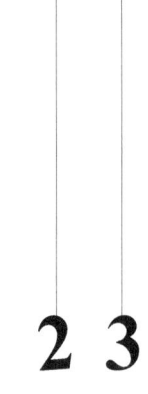

23

"WHAT'S THAT AROUND YOUR NECK?" Marsha demands as she takes my plate. "Looks like a frickin' doily."

"It's a scarf."

"Well, be careful you don't hang yourself with it. There's people who've got it in for you." She plunks a barbecued chicken breast and a few roasted potatoes on my plate.

What she says doesn't compute. "What are you talking about?"

She waves a hand. "Next!"

Since she's clearly not giving any more details, I pay at the till and head for our table. Somebody has it in for me? I look around the cafeteria, but I see only what I usually see—students talking, laughing, texting.

"Did you hear Greg Kolenick got expelled?" Kathy asks as soon as I sit down.

"Really?" Teneil asks. "You can get expelled for being a loser?"

"Apparently he got caught trying to steal an exam," Erica explains.

"I bet Greg will be back at school by Monday," Miranda says. "His dad—"

"Not this time," Brooklyn interrupts. "Greg's used up his nine lives."

My appetite vanishes.

"You gonna eat that chicken or wait for it to grow feathers?" Miranda asks, picking up my fork.

I push my tray over to her. "Go ahead. Help yourself."

The girls exchange details they've gleaned about Greg's suspension. I'm glad Kim's already done with him. Then Marsha's warning echoes in my brain. Was she talking about Greg?

"So what's Greg going to do now?" I ask.

"Who cares?" Kathy says. "Who cares what any guy is doing?"

"Well, Parker, I know what the ref was doing when we played Weyburn a few weeks ago." Erica pulls her chair close to Kathy and places her head on Kathy's shoulder. "He was thinking, 'Damn, I gotta get me some of that 18.'"

Kathy pushes Erica away. "Get real!"

"Yeah, how come you got a point for every goal, even when you weren't on the ice?" Brooklyn asks.

"Okay. Okay. So maybe I gave him my phone number," Kathy says.

Erica puts two fingers in her mouth and wolf whistles.

"Well, he asked for it first!" Kathy blushes and tucks her blonde hair behind her ears. I enjoy seeing her this uncomfortable. "Are you guys going to the Winter Wonderland Dance?" she asks, in an obvious ploy to divert our attention.

"Why? Is the ref coming?" Erica ducks to avoid the banana peel Kathy wings at her.

"When is it?" Teneil asks.

"Last Friday in November. The week before the Regina tournament," Brooklyn says.

"It's semi-formal," Jennifer says.

Erica gives her D-partner a shot in the arm. "Remember the tux I wore last year?"

"It wasn't a tux," Brooklyn informs us. "It was a plaid leisure suit. Yellow and black plaid. Trés ugly."

"I'm wearing it for grad," Erica announces.

"You are not!" Brooklyn says. "You'll get yourself a poufy dress like everybody else!"

Thus ensues a lively discussion about whether or not wearing a poufy dress at Grade Twelve grad constitutes conformity.

I listen with half an ear because I'm thinking about Kim again. I wonder when she started cutting. Was it after she and Mark broke up? Or when she didn't make the senior volleyball team? Or when Greg started hitting on me?

So often I think I know what's going on behind someone's face, and then I find out I don't know them at all.

"Here comes Michelle," Kathy says. "Are you going to the dance with her? Or with us?"

I don't like her tone. "That sounds like an ultimatum."

"Look, Jessie. You must know she talks too much. She's driving us crazy," Teneil says.

"I'll talk to her," I say.

"There was another girl like that." Teneil gazes at me. "Never listened. Just talked about her life in Saskatoon. Remember her?"

"Yeah, I remember," I say. "I wasn't aware that you noticed."

"I noticed all right," Teneil says. "Everyone noticed. My grannie always says, 'Teneil, you don't learn nuthin' by talkin'.'"

"Learn anything," I correct her.

"You know what I mean."

Michelle plunks beside me. "Hey, guess what? I'm doing a solo at the Optimist Festival!"

"That's nice," Kathy says.

Michelle starts talking about the songs she has to practice. The girls pack up their stuff and start to disappear. Michelle keeps chattering about jazz band, her piano teacher and a new song she's writing until it's only her and me.

"Michelle, you should eat before it gets cold," I say when she pauses to take a breath. I know lunch is the highlight of her day. It pains me to hurt her feelings. "There's something I need to talk to you about."

Her wide eyes make my stomach do a flip. Maybe I don't need to say anything. Maybe I can let it ride. But when I think about Kathy's expression when she left the table, I know I need to do something before someone says something mean to Michelle.

I take a deep breath. "Hey, Michelle, when you sit with us, you need to listen more and talk less."

She slumps in her chair and hangs her head.

"Michelle, are you okay?"

"You hate me," she says. "You hate the fact I don't play hockey."

I put a hand on her arm and squeeze. "You're one of my best friends. I don't hate you, and I don't care about you not playing hockey. I wish you didn't always try to steer the conversation away from hockey."

"I talk too much." Michelle wipes her eyes with the back of both hands. "I'm sorry."

I know she is.

And I'm sorry for telling her.

On Wednesday morning, I go to the Remembrance Day Service at ECS with my parents and Courtney. We go out for lunch, and then Dad lets me drive over to Michelle's to pick her up for the hockey game.

"Call us when the game's over," Dad says as he climbs into the driver's seat.

I feel crappy about what I said to Michelle at school. She's hardly said a word since. Is she mad at me? Embarrassed? Depressed?

I open the arena door for her and pay her admission to the game. When she protests, I say, "My dad told me to pay your way. You want a pop or something?"

She nods.

I pick up a program and some drinks from the machine and make my way towards the stairs. Meanwhile I'm pouring through the Broncos' roster, looking to see what number Mark is wearing. There he is. 28. He's listed as 6'1", 185 lbs. Defence. Previous team—Estevan Bruins.

We've missed the warm-up, which ticks me off. It would have been a chance to see Mark interacting with his teammates. I hope he's doing okay in Humboldt.

"You excited about seeing Mark again?" Michelle asks.

"Uh-huh." I try to recall how much I've told her about Mark. Not a lot. For a long time, the topic's been too painful.

When we get upstairs, the first person I see is Mark's dad. Mr. Taylor's easy to recognize because he's tall with this awesome silver hair. I used to bug Mark about his dad being the Silver Fox, and I never knew why Mark didn't find that funny. I guess I know now.

Mr. Taylor's standing at the rail by himself. That strikes me as strange, but then, he's never lived in Estevan, so he doesn't have any friends in town. Mark and his mom moved here after his parents split up. I'm uncertain about approaching Mr. Taylor, but since no one else is going to fill me in on the last two months of Mark's life, I decide to make an effort.

"I'm going to talk to Mark's dad," I say to Michelle. "Can you keep quiet for ten minutes? It's important."

"Mark's dad," she says. "Isn't he the one that's . . ." Her voice fades as she catches my look. "Got it." She makes a zipper motion across her lips.

I tap Mr. Taylor on the shoulder, and he turns around. He's got his phone to his ear, but he waves me closer.

"I was listening to my messages," he says. "How're you doing, Jessie?"

It's cool he remembers me. I only saw him maybe three or four times when I was going out with Mark. I take his extended hand and shake it. "I'm great. Mr. Taylor, this is my friend Michelle Purdy."

He shakes hands with Michelle. We chit-chat for a while. By the time the Broncos step on the ice, we've covered the weather, the upcoming election, the cost of real estate in Estevan, and the Xtreme. I'm looking for Mark on the ice, but I don't see his number—or anybody who skates like him.

"Sorry to hear your team's having a tough year." Mr. Taylor smiles. "You lost a fine coach when Steve moved away."

"How does Mark like Humboldt?" I ask. "Does he have good billets?"

"Yes," Mr. Taylor assures me. "He likes the school and his teammates and his mom being close by. But I think he especially likes being near Holly."

I didn't think an offhand remark like that would bother me, but it does.

"That's good." I shove my hands in my pockets, hoping I'll find a tissue, because my nose has started to run.

"Too bad things didn't work out between you two," Mr. Taylor says. "He liked you a lot."

I clear my throat. "Yeah, I liked him too."

"Speak of the devil." Mr. Taylor says.

Mark's wearing a black suit, white dress shirt and dark green tie. A tablet is tucked under his arm. His hair is shorter, but I'm glad to see he hasn't dyed it a silly colour. He looks like a million bucks.

"Hey, Dad." Mark hugs Mr. Taylor. "Sorry I'm not playing."

"How's your knee?" Mr. Taylor asks.

"Just a tweak. Coach wants me to rest it though. Big home-and-away coming up against Nipawin."

"No problem, Son." Mr. Taylor looks back and forth between Mark and me, clearly not sure how to proceed.

I know one thing. Mark's not going to get the best of me this time. "Mark, this is my friend Michelle."

Mark nods at Michelle. "Hey, Michelle."

Michelle smiles at Mark. For a split second I think she's going to say something, but she snaps her mouth closed.

"How's Holly doing?" I ask. "I've been following her wrestling team on the U of S website." This is a blatant lie. I've never looked up Holly's wrestling stats.

He looks confused. "She's doing fine," he says.

"Say hi to her for me." It's not so hard to sound breezy when you put your mind to it. "Talked to Tara lately?"

"Not this week." His forehead wrinkles, like he's trying to do a mental math calculation.

"Well, I'll leave you and your dad to talk." I start to back away. "I imagine you've got lots to catch up on—or are you doing stats during the game?"

Mark looks at the tablet like he's never seen it before. "I'm recording turnovers."

"Good luck with that—and with your season too. Nice seeing you again, Mr. Taylor."

As I walk away, I don't know whether to kick myself for not staying longer— or do a handspring for not making a fool of myself.

"How did I do?" I whisper to Michelle. "Did I look mature and confident?"

"Oh, yes," Michelle says, "and more importantly, you looked like you were way over him."

Which is great, because after only two minutes in his company, I'm sure I'm not.

We find our seats, and I pretend to watch the game. Frankly I couldn't care less who wins, now that I know Mark isn't playing. I steal glances in his direction, hoping I'm not being obvious. Then I realize someone has sat down behind us.

Jordan, Jodi's on-again, off-again boyfriend, leans over my right shoulder. "Hey, Jessie. How's it going?"

"Okay." I keep my eyes on the ice.

"Greg's wondering what you're up to this weekend. Thought you and him and Jodi and me could get together. Go to a party or something."

Fear wriggles in my gut. What're these guys up to now?

"I have hockey this weekend," I tell him.

"Jodi says you don't." Jordan leans closer and turns his head towards Michelle. "Do you like to party with Jessie too?"

I know he's charming her to get to me.

"I like to write music," she says.

"You do?" This is clearly not the answer he was expecting. "About what?"

"Okay, so I don't have hockey," I interrupt. "That doesn't mean I'm going anywhere with Greg." I force myself to look him in the eye. It's not easy because I'm shaking in my boots. I keep thinking about what Marsha said.

Jordan drums his fingertips on the back of my seat. "Jessie, I saw you talking to Mark. But you know it's over." He turns to Michelle. "Time for Jessie to move on, right? Make some music of her own?"

Michelle nods uncertainly.

I take a deep breath. "Would you mind leaving us? We're discussing something important."

Jordan's eyes are hard as flint. "Be careful, Snow Queen," he whispers in my ear. As he stands up, he says to Michelle. "You should party with Jessie sometime. I guarantee you won't forget it."

After he's gone, Michelle says, "That was kind of weird. He's cute though."

"You definitely do not want to go to one of his parties," I tell her.

"You won't let me hang out with any of your friends." She sounds hurt and angry.

"How about I buy you a popcorn?" I offer.

For the rest of the game I try to forget about Mark and Mr. Taylor—and Jordan.

What Jordan said wasn't that bad. But the look on his face was something scary indeed.

2 4

The following Tuesday, our team meets in the parking lot behind the Blue Goose to take the Beastie Bus to Notre Dame for a rematch with the Hounds. Mr. Kowalski can't make it due to parent-teacher interviews, but Sue has agreed to coach. She checks off each name on her roster as we board. Most of the girls come straight from school. Even Jodi makes it with a few minutes to spare.

"This'll be the first time Brittni and Cory have gone head-to-head with Sue," Jennifer says after we toss our equipment in the back of the bus and grabs some seats. "I wonder who'll come out on top?"

"If Sue says as little as she's said so far, they'll walk all over her," I reply.

3:55 rolls around, and Sue does a quick head count. Brittni and Cory are missing.

"Did they say if they're coming?" Sue asks Jodi.

"We're supposed to pick up Cory in Midale at 4:30," Jodi says.

"Text Brittni and find out where she is," Sue replies with a frown. "Tell her the bus will leave on time—whether she's on it or not."

Kathy sits behind Jennifer and me. "Wanna bet we leave without Brittni?" she murmurs.

"Not a chance," I reply.

"Brittni says she's going to be a few minutes late," Jodi reports to Sue. "She says to wait for her."

Sue checks her phone and gives Mrs. Omalu the nod. With a hearty chuckle, Miranda's mom wheels the Beastie Bus out of the parking lot at precisely 4:00. Without Brittni. We hit a big rut and everyone screams in surprise.

"Hold on, girls!" Mrs. Omalu shouts and chuckles again.

"Sue means business," Kathy says as we pass in front of the Leisure Centre. I look for Brittni's black Jeep, but I don't see it anywhere.

"I bet Cory won't be at the Quik Stop either," Jennifer predicts.

"I'll take that bet," I challenge her. "Cory's been saying for weeks she wants to fight the Notre Dame captain. She won't miss her ride."

When we reach Midale, Mrs. Omalu doesn't pull onto the service road though she does brake so we can check the vehicles parked beside the Quik Stop. We pile up on the right side of the bus with the windows pulled down and our heads sticking out.

"I don't see Cory, Mom!" Miranda yells.

"Me neither!" Kathy calls.

"Windows up!" Mrs. Omalu accelerates, and I hang onto Jennifer, so I won't be thrown off my seat.

"Keep your ruddy arms and feet inside the bus at all times, mates," Brooklyn quips.

I tuck my hands in my armpits to warm them. "Do you think Steve would've left one of us behind if we were dragging the team down?"

Kathy shrugs, clearly not interested in hearing me talk about Steve again, so I think about him on my own. He never gave up on Kim even when she criticized his coaching. Then again, Kim was never late for games or practices, and she never missed them for lame reasons.

I hear Jodi laughing and teasing the younger girls. If it bothers her that Brittni and Cory aren't along, she gives no sign. I turn around to see if she's got her water bottle.

She does.

When I turn back, Jennifer raises her thick eyebrows. Seriously—she should wax those. I shift my body so I'm not looking at her and close my eyes. Jodi's not my problem. Look what happened when I meddled in Kim's life.

Because of Amber, we stop for a pee break in Weyburn. After that most of us sprawl all over our equipment in the back of the bus. It's more comfortable than sitting in the seats, which hardly have any padding. We hit this big bump in the road and Amber goes flying and hits her head on the roof. Not that she gets hurt or anything. It's pretty much the most hilarious thing we've ever seen.

Just before 6:00, we roll into the tiny prairie town of Wilcox. The sandwich I ate an hour ago is long gone, and hunger pangs gnaw my stomach, but I know better than to choke down some greasy rink food before a game. Instead, I buy an energy bar at the concession and wander around the rink lobby with Kathy, looking at the pictures of all the famous hockey players who graduated from Notre Dame. There's a big display case with memorabilia about Père Murray, the priest who arrived at the school in 1927. He took boys and girls and groomed them into men and women through faith, academics, and sport. Some NHL stars played at Notre Dame. Lots of female athletes have gone on to play at American Ivy League schools like Yale and Cornell.

"Makes you wanna have your picture up there, doesn't it?" Kathy says behind my right shoulder.

I turn around. "Would you ever move away from home to play hockey?"

Kathy shrugs. "If a school wanted me, I might."

"But you'd have to move away from your favourite referee," I remind her.

"Whatever," she says.

"How's it going with Brett?" I ask.

She sighs. "I thought I could handle him being a ref. But it's too weird. Don't get me wrong—he's nice and everything—but when I went out with him and his buddies the other night, all they talked about was officiating."

"What's wrong with that?"

"They talk about *reffing* hockey the same way we talk about *playing* hockey. It was creepy." Kathy sighs. "I think our worlds are too far apart."

"Let's go get dressed," I say.

She follows me down the first set of stairs. When we turn the corner, Sue stands on the landing with Jodi, and Jodi looks pissed. Sue narrows her eyes at us and checks her sport watch.

"Sorry, Coach," Kathy says. "We lost track of time."

"Mental preparation is as important as skill," Sue says.

"Oh, brother," I mutter under my breath, when we've moved past them. "Who does she think she is?"

"The coach," Kathy says. "Cut her some slack. She's the best thing that's happened to us this year."

I know better than to argue with her. "What do you think she's talking to Jodi about?"

Kathy pushes open the dressing room door. "Isn't it obvious? It's about time somebody did something about Jodi."

We walk right into the middle of a discussion about the SaskFirst camp to be held in Carlyle, where U18 female hockey players from the southeast corner of the province will assemble in a few weeks. The team picked at Carlyle, along with seven other teams, will complete in Humboldt at the Saskatchewan Winter Games in February. The Games are a terrific opportunity for us to play a higher calibre hockey and be exposed to university scouts. It's a hot topic, especially since Sue's going to help coach the Zone One team.

"How come none of you tried out last year?" Amber asks.

"We did," says Erica, pointing to Brooklyn, "but we didn't make it."

"Jodi would have made it," says Kathy, "but she broke her collarbone."

Amber jams her helmet on her head. "Are you trying out, Jessie?"

"Yeah, but I'm not sucking up to Sue to get on that team."

"No one's telling you to." Kathy unzips her bag and starts unpacking her equipment.

"If you keep giving her attitude, she's not going to pick you," Jennifer says.

I pull my hoodie over my head and hang it on a hook. "I don't give Sue attitude."

"Right." Kathy yanks off her socks. "You keep talking, and maybe you'll convince yourself." She looks at Amber and asks, "Amber, what's with your helmet?"

Amber, who's spent the last few minutes wrestling with it, is red-faced. "I don't know! It doesn't fit anymore! It's squeezing my head!"

Kathy crooks a finger. "Give it to Auntie Kathy."

Amber hands it over. While Kathy bends it back to its proper shape, Crystal tries to jam her own helmet on.

"Mine's bent too!" she complains.

"It's because we were sitting on our equipment!" Larissa says. "We squished them!"

"You know what that makes us, don't you?" Brooklyn asks Erica.

"Head cases," Erica says.

We're still laughing when the door flies open, and Jodi barges in. Her cheeks are purple.

"Hey, Jodi, what's up?" Crystal asks.

Jodi grabs her equipment and storms out without a word.

"What's with her?" Brooklyn asks.

"Do you think Sue said something to her about—" Jennifer raises her hand and tips back an imaginary bottle.

"No doubt," Erica says.

"About time," Brooklyn says.

I like Erica and Brooklyn, but it bugs me they don't show more leadership. They could say something to Jodi about not drinking during a game, but they never do. Isn't that their job as veterans? We can't count on Brittni or Cory to do anything about it.

After we're dressed, Sue and Mrs. Omalu come into the dressing room. Sue sits next to Miranda, and she looks calm and confident as she scrolls through her tablet. She's not like Mr. Kowalski, who's always nervous, or Mr. Scott, who's one rant away from a coronary. After a few minutes, she closes her tablet and stands up. She starts talking about the "Big Ice" factor at Notre Dame.

"If you get drawn out of position, it's a long way to get back, especially on PK. You wingers have a bad habit of playing too deep. Cover the defence like you're supposed to."

Now that's something I agree with.

"And stay out of the penalty box." Sue looks at Kathy. "Don't get drawn into shoving matches after the whistle. When the Hounds trash talk you, skate away."

Sue's pretty naïve if she doesn't know how much verbal abuse some of us dish out. Brooklyn and Erica have been working on their insults all week.

"Who's playing on Jodi's line, Coach?" Kathy asks.

Sue gives Kathy a tight smile. "Jodi's sitting this one out."

While we're digesting that tidbit, Sue goes on to draw up our power play, illustrating a breakout that makes perfect sense in light of our limited resources—which are getting more limited by the minute.

"But why isn't Jodi playing?" Crystal asks when Sue opens up the floor for questions.

"Never mind." Sue tucks her tablet under her arm. "I know you girls look up to her, and some of you think we can't win a game without her. But today you're going to have to try."

She stands at the door and smacks each of us on the helmet as we file past.

"I can't believe Sue benched Jodi," I say to Kathy. "She hardly says anything while Mr. Kowalski's around."

Kathy says, "Mr. Kowalski's the head coach. She probably doesn't think she has the right."

"Well, today she tackled the three biggest problems on our team," Erica says. "She's got my vote."

Behind me Jennifer whines about losing another player. Is this the same girl who didn't want more bodies last year because it would affect her own ice time?

We struggle with the drills in our pre-game warm-up. Everyone seems rattled by the Notre Dame vibe. The stands are nearly full of students wearing white and red. Then there's the banners. The Notre Dame legacy of excellence is long and rich. Sue stands on top of the bench, making small talk with the Hounds' coach. I don't see Jodi anywhere.

When the clock runs down, Sue sends Crystal, Amber, Teneil, Jennifer, and me for the opening faceoff.

"Look who's here," Jennifer says, pointing.

Jodi sits alone in the stands above and behind our bench. Her eyes and fingers are glued to her phone.

"I bet she's messaging Brittni," Jennifer says.

Good thing I'm in good shape because between the big rink and our nine skaters, we get plenty of ice time. Since we're short a forward, Sue puts Brooklyn on the wing with Kathy and Larissa. That means we play the game with only three D—Erica, Jennifer, and me. I get lots of practice learning my position.

Kathy scores first on a beautiful backhand. Jennifer pinches in for the second goal, calling for the puck, which Larissa throws out to her, and she bangs it in glove side. Then the Hounds score three power play goals. Shauna's is a high wrist shot from the point that sails past Miranda's glove, top right corner. But even strength, we are able to hang in there.

In the dressing room after the second period, we start convincing ourselves we might even be able to beat Notre Dame. After all, we beat Swift Current.

The Hounds score two quick ones in the top of the third, pulling in front 5-2. That's when I start getting frustrated. With seven and a half minutes left in the game, I get beat—again—and cross-check 6 into the boards, hitting her right in the numbers. She goes down face first and doesn't get up for a long time. The Notre Dame trainer and an EMT come out on the ice.

I earn my team a five-minute major and get escorted to the gate by the linesman. I restrain the impulse to smack my stick against the boards as I exit, knowing full well I'll sit out our next league game too.

The Hounds score two more power play goals while I'm sitting in our dressing room, contemplating my future on defence. Now that I have time to think, I realize how stupid I was to cream that girl. When the game's over, my subdued teammates file in.

Erica murmurs, "Tough one, Jessie. She turned at the last minute."

"I hit her when she was vulnerable," I say. "I deserved it."

Thankfully, Sue doesn't say a word to me or about me during her post-game analysis. She's low-key—focusing on what we did right, instead of dwelling on the negatives. Still, the thing she *doesn't* talk about hangs in the air like a huge billboard which reads, "Jessie put the final nail in our coffin."

Jodi pouts.

I'm ashamed. All I want to do is get out of here. I'd rather hitchhike than ride home in the Beastie Bus. I shower quick and head for the lobby, where Jodi's talking to some older boys wearing red leather jackets. Shauna's with her mother, boyfriend Brian, and a few other Hounds. She hugs me, and we visit for a bit. She asks how Kim's doing, but there's not much I can tell her that's not just a rumour.

"You played well on defence," Shauna says at last.

"No I didn't."

"Everybody has to start somewhere," she says. "You did all right."

"Thanks."

"What's with Jodi?" she asks. "She hurt or something?" Shauna's emphasis on the last word says it all. She knows what Jodi's like.

Before I can answer, Kathy thrusts her head in between us and throws an arm around our shoulders. "Who's in the mood for taco-in-a-bag?"

I shake my head.

"Aw, come on, Mac," Kathy says. "You think you're the only person who ever got suspended?"

"I could have hurt that girl." Tears burn the back of my eyeballs.

"She played a couple of shifts after you left," Kathy says. "Don't let it bother you."

I know I'll feel crappy later, but right now I need a solid infusion of cheese. I pull a twenty out of my jeans pocket. "I'm in, and Daddy McIntyre's buying."

"Two nights in a row on Daddy McIntyre," Kathy coos, not missing a beat. "Did I tell you about our hot date?"

I grab her toque and run with it, egging her on, while Shauna laughs.

Maybe getting suspended isn't the end of the world.

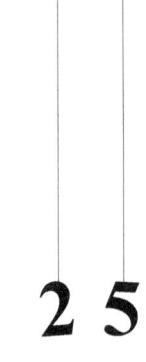

2 5

At Thursday practice, there are three noticeable absences—Brittni, Cory, and Jodi.

"Brittni's not throwing in the towel," Kathy says while she's unlacing her skates. "You can bet on it."

When I come out of the dressing room, a tall woman with elaborate streaks in her hair and eyelash extensions confronts Sue.

"You've got no right to stop her from playing!" Her voice echoes in the hall.

"She missed the bus," Sue says.

"She was late! Would it have been a crime to wait for her?"

I'm the one who feels like a criminal for standing here eavesdropping. I can't slip past them because of my hockey bag. Should I go back in the dressing room?

"We had a tight schedule," Sue says. "I'm sorry Brittni missed the game."

Then Kathy comes out, and her bag blocks my retreat.

"Brittni lives for hockey! It's not fair to take it away from her for such a lousy reason!"

Kathy and I freeze like a pair of statues.

"I'm glad we had this chance to talk," Sue says.

Brittni's mom eyes her suspiciously.

"I'm wondering why Brittni only seems to show up for home games. Whenever we go on the road—"

"Brittni has an active social life," her mom interrupts. "I'm sure you did too when you were her age."

"When I was Brittni's age, I was trying to get a college scholarship. I didn't have time for a social life."

"Surely you don't expect the same kind of commitment from these girls!"

"Of course not," Sue says. "That would hardly be fair to Brittni."

Brittni's mom snorts.

"Can I ask why you don't come to more of her games?" Sue continues. "It would mean a lot to Brittni to have you cheering for her."

Mrs. Wade's perfectly outlined bronze lips make an O.

"Brittni's a talented player," Sue says, "but I'd like to help her work on her team skills too."

Mrs. Wade wipes her nose with the back of her hand and digs in her designer handbag.

"Here's a tissue," Sue says, pulling one from her coat pocket. "Why don't we find a place to talk in private?"

Brittni's mom blows her nose and follows Sue into the empty dressing room across the hall.

"Wow," I say.

"Wow is right," Kathy says.

"Think this'll make a difference with Brittni?" I ask.

"Not a chance."

On Friday after school, I clean out my locker. Mom's been after me for weeks to bring home my gym clothes to wash, and from the way the girls have been wrinkling their noses at me in PE class, I know it's time. Around me, everyone's humming about the weekend. Some kids—like me—are going to the Winter Wonderland Dance while others are headed to house parties. Before long, the hallway's a graveyard. I've just finished rearranging my locker when Brittni and Jodi walk up.

"We were waiting for you outside," Brittni says. "Nice jacket."

"Thanks." What the hell is she up to?

Brittni flips her long blonde hair over her shoulder. "Hey, what are you doing right now?"

"Walking to the Civic to watch my sister."

"We can give you a lift," she offers.

Hell must have frozen over. I glance at Jodi, but she stares down the hall. Is she avoiding eye contact?

"We can stop at Sevie on the way," Brittni adds.

"Thanks, but no thanks," I tell her.

"You must feel bad about getting suspended in Notre Dame," Brittni says. "I know I feel awful when that happens to me."

I can't imagine Brittni feeling awful about anything. I slam my locker and attach the lock.

"We've got an idea," Brittni says, lowering her voice. "We know you don't like that blonde dyke any more than we do."

Nasty Brittni has returned.

There are two other blonde girls on our team, but I know she isn't talking about Crystal or Kathy. I may not like Sue much, but there's no way I'd talk about her that way.

"I don't mind Sue," I say.

"You don't have to lie for my benefit," Brittni says.

Jodi still won't look at me. She's staring at the floor now.

"Cory figured out a way to get her off our cases," Brittni says.

"I don't want to hear this." I pick up my backpack and bag of clothes. "Whatever it is—I'm not participating."

"But we can't do it without you," Brittni says. "Won't you at least listen?"

I stand there, heart pounding, while she outlines a scheme to get Estevan Minor Hockey to ban Sue from coaching. Brittni wants me to tell my parents that Sue's been "making advances."

"You can tell them Sue saw pictures of you and Jodi on Instagram, and she's been hitting on you ever since," Brittni says.

"Are you going along with this?" I ask Jodi.

"I will if you will," she mumbles.

She's lying. I know it. It'll all be on me. I step around Brittni. "I'm outta here."

"But you'll think about it, right?" Brittni calls after me. "We're counting on you, Jessie! In fact, the whole team is!"

It's all I can do not to break into a run. How in the hell do I get myself into these messes?

2 6

"YOUR HAIR LOOKS NICE LIKE THAT," Courtney says.

It's later that night, and I'm getting ready to go to the dance.

Courtney's lying on her stomach on my bed, her face cradled in her palms. "You should do it like that all the time."

"Too much work." Sitting on the edge of my bed, I check the dryness of the dark green nail polish on my big toe.

"Where'd you get the curlers?" she asks.

"From Teneil."

"Doesn't she use them?"

"What's with all the questions? You're like Breanne!" I tell her. "Teneil got her hair cut short, so she doesn't need them anymore."

"Can I use them?"

I reach back and tug on her blonde ponytail. "Not unless I help you."

"Why not?"

"Cause you'll burn yourself."

"Will not."

"Look, I'm not arguing with you. Promise me you'll let me put them in, okay?"

I stand and tug on the hem of my stretchy black skirt. I can adjust the length to pass Dad's inspection and then hike it higher when I get to the dance.

"Okay." She rolls over onto her back and stares at the ceiling.

I look at her out of the corner of my eye. I can tell she's thinking hard about something. What now?

"Jessie, do you get bugged at school anymore?" she asks at last.

I consider her question. I don't get teased as much now that Greg's been suspended. There's plenty of other drama at the Comp to keep me out of the limelight. I've settled into a daily routine, and life's pretty good for the most part.

"No, why?"

"What did you do to make it stop?"

I notice a tear drawing a line from her eye to her ear. "What's going on, Court?" I plop down beside her and place my hand on her stomach.

She crunches into a ball, hugging the pillow to her face. "It's the new girl," she mumbles.

I realize how completely I've been out of touch. "Tell me."

"She doesn't like me." She pulls the pillow down to her chest. "She says I'm spoiled and prissy. She says figure skating's stupid."

There are a handful of girls in Courtney's Grade Five class, and Courtney is the only one who figure skates—or does much of anything. Mom's told me about how these girls dress and the makeup they wear. It's ridiculous behaviour for ten-year-olds.

"What kind of parents let their daughters go around dressed like tarts?" Mom has said more than once.

"Have you told Mom?"

Courtney buries her face in her pillow again. "No."

"Why not?"

Courtney yanks away the pillow and glares at me. "Because Mom will make it worse!"

"No, she won't."

Courtney sits up. "Yes, she will!"

She's right. I didn't tell Mom anything last year for exactly the same reason. But when Kim needed help, I went to Mom, so—

"I don't want Mom to know," Courtney says. "Please don't tell her."

"Okay," I say, knowing it's the wrong promise to make. "What's the new girl's name?"

"Ashley."

"So Ashley is probably trying to fit in, and the only way she knows how is to make all the girls dislike you."

"But why me?" Courtney's face crumples, and I wrap my arms around her. "I never did anything to her."

I lick my palm and smooth down the blonde, staticky hair sticking to my nose.

"She makes fun of me when the teacher's not in the room," Courtney sobs, "and she won't let Lana or Peyton talk to me at recess. I don't even want to go to school anymore. What do I do to make her stop?"

"Let me think." The Ashleys of the world don't always change their ways when a teacher talks to them. They only get sneakier. I hug Courtney closer. "You need to show Ashley her nasty remarks don't bug you."

"But they do!"

"For the next few days, pretend they don't. When you see Ashley on Monday, walk right up to her and say 'hi.'"

"What if she says something mean to me?"

"You could just agree with her. Say 'I guess I am.' Or 'Wish I could do something about that.' Then talk about something else. Then end the conversation when you want to. Take control."

Courtney pulls out of my arms and crawls off the bed. "Is that the best you can do?"

"On short notice, yes." I grab her hand and squeeze it. "Were you hoping I'd offer to kick the crap out of her?"

Courtney laughs for the first time since she came into my room. "Maybe!"

"Look, Courtney, girls like Ashley don't know who they are or what they want. But you know who you are, right?"

Courtney nods.

"You can talk to me any time. In fact, on Monday after supper, we'll meet here and talk about how things went and plan strategy. You're not in this alone."

Courtney wipes at her eyes with her free hand. "Okay."

There's a knock on my door, and Mom looks in. "Michelle called, Jessie. She says she's too sick to go to the dance."

"That's funny. She seemed okay at school." I think back to ELA class. She was all right then, but I never saw her after that because she didn't join us at lunch. I had good intentions about texting her and asking why, but I never got around to it. "I wonder why she didn't send a text." I check my flip phone.

Mom eyes my skirt. "Do you want your dad to drive you?"

I tug the hem lower on my thighs. "Would it be all right if I called Kathy or Teneil?"

I know there'll be a Breathalyzer and other hoops to jump through when I get to the school, and I'd rather not jump through them alone.

The arrangements are soon made. Mr. Parker will pick me up, and after the dance, I'll spend the night at Kathy's. A damn near perfect plan because the Parkers don't make Kathy abide by prison lockdown rules.

When Mr. Parker pulls up in front of the house, Dad's watching the hockey game, clutching the remote and scowling. He takes one look at my outfit and asks me if I'd consider wearing a set of insulated coveralls.

"I thought you like it when I dress up," I say as I pull on my Xtreme jacket. He grunts.

"Be careful, Jessie," Mom says in my ear as she hugs me goodbye.

As I walk down our front steps, Mr. Parker leans against his car, puffing a cigarette. "You look nice," he says. "Hardly recognized you without the shoulder pads."

The front passenger window descends, and Kathy's grinning face appears. I hardly recognize *her* without her signature skater toque. "Nice shoes."

I look down at my beat-up, old runners. My stilettos are tucked in my backpack along with a change of clothes, sleepwear, and makeup kit.

Mr. Parker drops his cigarette, steps on it, and opens the back door for me. I climb in beside Miranda.

"Where's Teneil?" I try to recall the last time one of them went anywhere without the other.

Miranda winks. "Teneil's snagged herself a Bruin."

Seems like everybody's got a fella these days. Everybody except me. "Really? Which one?"

Kathy pokes her head between the bucket seats and gives me the details while Mr. Parker negotiates the slippery streets.

"Poor Miranda," I say when Kathy's done. "What are you gonna do without your trusty sidekick?"

Miranda winks. "Maybe I'll get a man too."

"Maybe you should start with a boy," Mr. Parker says.

We all laugh.

"How come Brett isn't coming to the dance?" I ask Kathy.

"He's linesing a senior men's game."

"Next stop, NHL," I tell her. "You can only hope to contain him, Parker."

Miranda and I give Kathy the gears all the way to the school. Her dad seems to enjoy it.

"Have fun, ladies. Call me if you need a ride." He waves through the open passenger window as we climb out and pick our way up the icy sidewalk towards the main entrance.

"Why did he say 'if?'" I shiver under my light jacket in the cold November night. "Isn't he coming to get us after the dance?"

"We thought we'd go to a party after," Kathy says.

"Whose party?" I hate to sound like the Fun Police, but I have a lot at stake here. There are people I don't want to see.

"I don't know," Kathy says. "Do you plan every minute of your day?"

"You're talking to the Queen of Spontaneity. Guess how many times I've gotten myself into trouble by not planning my day?"

"I hope you both studied for the test," Miranda says, opening the door.

I'm confused. "What test?"

Miranda leads us to the lineup at the Breathalyzer. We pass with flying colours and head up the steps to the gymnasium, where we hand in our tickets and admire the decorations the SRC has been working on for weeks. White, red, and green LED lights wink along the walls and across the ceiling. Ms. Peters serves mocktails at a long table. Kathy buys Miranda and me some fruity concoctions with tiny umbrellas, and we walk over to the cut-outs of Santa and Rudolph to get our pictures taken. The photographer and assistants are dressed like elves, and they pop a red clown nose on Kathy when she puts her face through the Rudolph cut-out.

Erica and Brooklyn show up just before 8:00. Erica sports her yellow and black plaid leisure suit, along with a yellow bow tie and a black fedora.

Brooklyn says, "Guess what? Erica bought a grad dress in Regina, and it's pink. In fact, it's *fuchsia*."

"No way!" Miranda says. "You caved!"

Erica shrugs. "I didn't know I look pretty in pink."

That gets Kathy and Miranda talking about their dream dresses even though graduation is two-and-a-half years away. It makes me wonder what Mark will wear for his grad—and if Holly will wear a dress to match his tie. I push the thought aside and try to concentrate on having a good time.

We group dance for most of the fast songs. A guy I don't know asks me to slow dance, but I can tell from the smirk on his face that saying 'yes' would be a mistake. Funny how a couple of stupid pictures can bring out the worst in people.

Then Evan ambles over and asks me to dance. I feel safe wrapped in his long arms, with my chin barely reaching his chest. All my problems seem far away. When the song's over, he asks me to go to a concert with him, but I tell him

I have Zone One tryouts that weekend. Then he asks me to go for supper on Sunday night.

"Can't we just be friends?" I ask. "It's not fair to go out with you if I still like Mark."

"Why don't you go out with me and I'll let you know when I can't handle it?" Evan suggests.

"I'll think about it," I say. "Can I talk to you about something else?"

The music's too loud to have a decent conversation, so we go into the hallway. Two teachers lean against the wall, deep in conversation, but I don't mind them being around as long as they don't overhear us.

With the music pulsing behind us, I unfold Brittni's scheme to sabotage Sue's reputation.

"You're kidding me, right?" Evan says when I'm finished.

"I'm not." I reach down and unbuckle the straps on my stilettos. My toes and calves are killing me.

"They must think you're pretty stupid. You're not going to do it, are you?" he asks.

"Evan!"

He leans against the wall. "You better talk to your coach."

"Sue's not very approachable."

"That's no excuse. She deserves to know what's going on." He looks me in the eye. "Would you like to pray about it?"

Typical pastor's son. "Actually, I don't. I think God has more important concerns. But I *will* talk to Sue." I bend over and pick up my shoes. "Let's go back in—before the girls start talking about us." As we retrace our steps, I tug on his arm and say in his ear, "You know—if there was just Brittni *or* Cory, the Xtreme would be okay. It's the two of them combined that's bad. And they're dragging Jodi down with them."

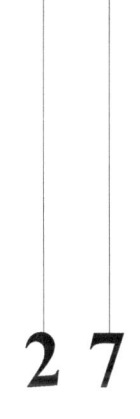

2 7

AFTER THE DANCE, ERICA AND BROOKLYN go home since they both work tomorrow. Evan gives Kathy, Miranda, and me a ride to the house where Teneil's boyfriend and another Bruin are billeting. Their billets, who are out of town, apparently don't mind if the boys have a "few friends over" after the game.

The Bruins start trickling in shortly after we get there, all pumped up by their five-game winning streak—something the Xtreme can only dream about—and the fact they don't have another game until Tuesday. Everybody ends up in the basement, which has an awesome party room. There's a wet bar in the corner and a pool table and a huge sectional sofa. Within an hour, it's standing-room-only. Kathy, Miranda, and I lean on the bar while Teneil plays pool with Mike, her Bruin.

"Is your mom okay with you being here?" I ask Miranda.

"As long as I only have one drink an hour and get home before 2:00."

I feel guilty because my parents think I'm at Kathy's. What if they call her place to talk to me, and I'm not there?

"Quit worrying about your parents," Kathy says, reading my mind. "They've kept you locked up long enough. You're fifteen now."

"Just the same, I'm not drinking," I tell her. "And I don't need to tell you why."

"Nope," Kathy says.

I watch Teneil flirt with Mike. Whenever he says something funny, she clings to him, laughing like it's the funniest thing she's ever heard. I watch his face when she does it. He looks embarrassed.

I also keep an eye on the Bruin who's bartending. He has a heavy hand when he tops up my friends' drinks.

"Pourin' triples, seein' single, and actin' double," Teneil giggles, bumping me with her hip.

"I don't think that's how it goes," I tell her.

"You should have a drink," she says.

"Sure thing. Evan, can you get me a coke?"

At least I can trust him not to mess with it.

Evan tells me about his conversations with university basketball coaches. I don't know a whole lot about playing sports for Canadian universities, but I do know athletes have five years of eligibility. Evan can practice with the basketball team for a year or two while he's taking classes, and as long as he doesn't play any games, he can maintain his full eligibility. Evan wants to be a doctor, which means he'll be in university for a long time. When he isn't playing or practising with the ECS Elecs, he's running, working out or making healthy meals.

"I'm not going to screw up my body by putting poison in it," Evan tells us. "I'd lose a whole week's training by going on a bender on the weekend."

Kathy doesn't have any of Evan's reservations about drinking, and Teneil and Miranda seem to be in a race to see who can get the drunkest quickest. I'm disappointed in all of them. But I can't do a thing about it.

After a while, Miranda starts complaining her head hurts, but I'm pretty sure her stomach's the problem. I ask Evan to give her a ride home since everyone else I know is too plastered. I'd like to go home too, but somebody has to keep an eye on Kathy, and she's not ready to leave yet.

Then Jodi and Jordan show up, and I can tell Jodi's got a head start on everybody. She stumbles and giggles her way down the carpeted stairs and nearly falls into the guys at the bottom. She saunters over to me, holding a mickey of spiced rum in her left hand like a martini glass.

"Hey, it's Jessie Mac." She pauses to take a swig. "Remember when you and me were bosom buddies?" She laughs and snorts.

I'm too embarrassed to say anything.

"Didn't think you'd be here, Jessie," Jordan says, pulling out his phone. "You've been such a Snow Queen the last few months."

I know he's texting Greg.

"I'm going as soon as Kathy's ready to leave." I'd like to tell him a few other things, but I know the words will be wasted. Instead I ask Teneil where the bathroom is, so I can change.

"Aw, but you look so pretty." Jodi slips an arm around me. I can smell the rum on her breath.

"Thanks. But I'm still going to change."

I make my way through the crowd in the hallway, grabbing my backpack from under the stairs. Once I'm in the bathroom, I lock the door and lean against it. If Greg's coming, I definitely need to get out of here. When Evan comes back from dropping off Miranda, I'll get him to drive Kathy and me to her place. I start unpacking my change of clothes.

I hear a commotion outside the bathroom door, and at first I think somebody's trying to bust in. I put my ear against the door, but I can't make out what anyone's saying. I hear Jodi's name a few times. Then I realize everybody's going upstairs. That can't be good.

I pull off my skirt and top, cursing my gel nails for getting in the way, and yank on my jeans and T-shirt. By the time I'm packed and out the bathroom door, there's not a soul in the basement.

The only people upstairs are Brittni, Cory and a handful of Bruins. They're sitting around the kitchen table, playing poker. I hesitate at the top of the stairs, but they don't notice me. Through the screen door, I can see a crowd gathered on the front step and yard. Everyone's turned in the direction of the neighbours' driveway.

When I step outside, I spot Kathy and Teneil standing at the edge of the crowd. "What's going on?"

"Jodi's doing a backflip." Kathy punctuates the statement with a loud hiccup.

"Where?"

"Off Jordan's truck," Teneil says.

"And you're just going to let her?"

Kathy dismisses my concern with a wave of her hand and a backwards stumble.

"She's done it before."

"You're both wasted." I look around and wonder if I'm the only sober one left at this party. Heart pounding, I push through the crowd.

Everyone's chanting, "Jodi! Jodi!"

She's poised on the truck's open end gate, her arms raised like a platform diver.

"Jodi, please get down from there!" I call to her.

She looks in my direction, and she smiles—like a high priestess acknowledging her worshipper. Then she bends her knees, takes a breath and launches herself into the air. Or nearly launches herself. Her bare foot slips on the metal and she goes down hard. The back of her head hits the pavement with a sickening thunk, and she lies there like a sack of flesh.

No one is chanting now.

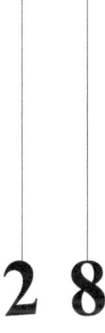

2 8

IT'S A BRUTAL WEEK. HOURS OF WAITING for news about Jodi's condition until her specialist in Regina upgrades her ICU status from "critical" to "serious but stable." Jodi's in a medically induced coma, but at least she's breathing on her own. Larissa explains that her doctor is keeping her unconscious so her swollen brain has time to heal.

Our Tuesday practice and Thursday game in Carnduff are cancelled—not that I'd go anyway. Apart from school, I'm under house arrest. My parents are so angry they're not even speaking to me.

They say, "Courtney, will you tell your sister it's time for her to go up to her room and do her homework?" and other nonsense.

I've tried to point out that God wanted me at that party. If I hadn't been there, who would have stopped a hysterical Jordan from throwing Jodi in a truck and driving her to the hospital? Who would have sent for Brittni, who knows First Aid and who was sober enough to follow the instructions from the lady on the phone after we called 911? Who would have gotten Cory to bring blankets from the house to keep Jodi from going into shock? Thank goodness Evan came back in time to help out. He and Brittni's boyfriend made the Bruins form a circle to keep everyone away from Jodi.

When I phoned Mrs. Palmer this week, she told me I'm "Jodi's angel," but I don't feel angelic. For one thing, I forgot to ask Courtney about her first day of our anti-bullying campaign.

"I thought you were going to help me," Courtney said when I finally remembered. "What you told me to do didn't work. Ashley said I was just sucking up to her."

When I tell her we need to talk to Mom, Courtney cries and begs me not to say anything. I'm so worried about Jodi I let Courtney talk me into it.

Things aren't any better at school. I bring my lunch and eat it beside my locker because I can't picture myself walking into the cafeteria and hearing all the gossip about what happened at the Bruin party or sitting down with the rest of the girls and pretending nothing's wrong.

Everything's wrong.

I'm furious with Kathy and Teneil. Sure, they were drunk, but how could they let Jodi do something so stupid?

Michelle's decided she's not talking to me either—or sitting with me in ELA, which will make it hard for us to present our partner project on Portia, the heroine from *The Merchant of Venice*. Not that I care much about Shakespeare right now. Those famous words about having a "pound of flesh removed from the region of my heart" resonate way too much.

I've apologized to Michelle more than once about telling her not to talk so much around the team. I've apologized for not phoning her back on the night of the Winter Wonderland dance.

"You couldn't wait to go with the other girls instead of me," Michelle told me earlier in the week. That's when she was still talking to me. "You were glad I couldn't come."

Frankly, I don't think Michelle was sick. I think it was a test—which, unlike the Breathalyzer—I failed.

Evan's the only person I feel like talking to, except for Tara and Shauna, who each call me the week after Jodi's accident. Accident. Now that's a funny word to use to describe something so preventable. Anyway, it was great to hear their voices. I talked with Tara for over an hour, and we cried most of the time because we're both so scared for Jodi.

The only good news I've heard all week is that Estevan is hosting the SJHL All-Star game at the end of January, and there's a good chance Mark will be playing in it. That means he'll be around all weekend, so when he ignores me, at least I'll have another reason to be miserable.

And then—miracle of miracles—he calls me.

Yeah, Mark calls to say he's sorry about Jodi.

Naturally I miss the call. The most important phone call of the decade, and I'm babysitting Breanne. I don't find his voice mail until a day later. I listen to it twenty times. But no matter how many times I listen, he never says anything about me—just Jodi and our team. He's doing what a person has to do in a situation like this. He's ticking off a box. It doesn't mean he cares about me. After two days, I delete the message. It'd be better if he hadn't called at all.

On Friday after school, Dad drives me to Carlyle for Zone One tryouts. On the way, I try to get him to loosen up by talking about the Saskatchewan Winter Games tournament.

"When is it, anyway?" Dad stares at the snow drifting across the black pavement of Highway 9.

"February break."

"Think hotel rooms will be hard to come by?"

"Forget the hotel rooms, Dad. I'm not making the team. Kathy says the competition will be tough."

"Then it's a good thing you're trying out as a forward," Dad says. "You don't know how to play defence yet, and you're a liability in your own zone."

He's so encouraging. "Thanks, Dad." We drive in silence for a few minutes. "I never thought I'd like playing defence. But I love the way I can speed up or slow down the play."

"Ever feel like the Hounds of Hell are barking at your heels?" he asks.

"Sure—in Notre Dame."

He laughs. Mission accomplished.

When we get to the rink, a lady at the registration table gives me a red jersey. The girls trying out are divided onto three groups—Team Red, Team Yellow, and Team Green. Jennifer and Shauna are on Team Yellow. Miranda and Teneil are on Team Green. I'm glad to see that Carla Stonechild, who played with the Xtreme last season, is on Team Red. Kathy's also on my team, but I'm not so happy about that. I've hardly talked to Kathy since the Bruin party.

Kim isn't listed at all. She could be trying out for Zone Two—Regina. But who knows if she's even playing hockey? It's like she fell off the edge of the earth.

Carla is the first person I see as I enter the Team Red dressing room. She gives me a big grin and a hug and clears a spot next to her on the bench.

"I can't believe we get to hang out together for the weekend," I say.

"Hopefully we'll both make the team," Carla says.

"You will for sure, but I don't stand a chance."

"You're just saying that so we'll tell you how great you are," Kathy says from across the room. She doesn't sound like she's kidding. She would never have said that to me a week ago.

"How's Jodi doing?" Carla asks. "Is she still in the hospital?"

"Yes," Kathy says. "We're worried sick about her."

That does it.

"You're saying you give a rat's ass about what happens to Jodi?" I demand.

Kathy swears and yanks off her toque.

"You knew what she was doing was dangerous! Why didn't you stop her?" I know my voice is too loud.

The other girls, most of them strangers, stop dressing and stare at us.

"Easy, Mac," Carla says. "You too, Parker. Ripping each other to pieces won't help."

Silence.

"I'm sorry, Kathy," I say at last.

"I was drunk." Kathy sounds heartbroken. "I wish I wasn't, but I was."

I put my head in my hands. "It shouldn't have happened. It was a stupid thing for her to do."

"Yeah, it was stupid," Kathy says. "We were all stupid."

It's the same feeling I had when my relationship with Mark went off the rails. I want to turn back the clock and change things, but I can't.

"Are you talking about Jodi Palmer?" one of the other girls asks. It turns out she played some AAA summer hockey with Jodi in Regina. "It's too bad she's not here," the girl says. "She was a hell of a hockey player."

Was.

What's going to become of Jodi?

As soon as I get on the ice, I push her out of my head and try to focus on the skating and puck-handling drills. But it's hard to forget about the young women in the stands, watching us and making notes on their tablets.

"Who's doing the evaluating?" I ask Carla.

"Some players from the University of Regina," Carla says, then points at a girl ripping slapshots at the other end of the ice. "But that one plays at U of S."

I've heard the girls on Team Red talk about the AAA U18 League expanding to include Weyburn, Swift Current, and Prince Albert next year. That could put a nail in the coffin of our league. Still, it would be exciting to have a AAA girls team in Estevan one day, especially if my friends and I are playing on it.

Sue and the girl from U of S run the practice session while Bud Prentice, the other Zone One coach, sits in the stands with the other evaluators. From what Carla says, the SHA selects coaches who are not affiliated with girls teams within their zone. That way they're impartial when they're selecting the Zone team. Apparently Sue committed to coaching Zone One before she started helping Mr. Kowalski coach us. That means she'll have no input in picking her team.

"What's Sue like?" Carla asks me, as we're coming off the ice.

"She's okay. She doesn't smile much."

"Does she know her stuff?"

Kathy jumps in. "I've learned lots from her, and she's only coached a couple of games."

"Is she as good as Steve?" Carla asks. "Be honest now."

"Nobody's ever gonna be Steve," Kathy says. "But Sue's great."

"Well, if she coaches the U18 girls next year, maybe I'll be back," Carla says.

"That's the best news I've heard in a long time," I say.

"Our D has been hurting all year," Kathy says. "I'll put in a good word with Sue about you quarterbacking our power play."

"Thanks," Carla grins. "Hopefully you've got more pull with Sue than you had with Steve."

I have a few words for Sue myself. As soon as we're back in the dressing room, I strip off my equipment and throw on my clothes, not bothering to shower. I pull my hair into a ponytail and head out the door.

Sue came out of the referee's room earlier, so I'm guessing she uses it for changing. I knock on the door, and I'm relieved—and anxious—when I hear her voice call out, "Come in!" When I enter, she says, "Leave the door open. Any update on Jodi?"

I shake my head. "That's not what I came to talk to you about."

She raises a blonde eyebrow.

I tell her about Brittni's and Cory's plan to get her banned from coaching. I don't tell her about "that night." I haven't spoken more than a handful of words to Sue in the time she's stood behind our bench. I'm sure as hell not telling her about the time I got drunk and necked with my ex-best friend.

Sue listens with arms folded. "Thanks for telling me," she says when I'm done. "Is that everything?"

Everything? Is she for real? "I guess so."

"Good. I have a meeting with Bud and the other evaluators." She glances at her phone. "I'm already late."

"Do you understand what I'm telling you?"

"Of course I understand." Sue digs around in her briefcase. "Ask me if I'm surprised."

Okay, I'll bite. "Are you?"

"No." She pulls out a folder and quickly flips through a few pages.

"Coach, you could be in trouble," I say. "They're gunning for you."

Sue slams shut her briefcase and fastens the snaps. "Look, I don't need this. I have a full-time job and a life of my own. Whatever game you girls are playing, you'll have to play it by yourselves."

"I'm not playing a game. I'm just warning you what's going on."

She locks eyes with me. "You think it's easy being a coach nowadays? I can't ever be alone with a player—even when we're the same sex." She jerks her head at the door. "That door has to stay open because you could accuse me of being a sexual predator." She picks up her briefcase and the folder. "I appreciate you coming, Jessie. I'll see you during the scrimmage."

Sue leaves for her meeting—just like that. She's one cool customer.

⚓

We're at the rink all day Saturday because Team Red has a practice session in the morning, and then a scrimmage at 5:00 p.m. It's a long day watching Team Yellow and Team Green on the ice, measuring myself against them in skating, passing, and shooting. There are lots of girls who have serious skills, and I know in my heart I'm not going to get picked.

All the instructors are helpful. It's obvious they love the game as much as we do. Robbie, the one who plays for the University of Saskatchewan Huskies, gives me pointers on my hand position and weight transfer to help my slapshot.

I get to showcase that slapshot in our scrimmage against Team Green. Even though I'm playing on a line with two girls I never knew until yesterday, I get an assist and a goal. But halfway through the second period, Miranda takes her turn between the pipes and shuts down our scoring. After the scrimmage, Coach Bud tells me he likes the way I work the corners.

"You're strong on your stick, Jessie, so don't be afraid to fire the puck at the net instead of looking to make a pass. Have some faith in your own ability to score." He tugs on his waistband where his wind pants are waging a war with his pot-belly.

I like Bud. He's definitely old school.

"Hockey is a simple game," he tells us. "You skate, and then you pass or you shoot. It isn't rocket science. It's geometry. It's knowing your angles and predicting where the puck will go. Get to know the boards because they're your best friends."

Sue doesn't say anything to me all day. I begin to wonder if she's ticked off because of what I told her about Brittni and Cory.

The next day I miss church so I can catch a ride to Carlyle with Mr. Parker and Kathy for our final scrimmage against Team Yellow.

"I've got some good news about Jodi," Mr. Parker says as soon as I get in his SUV. "Her mother called this morning. Jodi's come out of her coma."

"That's great! Is she gonna be okay?" I ask.

Kathy jumps in. "She didn't remember anything about the party, but she knew her parents. And she was pissed about missing the tryout for Zone One."

"That's a good sign, isn't it?" I ask.

"It sure is," Mr. Parker says.

I have wings on my heels during our final scrimmage, and I get four shots on net. Okay, so three of them hit the goalie square in the chest, but no goals are scored while my line is out.

"I'm going to see Jodi as soon as she's well enough," I tell Kathy after the scrimmage. "Wanna come with me?"

Kathy nods.

No phone call for me from Coach Bud on Sunday night. I spend most of the evening in my bedroom, trying not to leap when my phone buzzes. But it's only Kathy—and later Miranda—letting me know they made the team. They're super excited, and I try to be excited for them.

"Shauna and Carla made it too. But not Jennifer or Teneil. They're bummed," Kathy says.

"There's still next year," Dad tells me later. "Don't be too disappointed." But he looks as crushed as I feel.

I always knew it was a long shot. Then again, if I have to choose between Jodi being okay and me making Zone One, I know which one's more important.

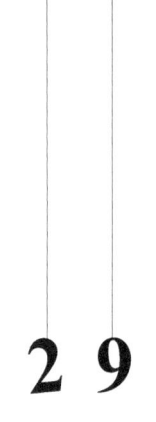

2 9

ON TUESDAY NIGHT, WE HOST CARNDUFF. Brittni and Cory look daggers at me the minute they walk in the dressing room.

"You let the whole team down, McIntyre," Cory says to me.

"Jodi especially," Brittni adds.

Everyone looks confused. It's all I can do to keep my mouth shut. What can I say to a pair of girls who are willing to ruin someone's coaching career—maybe even her life?

"I'll bet Sue had a good time at the camp," Cory says, "helping all those girls work on their skills."

Brittni laughs, but no one else does.

Certainly not Jennifer or Teneil. They've had a pout on ever since they didn't make the Zone One team.

"It's not fair," Jennifer says. "I see the ice just as well as Shauna and Carla do."

That's not true, although I don't tell Jennifer. She has a bad habit of losing track of the opposition, which means I need to stay way back to cover the cherry pickers. I'm getting lots of practice at being a "defensive" D-partner. As for Teneil, she's a great skater, but she's not that strong on her stick.

It's not a good day to finally get our new uniforms, which are sponsored by

Teneil's dad's company. We're not the Xtreme anymore. We're the Rafferty Rage. How appropriate.

"The what?" Cory asks, holding up a red-and-black jersey. There's no mistaking the scorn in her tone.

"Rafferty—like the reservoir," Teneil explains.

"We *know* where the Rafferty is," Cory says. "It's one of our favourite drinking spots. Right, Britt?"

"I went tubing at Rafferty last year," Crystal says. "I screamed like a little girl."

"Crystal, you *are* a little girl," Erica says.

"Don't we get matching socks?" Brittni asks.

"Next year," Mr. Kowalski says.

"That sucks," Cory says.

Everyone else seems thrilled with the jerseys. The logo in the middle is a howling coyote with fiery red eyes. I liked the Xtreme ones better, but I have the intelligence not to say that in front of Teneil. Not that I get to wear my new uniform just yet. I'm sitting this one out because of my checking-from-behind penalty at Notre Dame.

When the coaches come in, Sue steps into her "I'm just the assistant coach; let Mr. Kowalski call the shots" routine.

"Try to stay out of the penalty box," Mr. Kowalski tells us.

If it weren't for Jodi's accident, we'd be getting primed for the Regina tournament. Mr. Kowalski pulled our team since none of us felt like going. He hasn't even breathed the word "provincials." With our current record of one win and numerous losses, who would expect him to?

"So who came up with a stupid name like Rafferty Rage?" Cory asks.

"Why does she have to ruin *everything*?" Amber murmurs in my ear.

Mr. Kowalski looks hurt. "Steve and I dreamed it up last year. We thought a new team in a new league should have a new identity. You aren't all Estevan girls, so we picked a regional name."

"Figures," Cory says, moving towards the door.

Sue pulls me aside while everyone's leaving the dressing room.

"So you didn't make Zone One?" she asks.

"No."

"You know I couldn't take part in picking the team," she says. "Did you give Bud any reason not to pick you?"

"No. I listened to the instructors. I got along with everybody."

Sue shakes her head. "Jessie, I'm disappointed for you. You deserve to be playing in that tournament."

As we walk together towards the ice surface, my happy heart putters. Somehow her endorsement makes it better. Maybe I should be angry because she thought I should make the team, and Bud didn't. But, it's the opposite.

"Sue, do you think I could make the Zone team next year on defence?"

She unlatches the gate and pulls it open. "Each team only has six D, so your chances are slimmer." She smiles and slaps me on the shoulder. "But keep working hard, Jessie, and good things will come your way." She slams the gate and makes her way across the ice.

Wow.

"Hey, rich girl, where's *your* une-i-form?"

"Hello, Marsha," I say, still watching Sue.

"Aren't you playing?" Marsha asks. "I wanted to see somebody elbow you in the head or set you on your skinny ass."

Even Marsha's not going to ruin my improved mood. "Sorry to disappoint you."

"Where do you usually watch from?" she asks.

I point at the box of girls in red and black.

"I know that!" Marsha says.

I walk towards the stands on the west side of the ice. I'm on my own tonight since Mom is helping Courtney study for a test, and Dad has a Kinsman meeting. I could have brought Michelle to keep me company, but she's still not talking to me. I step onto the top row and Marsha steps up beside me, along with a guy I don't know. His dark hair covers most of his pale face, and his eyes are outlined in black. He's wearing skinny dark jeans and white sneakers that are totally at odds with Marsha's baggy clothes and wool toque. I hope Marsha and her friend will behave themselves.

"So how come you're not playing?" Marsha asks.

"I'm suspended."

"Ooo, suspended. So what happened?"

After I finish my explanation, the guy asks, "Was the other girl hurt?"

"No."

"That sucks," he says.

He clearly doesn't get it, but I'm not going to waste my breath setting him straight. I smell chlorine, and a mittened hand slides into mine. I look down at Breanne. She's wearing a white toque, but the tips of her pigtails are wet.

"Hey, Short Stuff." I give her hand a squeeze. "Were you swimming?"

"Yes." She screws her little mouth into a frown. "Why aren't you *playing*? I came to watch you."

"Long story," I tell her. "Is Evan here?"

"He's got basketball," she says. "I came with Mom, but we're leaving right away. Guess what?"

"What?"

"I learned to skip. Want to see me?"

She skips back and forth in front of us to demonstrate. Even Marsha and her friend look impressed.

"Cute kid," Marsha says to me. "She your sister?"

"No, I just babysit her sometimes."

The Rage and Carnduff line up at centre. Brittni is on a line with Kathy and Teneil while Cory is playing with Larissa and Amber. I question the wisdom of the latter combination, since Cory rips us a new rectum every time we make a mistake.

"I'm sure glad not to be wearing Amber's skates," I say.

"Why would you wear her skates?" Breanne asks.

"Never mind." I look back at Marsha. "Just so you know, we're going to get hammered."

Her friend laughs. "That's why we came!"

Breanne tugs on my hand and whispers, "Why're they so mean?"

"They're not as mean as they look," I whisper back.

The referee is Kathy's boyfriend Brett—or should I say ex-boyfriend. Kathy broke up with him last week, citing "irreconcilable differences."

From the moment Brett drops the puck, something miraculous happens to our team. I don't know if it's the new une-i-forms or the alterations to the lines, but the Rage play out the first period like their lives depend on it. They beat Carnduff to the puck and win the battles on the boards.

"WTF?" Marsha says halfway through the period. "When's somebody gonna get creamed?"

"There's no body contact," I explain. "But keep your eye on 18. She might catch somebody coming across centre with her head down."

"Oh, Blondie," Marsha says, gesturing at Kathy. "I remember her."

"Is she your friend?" Breanne asks, pointing a mitten at Marsha.

I have no clue what to say. Thankfully, Mrs. Gedak shows up to take Breanne home.

Miranda plays a solid twenty minutes in net, and the period finishes up with no score and no penalties for either team.

Marsha pokes me in the arm. "I thought I was gonna see some elbowing and high-sticking." To my surprise, she adds, "Still, it's better than I expected. Those girls are pretty good skaters. Bet you slow them down, huh?"

"Yep." No point in arguing with her.

"So now what happens?" her friend asks.

"I'm going to the dressing room." I step down from the stands. "But you can't come."

"Aw," Marsha says piteously. "I guess I'll go for a smoke."

I lose them in the surge of people headed for the lobby. Inside the dressing room an entirely different drama plays out.

"We can't get any points if we don't play together!" Cory shouts. "It's like you want us to lose!"

"You should be prepared to play with every girl on this team," Mr. Kowalski says.

"Says who?" Cory demands. "It's my last year playing hockey! I deserve to play with my friends!"

"There's no 'I' in 'team,'" Amber says.

"Shut up!" Cory says.

"Cory is trying to play with Amber," Brittni points out. "But she's got no one to pass to."

Brittni and Cory dominate the dressing room while Sue watches, expressionless.

Jump in there, I think. Take a stand, like you did with Jodi in Notre Dame.

"If you don't put Brittni back on my line, we're walking," Cory says.

Mr. Kowalski turns white.

"You're not giving us any choice," Brittni says. As usual she makes it sound like she's the only adult in the room. "If I can't play with my friends, why am I wasting my time coming to practices and games?"

"And we won't be the only ones quitting, right?" Cory looks around the room for confirmation.

Everyone but Kathy stares at the floor.

"You've got to be kidding," Kathy says.

"You girls are playing so well," Mr. Kowalski says. "If you just—"

"We're not *scoring*," Brittni says, as if he's a small child. "It's simple. If Cory and I don't score, we don't win."

Mr. Kowalski caves. "Okay," he says. "You and Brittni can play together this period."

"No way." It's out of my mouth before I can stop myself. "No way, Mr. Kowalski. You can't let them bully you."

"Shut your face, McIntyre," Cory says. "It was your stupid penalty in Notre

Dame that got us into this mess."

"What are you talking about? You constantly miss practices and games. You pick fights with players from other teams. You're an embarrassment to all of us. You're both damn lucky we let you play," I tell her.

"Mac, once your mouth gets going, there's no stopping it," Kathy says. "But what you just said is one hundred percent true."

Brittni glares at her—then me. "I don't have to put up with this." When she looks at everyone else, they duck their heads. "This hockey team sucks. And it's sucked ever since these two took over." She jerks her thumb at our coaches.

"Yeah," Cory says. "The wimp and the dyke."

It's a you-could-drop-a-pin moment.

Mr. Kowalski looks crushed, but Sue's face doesn't change at all. What is she made of?

Then Sue stands up. "There's no need for name-calling. Cory and Brittni—you've played your last game with this team."

"You can't cut us! We *quit!*" Cory screams.

Brittni sits and yanks on her skate lace. "And so is everybody else. Right, girls?"

I feel like I'm back in Rosetown—with the entire future of our team on the line.

I look at Kathy. She puts her palms together as if praying. I nod.

We all sit in silence while Brittni and Cory strip and cuss us out. Kathy and Crystal are "f'ing puck hogs" while Amber is an "f'ing stupid rookie." Brooklyn and Erica are "f'ing pylons." Larissa and I are "f'ing do-gooders." Miranda is an "f'ing sieve."

Then they walk.

Sue and Mr. Kowalski give us a thumbs-up and exit too. The door scarcely closes behind them before Kathy stands up and lets loose a primal scream. We join in.

Except Teneil. "They never insulted me," she points out. "It's not fair."

I'd like to say the Rage go on to win that game against Carnduff. That we're all fired up, and we score a dozen goals.

We lose 6-3.

But the last period has one highlight we'll remember for a long, long time. The Rage catches a break on what should have been an icing call, and we get the puck in deep. Kathy and Larissa crash the net, and Larissa fires a shot at the Carnduff goalie, who gives up a juicy rebound. Kathy pokes the puck in as the net comes off its mooring. Brett blows down the play and waves his arms, indicating no goal.

Kathy starts to beak him. She's right in his face, pleading, then arguing, and Brett has no choice but to give her an unsportsmanlike. While the linesman escorts her to the penalty box, Kathy's still shouting at Brett. He stares at her with this pathetic look on his face.

All the while, Marsha and her friend pound on the glass, screaming at Brett. "You guys got robbed!" Marsha says to me. "That puck was so *in*!!"

The story doesn't end there. Three surprises await us in the school cafeteria on Wednesday.

First of all, Marsha produces a plate of Dino Buddies. "I found a bag in the freezer," she says. "But don't tell anybody."

When Brittni walks over to our table, we all paste big smiles on our faces. "I thought you'd want to know Jodi's been moved to the Estevan hospital," Brittni says.

"Have you gone up to see her?" Kathy asks.

"I'm going later today," Brittni says.

"That's good," I tell her. "You're one of the reasons she's still alive."

Brittni's perfectly plucked brows make two squiggly lines. "I don't get you," she says and walks away.

That's okay. I don't get *her* either.

Then a lady delivers a bouquet of two dozen red roses to our table, and Kathy gets tears in her eyes when she reads the card.

"Well, what does he say?" Erica demands.

"One dozen is for the goal he waved off, and the other is for the penalty," Kathy says, pulling one of the roses toward her nose and inhaling deeply.

"That guy's a keeper, even if he is a ref," Jennifer says.

"Kathy, you gotta forgive him. You just gotta," Erica says.

"Maybe I will," Kathy says. "Think I can draw another two minutes for body contact?"

While everyone howls, she grins her wicked Kathy grin.

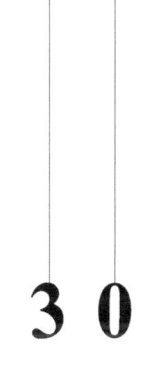

3 0

AFTER SCHOOL, I CALL JODI'S MOM.

"Jodi would love to see you girls," Mrs. Palmer says.

Frankly, I'm not so sure she will. Kathy and Larissa come along. Jodi's in a private room, and the nurse at the station warns us to keep our voices down.

"She's sensitive to noise," she says. "You can only stay for five minutes."

The room is dark. Jodi's propped up with pillows, but her head is swathed in bandages. Her eyes look like big, dark bruises, and she's pale as the sheets on her bed. Poor kid. Good thing Larissa's along. Dr. Bilku is Jodi's GP, and Larissa knows the medical lingo. I listen to Larissa's calm, muted voice. I don't have the faintest clue what to say to Jodi anyway, and apparently neither does Kathy.

There's a lapse, and the silence hangs around us like a thick, woollen curtain.

Jodi's eyes roll in my direction. She doesn't say a word. In fact, she hasn't said a single thing since we came in the room.

"Hey, Jodi." I step closer to the bed rail. "I hate to see you like this."

Jodi nods and winces. "I'm sorry, Jessie Mac," she whispers.

Why would she apologize?

"It's okay, Jodi," I reach over and squeeze her hand.

A tear seeps from the corner of her eye. That little trickle breaks my heart.

"I just wanted people to like me," she says.

"Everybody wants people to like them," Kathy says. "It's natural."

"Jodi, you never had to do anything," Larissa says. "Everybody likes you for who you are."

Jodi looks at Larissa, and it's plain she doesn't believe her. Then the dark smudges that are her eyes regard me again. "I messed things up for you too—at Shauna's."

"No, you didn't," I assure her.

"Yes I did. And I didn't even care."

"You didn't make me start drinking. I did that all by myself." I take a deep breath. "And yeah, things were messed up for a while, but I'm okay now. Maybe it's good it all played out the way it did. Who knows what I'd be up to right now?"

That sure didn't come out the way I intended.

Jodi shuts her eyes and says, "Can you get a nurse? I'm gonna get sick."

Larissa presses the call button near Jodi's hand. "We'd better go."

A nurse whisks into the room, and I start to step away from the bed. Jodi puts a hand on mine. Her grip is weak. "I meant what I said at Shauna's." Her voice is so soft I lean closer. "You *were* my best friend. I never had to impress you, Jessie."

We're all crying when we leave the room. Larissa says Jodi's going to have a tough time with her balance. It'll be ages before she can play any sport again—if she can play at all. And hockey is one big question mark.

I don't know how a hospital visit can make a person feel so good and so crappy at the same time.

Once Jodi's home, I go to see her once a week. Mom and Dad don't even complain about driving me to Jodi's farm west of Macoun—unless I'm the one doing the driving. Jodi won't be back at school until after Christmas holidays.

I sometimes spend the night at Jodi's place. I even stay there for a whole week during Christmas vacation. Normally Jodi would spend the holidays driving the hell out of her snowmobile, but she can't handle anything like that. She's dizzy, tired and nauseated most of the time, and her headaches won't go away. Most days she can't do anything but sit in the dark. It's a big deal when she's finally feeling good enough to go outside for a short walk.

We spend a lot of time talking. We talk about everything—and I mean everything. We talk about the Bruin who was too old for her.

"He thought I was immature, and he was right," Jodi says.

We talk about Jordan. Jodi isn't with Jordan anymore. Nothing new there. But this time it's for good. To his credit, Jordan tried to see her when she was in the hospital, but she didn't want any part of him.

"I don't wanna be that Jodi anymore," she says.

We talk about the old Jodi—who thought she had to outdo the last stunt she'd pulled. The one who thought she had to be wild and crazy all the time. She's hazy about some of these wild and crazy times. Larissa says Jodi's short-term and long-term memory may have permanent "blanks" between the lines.

We talk about me too. Mark. Courtney. My sister's battle for survival in her Grade Five classroom.

"Those little snots!" Jodi says after I tell her about Courtney's latest skirmish.

A few weeks ago, Ashley invited Courtney to a sleepover.

"I think Ashley's only inviting me so she can be mean," Courtney confided to me. But Ashley was so nice at school that Courtney eventually decided she would go.

On the night of the sleepover, not long after Courtney got to Ashley's house, two of the girls yanked down her leggings while Ashley took a picture of Courtney's underwear. Courtney managed to hold off a meltdown long enough to call my mom to come pick her up. That was the end of Courtney and me handling the situation on our own. We were fools to try.

Mom asked all three mothers to come over for coffee, so they could talk about a problem in Grade Five. She made all of them think it was the teacher. Then she dragged out the heavy artillery and started blasting.

"Mom talked to Courtney's teacher and the principal too," I tell Jodi. "They're doing what they can. But those little witches are pretty good at waiting until no one's looking. Mom calls them 'the Coven.'"

"Tell Courtney to hang in there," Jodi says.

"She is hanging in there. I'm proud of her. And Mom says she can change schools if she wants, but Courtney says she's not going to let them win."

Once Michelle starts talking to me again, I take her along to Jodi's farm. It's amazing how well Michelle and Jodi hit it off. They're about as different as any two girls can be, but Jodi loves listening to Michelle talk about music and the books she's read.

"How'd you ever get to be so smart?" Jodi asks her.

At least Michelle doesn't talk about hockey. I know enough to steer clear of that subject because it bothers Jodi.

Besides, our team record is 3-9-1. Even though we've won two more games since Brittni and Cory quit, the Rage is still last place in our league. It's a good thing all the teams get to participate at the final tournament in Caronport.

Since the "cancers" quit, winning or losing games has become less of a priority. We're making up for lost time in the "having fun" department. Every game there's a dance party going on. Without a doubt we're the happiest losers in the league.

"Mr. Scott told my dad we're a 'travesty,'" Kathy says one morning in the courtyard after Christmas break.

"Do tell," Erica says. "I'd love to hear what he thinks about our season."

"He says our team 'went to hell' after Kim left."

"You don't say!" Brooklyn smacks her cheeks with both palms.

"He says Mr. Kowalski and Sue need to 'crack the whip.'" Kathy makes little quotation marks with her fingers. "And get us to take the game 'more seriously.'"

"Someone needs to tell him we're getting better all the time," I say. "The scores are getting closer."

I try not to worry about the problems that still exist. Things will never be perfect. Jennifer's still bummed about not making Zone One while Kathy has the tact of Attila the Hun. Erica and Brooklyn will never skate any better, but at least they make less mistakes. We're learning how to coexist in spite of the differences in our abilities and priorities.

Like Sue says, "It takes all sorts of players to make a team."

And that's what we are. Win or lose. No matter who's on the power play or killing a penalty. We're a team.

31

"I'M NOT STICKING AROUND for Ryan's party," Jodi says.

I put down the book I've been reading to Jodi. Reading is one way I can help her with school. She never was a good student, and thanks to the trauma to her brain, she'll be lucky to finish her Grade Ten credits by June.

"What party?" I ask.

"The one after the All-Star game," she says. "I'm not going to the game either. I'm sleeping over at Michelle's place."

Jodi's older brother Ryan plays centre for the Nipawin Hawks. He was picked for the Northern All-Star team playing in Estevan against the Southern All-Stars on Saturday night.

I don't ask Jodi why she's not going. I know why. She hasn't been to a live game since her accident. Even focusing on the puck when she's watching a game on TV makes her nauseous.

Her brother's got a few offers from American universities to play south of the border next year. He's the first Palmer to be offered such an opportunity, and her parents are over the moon about it.

"I'm happy for Ryan," Jodi says.

But I know she's thinking she may never have that opportunity.

"I'm glad you're hanging out with Michelle," I tell her. Of course I'm glad. It takes the pressure off me now that Michelle has two friends.

Michelle's pretty smug about her friendship with Jodi. Like "you thought Jodi was your friend, but now she's mine" sort of smug. But as long as Jodi's happy, I don't care.

"Did I tell you Michelle and me are writing music together?" Jodi asks.

I shake my head, resisting the impulse to correct her grammar.

"That is, as soon as hearing my voice inside my head doesn't give me a headache."

"No, you didn't," I tell her. "Maybe the two of you will be famous recording artists one day."

"Doubtful," Jodi says.

I set the novel on her nightstand. "Enough reading for one day?"

Jodi nods.

I know the All-Star game is bad medicine, but I haven't seen Mark since Remembrance Day—over two months ago—and I need a fix. Watching the game isn't a problem. The issue is getting to the party at Jodi's farm.

When I ask my mom if I can go, she wrinkles her nose like she's smelled a fart. "Don't you have exams to study for?"

I'm prepared for her question. "Finals aren't for another week, and I'm sure to be fully recommended, which means I'll only have to write math. Everyone writes math."

She knows better than to tell me I need to start studying for math because I started prepping after Christmas holidays. I can tell she's trying to think of an excuse, but finally she says, "If it's all right with your father, it's all right with me."

I go downstairs to the room Mom and I call the BobbyOrrium. It's Dad's office, but the walls are full of every bit of Bobby Orr paraphernalia you can imagine. He's got a pair of signed jerseys—one Boston Bruins, one Chicago Blackhawks. He's got a blown-up picture of Bobby soaring through the air after he scored the winning goal against the St. Louis Blues during the 1970 Stanley Cup. Bobby Orr bobbleheads, coffee mugs and coasters line the shelf above his computer. Dad makes calls on a bright yellow rotary dial phone, plastered with Bruin stickers. If there were such a thing as Bobby Orr toothpaste, Dad would brush with it three times a day and keep himself smelling fresh with Bobby Orr deodorant. I'll say one thing—Dad's obsession with Bobby makes gift giving a no-brainer.

Dad's got on a pair of headphones, and he's humming some golden oldie rock'n'roll while he studies our league website on his computer screen. He clicks on the page that shows the stats for the defensive players from all the teams. I know I'm way down on the list.

"Hey, can I talk to you for a minute?" I ask.

He doesn't hear me, so I tap him on the shoulder. He nearly jumps out of his skin.

"What's the idea of sneaking up on me like that?" He's talking too loud because he's still got his headphones on.

I pull them off. "Sorry, Dad."

I know he's embarrassed I caught him stalking my stats. He exits the website and pulls himself together. "What's up?"

I tell him about the party at Jodi's after the All-Star game. His forehead gains another furrow with each detail of my master plan.

"So why her place?" he asks. "Is it Party Central again?"

I explain to him about Jodi's brother, then add, "Not all the hockey players will be there. Jodi says some of them will head home for the weekend."

"Will Jodi's parents be there?"

"I don't know."

Dad looks miserable. "I don't want you to go, Jessie."

"I know, but I'm not a kid anymore. And I can handle myself."

"If I say 'yes,' do you promise not to drink?"

"I promise."

"Who's bringing you home?"

"Evan."

Dad looks doubtful.

"Dad, you know Evan doesn't drink. He's ultra religious."

"It's all right with me if it's okay with your mother. But will you please call me if you need a ride?"

I crawl into his lap and put my arms around his neck. "You're the best." After a minute, I get back on my feet because I'm too big.

The big yellow phone rings, and Dad picks up. "Yeah, she's here," he says after a minute. He hands me the receiver. "It's Bud Prentice."

From the expression on his face, I can tell he's thinking what I'm thinking. I raise the phone to my ear with trembling fingers.

"Hi, Coach."

Bud gets right to the point. "You doing anything during February break?"

"I don't think so."

"One of my forwards broke her wrist yesterday snowboarding. Bad break too. She won't be playing hockey for a while. I'm calling to see if you want to play Zone One."

"I sure do," I say.

While he gives me some details, I think about what Sue told me: Keep working hard and good things will happen. She was so right.

3 2

EVAN PICKS UP MIRANDA, LARISSA AND ME on the night of the All-Star game. Naturally Larissa isn't ready when we get to her place. She's still eating supper, so we don't get to the rink in time for the warm-up. I knew I should have got Dad to drop me off. In only four months, I get my steering papers, and then I'll never be late for anything again.

"O Canada" is wrapping up as we climb the wooden steps to the arena entrance.

The stands are packed. I'm not surprised. There're three Bruins on the Southern team, so naturally there's great fan support. The fact that Jodi's brother and Mark Taylor are playing for the North doesn't hurt either.

I'd hoped to see Mark's mom and dad—and hopefully not Holly—but there's no way to find them easily in this crowd. We manage to locate some of the other girls from the Rage though.

After a few dignitaries give speeches and perform the ceremonial puck drop, the game begins. Mark isn't a starter, but he's on the ice for the next shift. It's tough to tell how he measures up against guys who are three years older than him because there's no hitting. Jodi warned me this would be an exhibition game, lacking in intensity.

"We could show these guys a few things about playing no contact," Larissa says.

"You're right about that," Evan says.

Mark coasts, like the other defencemen. I wonder if he's bored. The game is high scoring too. Ten minutes in, the Southern All-Stars are ahead 6-4. I only pay attention when Mark's on the ice.

Kathy comes to sit with us. If anyone's more excited than I am about my spot on the Zone One team, it's her.

"You're going as a forward, right?" Kathy asks. When I give her the nod, she says, "Maybe Bud will put us on a line together."

The SaskFirst philosophy is for the coaches to roll their lines, not shorten the bench to bring about a win. Everything is designed to keep the playing field fair, with each team allowed two ninety-minute practices prior to the tournament. I'll get the same ice time as anyone else on the team, no matter which line I'm on.

During the first intermission I spot Mrs. Taylor on the other side of the stands.

"I need to go talk to somebody," I say to Evan. "I'll be back in a little while."

When Mrs. Taylor sees me, she winces like she's trying to remember me.

Here we go. I'm slipping into obscurity already.

Then she exclaims, "Jessie, I hardly recognized you! You look so different!"

I guess I do. A few weeks ago, I let my mom talk me into getting my hair cut to my shoulders. I even let the stylist add blonde highlights and give me bangs.

"Good different or bad different?" I ask.

"Definitely good different."

"Is Mark's dad here?" I ask.

"He couldn't make it."

She doesn't elaborate, and I don't ask for details. The other adults gradually move away from us, and before long, we're alone. Perfect.

"So it's great Mark made the All-Star team, huh?" I say. "I mean, it's only his first year of Junior A. Has he made any plans for next year?"

"That's the problem," Mrs. Taylor says. "His father wants him to go to Calgary and try out for the Hitmen."

Wow. The Dub.

"And will he?"

"I want Mark to go to school right away and not get distracted by hockey. He's applied to some universities." She pauses to clear her throat. "When he went to Calgary last summer, he went with an 'I can accept this' attitude. But when he came back to Estevan, he was faced with so much ugliness."

"I heard."

"It wasn't the team. Just one of the players who tried out. I think you know which one."

Greg.

"But the others said nothing, and Mark interpreted this as agreement," she continues.

"Mark's going to be okay, Mrs. Taylor," I say. "You raised him right. The decisions he makes about his future will be good ones."

She hugs me. "Jessie, you're sweet and wise. Thank you for that."

I watch the entire second period with her. She doesn't say much about Holly, apart from the fact she couldn't come down for the weekend because of a wrestling tournament in Edmonton.

"That poor girl has classes all morning and labs all afternoon. And then she rushes off to the gym for wrestling practice and hops on a bus every weekend. I don't know how she does it."

I interpret this as meaning "Holly doesn't have much time for Mark."

Now that's a heartbreaker.

When the buzzer sounds to end the period, I say my goodbyes. I want to think about the things she told me. I walk down to the far end of the arena, where no one's standing, and lean against the rail while the Zamboni floods the ice. So maybe I'm not the only reason Mark and I broke up. It's obvious Mark's been dealing with a lot of stuff. Part of me feels sad I couldn't be the one to help him through it all. I feel a sharp twinge of jealousy that Holly got to do it.

After the game Kathy, Miranda and Teneil get a ride to the party with Teneil's older brother Jonathon.

"I'll take you there, but I'm not staying," Jonathon says.

"Why don't you guys come with me and Evan?" I ask Kathy. "He'll bring us home."

Kathy grins. "Two's company. Five's a crowd."

On the way to the farm, Evan hums while I stare out the passenger window at the dark countryside, spotted with white patches. Because of the warm weather this past week, we've lost most of the snow we had. Evan reaches across the console and takes my left hand.

The gesture makes me uncomfortable.

"You know how I feel about you, Jessie," Evan says.

"Yes." I wish I could explain how he makes me feel when he acts like this. Boxed in. Trapped.

After a few seconds I pull my hand away, zipping my hoodie up to my chin. I fold my arms and tuck my hands in my armpits. Life would be easier if I felt the same way about Evan as I do about Mark.

The party's already started when we get to Jodi's farm. Since there aren't any snowbanks, the vehicles are parked in the middle of the yard. Evan drives in, then turns around and pulls over near the lane.

"You planning on making a quick getaway?" I ask.

"We'll leave whenever you're ready." Evan starts to unfold himself from his seat. He should drive a bigger vehicle. Then he takes my hand again. "Jessie, there's something I want to ask you."

Oh, here we go again. I try to think of a variation on the phrase, "If we go out, it'll ruin our friendship," but my mind draws a blank.

"Will you be my escort for grad?"

The question takes me by surprise. I never dreamed he was thinking about it.

I have dreams of my own. Tonight Mrs. Taylor told me Mark's coming back to ECS when hockey season is done. Her artist-in-residence thing in Muenster is over at the end of February too. Part of me hopes I'll get back together with him in time to be his grad escort. Yeah, it's stupid. But there it is, just the same.

The yard light shines through the windshield, so I can see Evan's face. He's looking at me so hard I don't have the heart to refuse.

"Sure," I say. "That'd be nice."

I don't know many people at the party. Most of the guys, like Jodi's brother Ryan, are way older than me, and so are the girlfriends who've tagged along. Brittni's there because she's dating the guy picked as Game MVP for the Southern All-Stars.

Of course Brittni's the center of attention. I hear her mention Sue's and Mr. Kowalski's names a couple of times, so I move into the kitchen, out of earshot. Not before she glares at me from across the room.

I don't care what she tells everyone about the Rage, as long as she doesn't come back to play, and with only another month left in our season, that isn't likely.

Kathy, Miranda and Teneil finally show up. Teneil's not going with her Bruin anymore. She says she broke up with him, but from the way she ties into the booze, we know it's the other way around. Teneil turns out to be a weepy drunk.

"I did my best," she blubbers. "I just don't know what went wrong." She wipes away the snot and tears with the sleeve of her hoodie.

I look around for a box of tissues, but I don't see one. "You're too good for him, Teneil."

Her eyes glisten. "You think so?"

"Yes." There's no point telling her she was obsessed with him from the start. Mike was her first serious boyfriend, and he was all she talked about.

Mike is there too. He's downstairs where most of the guys are playing air hockey and video games. Guys like Jordan and Greg.

I haven't seen Greg for weeks. I didn't even know he was still around until I saw him walk in the back door, and I made damn sure he didn't see me.

"Greg's pissed about the way things turned out for him. Getting kicked out of school and stuff," Kathy slurs. Teneil's not the only one who's had too much to drink. "Now what's his daddy gonna do?"

I have a tough time feeling sorry for Greg. Most of the crappy stuff that's happened to him this year has been his own fault.

Then Teneil takes out her phone and takes a selfie of us. There's plenty of other picture-taking going on—and videoing. The theme's the same. Kids screaming and posing with their bottles of beer and plastic glasses. Sticking out their tongues. Making kissy lips. Licking faces. They'll Snapchat the photos with filters to commemorate the occasion. Just like they did last weekend—and the weekend before. I get a kick out of watching them.

I'm waiting for Mark after all. I heard someone say he's coming, so I can wait all night if I have to. Meanwhile Evan yawns in the corner, keeping an eye on me. He has a basketball tournament tomorrow, so he needs his sleep.

"Why don't you just go home?" I ask, trying to put him out of his misery.

"Not without you," he says.

"I'll be all right."

"How will you get back to town?"

"I'll call my dad." I look at Kathy, Teneil and Miranda, giggling as they pour their refills from the assorted bottles on the kitchen counter. They don't show any signs of slowing down. "He'll give us all a ride."

"I'm not leaving without you," Evan repeats.

Something about the way he says it irritates me. I've told him over and over I'm not his girlfriend, and I just agreed to go to grad with him in spite of it. My first obligation is to my friends.

"That doesn't make sense." I try not to sound annoyed. "You've got to leave for Weyburn in six hours."

We go back and forth for a while, and he finally concedes.

"All right," he says. "Be careful, Jessie."

And then, just as Evan's walking out the back door, Mark walks in. It's late, but here he is—large as life. His dark blonde hair, tucked behind his ears, sticks out beneath his ball cap, the way I like it. I don't know the two guys with him. They must be from Humboldt because they're wearing dark green jackets like his. Mark introduces them to Evan.

Miranda's in my ear right now, telling me what she knows about the other goaltenders at the Winter Games. She leans close and spills her rye and coke on my socks while I inch backwards, closer to Mark and his friends. I'm not listening to her though I try to nod in the right places. I move close enough to catch some of the guys' conversation. This is the last year in the SJHL for Mark's two friends. Their hockey futures are uncertain, and they're discussing their options. Mark and Evan aren't saying much.

I wonder if Evan's ever going home, but finally he calls out, "See you, Jessie!"

I turn around. "See you!"

That exchange gets the attention of the two older guys while Mark's eyes sweep over me. Then he brushes past.

He's not getting away that easily.

"Hey, Mark!" I call out.

He turns. He's looking at me now.

"Sweet goal," I say.

One of his buddies sets his forearm on top of my shoulder. "Which one?" He's got red hair and a crooked nose punctuated with freckles.

"The second. When he cheated in from the point and went bar down." I turn back to Mark. "Sorry I missed your call after Jodi got hurt. That was nice of you—to call."

"You're welcome." He gestures to his friends. "Let's find Ryan."

"That'll take some doing," I say. "Last I heard, Ryan and his girlfriend were making out in the hot tub."

"Is that right?" Crooked Nose gives me a warm smile. "Do I know you?"

I consider taking a stab at making Mark jealous, but I know better. Instead I lift the guy's arm off my shoulder. "Sure you do. I was the little girl playing on the monkey bars the day you left home to play in the SJ."

"Shut down!" his buddy says, smacking Crooked Nose on the back.

Crooked Nose salutes me and follows Mark down the basement stairs.

Miranda pouts. "I kinda liked the tall one, Mac."

I shake a finger at her. "He's way too old for you."

She wanders off to find Teneil and Kathy, who are playing beer pong in the solarium. I hang out at the top of the stairs for a bit, listening to the sounds rising from the basement, scarcely believing Mark and Greg can be in the same room without punching each other's lights out. But I don't hear a single angry word, only the usual chirps and curses made by a roomful of guys playing an NHL video game.

I'd like to keep on hanging out here, but two cokes and a bottle of water have taken their toll. I need to pee. I can't possibly plan my next foray into Mark's world on a full bladder.

Three girls hover outside the upstairs bathroom, and from the way they're pleading through the door, it's clear the girl on the other side is having a meltdown. I know there's a bathroom in Jodi's parents' bedroom, but that door is closed.

I've drawn enough attention to myself without walking in on—

Never mind.

That leaves the bathroom in the basement. I walk halfway down the stairs, but once the entire room is visible, I chicken out. Greg's holding court in front of the bathroom door with Jordan and some guys I don't know. There's no way I'm running that gauntlet. I weigh my options, then retreat.

The girls are still beseeching whoever's in the bathroom to come out while my own call of nature is fierce. Time for drastic measures. My shoes are at the garage entrance, but I recognize a pair at the front door that look like Kathy's. I slip them on and head out, making my way down the icy steps. It's cold out here in my hoodie, but what I have planned won't take long.

I'm nervous about yanking down my jeans this close to the house. Knowing my luck, my bare butt will end up on Instagram. I consider peeing between the cars parked in the yard, but a player and his girlfriend come out of the house and head towards a truck. I keep walking, stiff-legged and biting my lip, until I've reached the barn. As much as I'd like to, running is out of the question.

Ducking behind the dark bulk of the building, I fumble with the zipper of my jeans and pull them down to my ankles and squat like a hen laying an egg. Sweet relief. When I'm done, I grope in my jacket pocket for a tissue, and finding none, I straighten and hike up my jeans. I'm in the process of closing the zipper when Greg steps around the side of the barn.

He doesn't look surprised to see me.

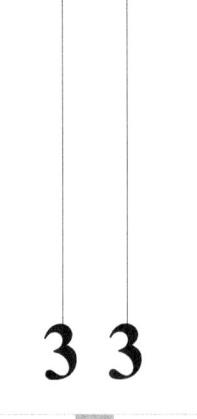

3 3

"HEY, JESSIE." HIS VOICE IS SMOOTH, almost polite. He holds a half empty liquor bottle in his left hand and his phone in the other.

"Hey, Greg." My hands shake as I button the fly. I'll have to walk past him to get to the house.

"Need some help with that?"

"No, I'm fine. Thanks."

"Will you hold this for me?" He tucks his phone in his pocket and extends the bottle.

"No way," I tell him.

He hiccups. "I just wanna get some chew."

He's drunk. I can always hit him with the bottle and outmaneuver him if I need to. I move closer and take the bottle from his hand, then step out of reach.

He pulls a tin of chewing tobacco out of the pocket of his jeans. He scoops out the plug in his lower lip, discards it, and stuffs in a new one. "Nice night."

"Yeah, it's nice." After all that's happened, I can't believe we're talking about the weather.

"Have a drink," he says.

"I don't drink hard stuff anymore." In spite of the cool air, the palm gripping the bottle is sweaty.

He nods and holds out a hand. "Well, give it back then."

There's no way around it. I have two choices—hand him the bottle or hit him with it and run for the house.

"I'm not going to hurt you, Jessie," he slurs. "Give me the bottle."

When I step closer, he grabs my wrist and jerks me against him. I try to tear free, and he stumbles but manages to stay on his feet. I open my mouth to scream, but he covers it with his hand, and pushes me against the barn.

"If you promise not to scream, I'll take my hand off your mouth," he murmurs. "Okay?"

He's covering both my nose and my mouth, and I'm struggling to get any air. He's got my right hand trapped against the rough siding of the barn, and his big body is pressed hard against mine. I've still got a grip on the bottle with my left hand, but I don't know how much longer I can hold on.

"I just want to talk to you," he says.

I stop struggling, and he frees my mouth. I gasp and fill my lungs, then swing the bottle in an arc, booze running down my sleeve as I smack him in the side of the head. I don't hit him hard enough to break the bottle, but he lets me go, cursing and reaching for his ear. I dart around him, my borrowed shoes slipping on the ice. I manage to take three strides before falling.

I feel his hand on my ankle, and I roll on my back, pummelling him with both feet. I hear a crack when I connect with his nose. He makes this choking noise, and I remember the tobacco plug. There's no way I'm doing the Heimlich on this guy, but I don't want him to die out here. I scuttle out of reach and watch until he coughs up the chew and spits it out. He lies on his stomach, panting.

"Serves you right!" I snarl at him. "Do you know what a loser you are?"

I'm ready to explode from a crouch and run back to the house. Then I see Jordan hurrying across the yard towards us. He's concentrating on the phone, which illuminates his face. I freeze, hoping he doesn't see us. There's not another soul in the yard, and the only sound is the rhythmic throb of rap music. Even if I did call for help, nobody but Jordan would hear me.

Behind me a trashy hip hop tune starts up. I check on Greg. He's lying on his back, one hand on his nose, the other digging in his pocket. We make eye contact, and he makes a lunge in my direction.

I throw myself back and roll out of his reach, coming to my feet and blowing past him. The ground's not icy once I get away from the barn. Ignoring his curses, I run into darkness. The yard light's glow doesn't penetrate this shapeless void of earth and sky. As my eyes adjust, mounds of junk and scrub brush start to appear. The dead grass gets taller, and the ground gives way beneath my feet, and I realize I've reached the dugout. Another two steps and I would have been on top of it. I don't trust the ice, so I keep moving along the perimeter. I'll make an arc to my right and sneak back to the house by traveling along the west side of the farm buildings.

I soon reach the shop, where Jodi's dad keeps their snow machines locked up. No way I'll get in there. I walk beside the building, trying to stay in the shadows. I trip and land face first on the frozen ground. I bang my knee on something hard, and in my struggle to free my foot from whatever it's tangled in, I jerk out a wooden handle, probably from a spade or shovel. It was caught in some chicken wire. When I hear male voices behind me, I look for a place to take cover. An upright tractor tire leans against the junk pile, and I back into it, still holding the handle. I'm shivering with cold and fear.

"Jessie! Come out! We're not gonna hurt you!" It's Jordan.

I don't believe him.

"She must be out here somewhere," he says.

Greg spits some F-bombs.

Jordan's answer is lost when the air compressor inside the shop kicks in with a bang, startling me. I bite the flesh between my thumb and forefinger to stifle the sob in my throat.

The boys walk past while the compressor keeps banging away. I relax a little because I'm pretty sure they didn't see me. I count to thirty as I consider my next move. Do I backtrack or follow them? The air compressor kicks out with a long wheeze, and silence shrouds me.

Just when I decide to retrace my steps, I hear the crunch of feet on gravel, the swishing of jeans. Did they double back? I squeeze the length of handle with both hands, imagining a homerun swing. There are no voices this time, and I figure the two must have split up.

As soon as I glimpse a foot, I strike with all my strength, clubbing someone in the shin. Is it Jordan or Greg? The guy moans and collapses in a heap, swearing and holding his leg. I crawl out of the tire and try to smack him across the shoulders, but he rolls away, still moaning.

"Sucks to be you!" I hiss at him.

"Jessie," he groans.

I see the ball cap and longish hair and realize I've chopped down the wrong tree. "Mark, I'm sorry! I didn't know it was you!"

He curses.

I drop beside him, dripping snot and tears on his hockey jacket. "I'd never hurt you!"

Mark rolls onto his back and brings his knee up to his chest, rubbing his shin.

"I'm really sorry," I say.

"It's okay." He straightens his leg and looks at me. It's the first time he's really looked at me in a long time.

That's when I kiss him. I know I shouldn't. He's not my boyfriend anymore, but I can't help it. When he doesn't respond, I kiss his cheeks and his forehead and then I hug him, sobbing in his ear and telling him how sorry I am for everything.

He lies there and lets me do it. Then he pats me on the arm. "Jessie, stop it."

"I'm sorry." I sit back on my heels and wipe my nose with my hand. One of these days I am going to start carrying tissues. "I was scared. Greg and Jordan are out here."

"I know. I saw you come downstairs, and I saw Greg leave the basement right after you. Then Jordan left," Mark says. "One of the guys said you all went outside, so I figured they were up to something. Did they hurt you?"

"No." It comes out in a rush before I can stop it. "I still like you, Mark."

He starts to sit up. "Never mind that. Let's get back to the house before they show up."

"I'm sorry to drag you into this." I sniff. "I hate the way Greg treats you and your dad. I mean, he should know that just because your dad's gay, doesn't mean you are too."

Even in the darkness I can tell Mark's mouth is wide open.

A thought strikes me. "So you *are* gay?"

Now his eyes are as wide as his mouth. He doubles over and starts laughing. It's a beautiful sound.

I decide it doesn't matter if I can't ever go out with him again—if he never kisses me again. As long as he looks at me, talks to me and laughs like that when I ask stupid questions, I can live with that.

He rubs a strand of my hair between his fingers. He brushes my cheek with the back of his hand and with his thumb, wipes away my tears. "Jessie, I'm going out with Holly."

I sigh.

He places a hand on the back of my neck, pulls my head close, and kisses me.

It's not like any other time he's ever kissed me. There's hunger and desperation in his mouth. His breath warms me right to my toes. He's saying something, but I have no idea what it is, and I don't care. I let him push me down and roll on top of me, pushing my shoulders into the hard, frozen ground. If he wants me here and now, he can have me.

This is wrong, Jessie, my little voice says.

Just a while longer, I think.

Then his weight is gone, and he's standing over me. "We're going back to the house," he says, holding out his hand.

I take it because it feels so good to have its warmth wrapped around my fingers. "So what does this mean?"

He moves quickly, even though he's limping and sucking in his breath at the pain in his shin. I hurry to keep up. At first I don't think he heard me. Then he says, "It means nothing."

My heart sinks, but when I think about the way he kissed me, and I'm sure he's lying. If not to me—to himself.

"Mark, are you still angry with me?"

He's muttering to himself.

"What're you saying?" I ask.

He stops and pulls me behind him. Greg is walking towards us. He's holding his right hand in front of his face. The sight of him makes me queasy.

"Markie, why don't you head back to the house?" Greg's voice is nasal, like his nose is stuffed up. "Jessie and me have something to discuss." He points at me with his right hand. His nose looks like a big shadow from where I'm standing, but I can see the dark stain of blood above his lip and below his chin.

"Jessie, you're gonna pay," he says.

My heart is racing, but I know one thing. Mark didn't leave me for Marsha and her friends when he hardly knew me, and he's sure as hell not leaving me alone with Greg.

"No," Mark says.

"You're a faggot, Markie, just like your old man."

"Go back to the house, Jessie." Mark gives me a little push.

"No!" I try to grab his hand again, but he pushes me a second time, harder.

"Jessie, I can't do anything with you here. Get going!"

I start backing away towards the house, and then I spot Jordan, coming up behind Greg.

"Greg, hold on!" Jordan shouts.

"We're gonna kick your ass, Markie," Greg says.

Jordan shoves Greg, knocking him onto his hands and knees.

"What the hell!" Greg sputters.

"Are you crazy?" Jordan demands. "What the hell, yourself! Like I told you back there, it was fun to scare her a couple of times, but I'm not going to jail for assault."

"Assault?" Mark gives me a sideways glance. "Did they touch you, Jessie?"

"Who assaulted who?" Greg says, grabbing Jordan's arm as he stands up again. "Do you see my friggin' nose and my friggin' ear?"

"You deserved it! I'll bite off your *other* ear if you come near me again!"

"You did that to him?" Mark asks.

What Greg calls me next is something I'm never going to repeat.

"Shut up, Greg," Mark says before turning back to me. "Is that why you smoked me in the shin?"

"Why else would I be hiding in the junk pile?"

"She's right, Nicker. You got exactly what you deserved," Jordan says. "Haven't I been trying to tell you that for the last ten minutes?" He looks at me. "I came out here to stop him, Jessie. You gotta believe me."

I'm not sure what I believe.

"Don't listen to him, Jessie," Mark says. "Go to the house."

"No."

"Jessie and I were just talking out here, and she freaked on me. She's psycho," Greg says. "She's the one who should go to jail!"

"You can't be serious!" I shout.

"It's your word against mine." Greg sounds calmer now. "And I hope you've got a good lawyer, because my dad is. You don't want to mess with me."

"I do," Mark says.

"That's only going to make things worse." Jordan steps between Mark and Greg. "Trust me. I have the solution." He reaches into his back pocket.

"What the hell is that supposed to mean?" Greg asks.

"Want me to show Jessie your latest text?" Jordan holds up his phone. "Or maybe she'd like to see all the texts you've sent me about her?"

Greg swears at Jordan. I haven't heard such a string of cuss words since Brittni and Cory quit playing hockey.

"I'll take that as a no." Jordan hands me his phone. "Keep this as long as you need it."

"Jordan, are you crazy?" Greg demands.

"Get in the car, Greg," Jordan says. "Your nose is swelling. Could be broken. I'm gonna find somebody to drive us to the hospital."

Greg and Jordan have a staring contest. Then Greg turns his back and retreats to the vehicles parked in the yard. I can't believe it.

Jordan shoves his hands in his pockets. "Jessie, I'm sorry about the stuff I said to you in the Civic that day. Greg was getting his kicks out of scaring you—and

I guess I was too. But ever since Jodi got hurt, I've done lots of thinking." He clears his throat. "I never thought he'd go this far. When he texted me tonight, to say he had you cornered, I came out here to tell him to lay off."

"You expect her to believe that?" Mark demands.

"She can believe whatever she wants," Jordan says. "It's the truth."

"So why did you help Greg look for me then?" Now that the fear is gone, I feel only cold and anger. I'm shaking.

"Jessie, you need to go inside," Mark says, noticing. "You're going into shock."

"I don't want to go back to the house. I want to hear Jordan's answer."

Cursing, Mark yanks off his jacket and pulls it around me. It isn't lined, but it definitely helps. The arm wrapped around my shoulders doesn't feel half bad either.

Jordan continues. "I was trying to talk him out of it. The only reason I split up with him was because I thought I'd find you first and help you get back to the house."

"Sure you did," Mark says.

"Whatever," Jordan says. "You're one to talk."

Mark stiffens. "What's that supposed to mean?"

"I saw you crawling all over her out there." Jordan jerks his head in the direction of the barn. "You've got some serious issues *yourself*, Taylor."

Mark sucks in his breath while I blush right to my toenails. How much did Jordan see?

"You should go home, Jessie," Jordan says.

"I'll drive her," Mark says.

"You can do whatever you like, Jessie," Jordan says, "but take my advice— that's *not* a good idea. Now if you'll excuse me, Greg's got a date with an emergency nurse. I'll tell her he walked into a door."

"What do you want to do, Jessie?" Mark asks.

I stare at Jordan's phone. The thought of seeing the things Greg's said about me sickens me. "I want my dad."

3 4

A WEEK LATER I'M IN MY ROOM—under house arrest—doing homework after supper when Dad calls me. "Jessie, come down here."

Mark's standing at the front door. Dad looks like he's come face to face with his own executioner.

"Hi, Mark." My heart is racing, but I'm determined not to show it. Can this mean—can it possibly mean—

"Mr. McIntyre, is it okay if I take Jessie for a drive?"

Dad scowls. "I don't think that's wise. Not after what she's been through."

"It's all right, Dad." I hope I sound calm. Meanwhile I'm thinking— get outta my way, Dad. I pull my jacket from the closet and follow Mark out the door. Dad makes a grab for my hand, but I yank it back. "Dad, please!"

I'm elated as I hop in the front seat of Mark's truck. Just like old times. Right down to my dad standing in the doorway, looking as if he'd like to have me back in preschool.

"Shouldn't you be in Humboldt?" I ask.

"I came down to meet with the Comp staff to talk about finishing off my last semester here. Picked up a few books."

"Oh."

I'm not the main reason then. Damn.

We don't go far. He drives a few blocks, makes a U-turn, and parks next to the valley. It's the same place we parked when he broke up with me last June, only this time we're facing west, looking directly at the Boundary Power Station. We got some snow last night, so there's a sugar frosting on the grass and the sidewalks.

"So what are we going to talk about?" I ask before he's even got the truck shut off.

"Pressing charges against Greg. You told your dad, right?"

I take a deep breath. "I told him everything. Mom too. I even told them about me and Jodi making out at Shauna's party."

Mark whistles. "How'd they take that?"

"Oh, they were . . . surprised."

Surprised. What an understatement. Stunned is more like it. Shell-shocked. Freakin' near traumatized. I feel sick every time I think about how crushed Mom was to learn I'd been keeping things from her again. But how did I know that a drunken make out session with Jodi was going to lead to all this other crap?

"Then what?" Mark prompts.

"My dad made an appointment with Mr. Kolenick at his office."

"Oh really." Mark looks surprised—and impressed.

"Dad told Mr. Kolenick a kid's been stalking me for months. Even attacked me at a party. He asked Mr. Kolenick if he should go to the police, and Mr. Kolenick said he should. He said this kid's obviously got anger issues and he needs help before he hurts somebody."

"No way," Mark says.

"Way. Then my dad told Mr. Kolenick who it was. They went back and forth about that for a while until Dad showed him Jordan's phone. Mr. Kolenick said he'd take care of it. Dad said he'd better because he'd be checking back in 48 hours."

"Did he?"

"Yes. And then Mr. Kolenick told him Greg blamed everything on Jordan. Mr. Kolenick talked to Jordan and got his side of the story, which he believed. Mr. Kolenick said to my dad, 'What does a father do when he can't believe anything his son tells him?'"

"Good question."

"Mr. Kolenick said he'd get Greg help, and he guaranteed Greg would never come near me again."

Mark pounds his palm on the steering wheel. "That's ridiculous! Your dad didn't buy that, did he?"

"He did after Mr. Kolenick brought Greg to our house and made him apologize."

"Big deal," Mark says. "So he said he's sorry. Everyone says they're sorry when they get caught."

"Maybe you won't believe this, but I honestly think Greg knows how close he came to messing up his future," I tell him. "He looked scared. So did his old man. I don't want to go to court. I just want Greg to never come near me again."

Mark and I sit in silence. It's killing me. I want to tell Mark a thousand things, but I don't have a clue where to start.

I muster up the courage to say the only stuff I want him to know. "Mark, I'm sorry about what I did at Shauna's. I've never touched alcohol since. And I never said anything to Greg about your dad. I don't know how Greg found out, but it wasn't through me. And I'm so much more grown up than I was last June." I take a deep breath. "Isn't there some way we could—"

"No." He stares at the floorboards beneath his feet. He sounds exactly the way I do when Evan tries to get me to go out with him.

It's hopeless.

Then Mark says, "This is going to be hard for you, but I need you to be quiet for a bit."

Time drags. Rivulets of water run down the windshield where the truck's heater melts the ice.

How long are we going to sit here? Why are we sitting here? If it's hopeless, why am I here at all?

Then he starts to talk. He talks about stuff I never dreamed of. How Frank Taylor isn't his biological father. How his mother got involved with one of her professors, a married guy with kids, when she was studying art at the University of Calgary. Then she got pregnant.

"The jerk wanted her to have an abortion," Mark says. "He didn't have tenure, and he was afraid of losing his job and family. Mom went to see a doctor to arrange it, and on the way back from the doctor's office, she stopped in a coffee shop, where Dad worked part-time. He was a student too. She was so upset she couldn't get her order straight. Dad knew she needed help, so he took a break, and she poured out the whole story to him right there. Afterwards, he drove her to her apartment and gave her his phone number and told her to call him if she needed someone to talk to. They got married three months later. They helped each other finish their degrees, and they looked after me, with a little help from their own parents."

"That's amazing."

"Any way you look at it, my dad's more of a man than that other creep was."

"Did your mom know Frank was gay when she married him?"

"Yes, but Dad said it would have killed his parents if they'd known the truth. They were . . . religious. He thought he could put it all behind him." Mark pauses to clear his throat. "But he and my mom knew he was living a lie. And then Dad met Gary, and that was it."

"When did you find out he was gay?"

"Two years after they divorced. I was fourteen. I couldn't understand how two people who loved and respected each other so much wouldn't stay together. When Mom told me the truth, it all made sense."

"You never suspected?"

Mark shakes his head. "Until I met Holly, I never knew anybody—besides my mom and dad—that I could talk to about this. It's been eating at me for a long time. But Holly gets it. She's tight with her Uncle Gary."

I'm not happy to be talking about Holly. I hope she's not going to play a role in the rest of this conversation.

"You could have told me about your dad," I tell him. "I would have tried to understand."

"I know that now," Mark says. "I didn't give you enough credit, and I'm sorry."

"Thanks. When did you figure that out?"

"When I saw you talking to him at the Civic," Mark says. "You were the only person who did—apart from me. You showed a lot of class, Jessie."

I feel a warm glow.

"I realized something else that day," he says.

My heart starts to beat faster.

"I realized I still like you. But right now, I'm with somebody else. Someone I care about."

"So what are you saying?"

"I'm saying—I like both of you, but I'm choosing Holly."

Not exactly the news I was hoping for, but—this is strange—I'm not heartbroken. Things could be a hell of a lot worse.

"Does this have anything to do with me being fifteen and her being older?" I ask.

"She's very special, Jessie. I wish you could be friends."

"I hope you realize that's not going to happen." I watch a big man walk a Pomeranian along the street. What's a big man doing walking such a little dog? I give my head a shake. "Okay, I take that back. I know she's nice, but you're asking a lot." I take a deep breath. "That night at Jodi's place when you kissed me, what were you thinking?"

"I wasn't thinking," Mark says. "I'm sorry. I shouldn't have done that."

It's like a door opens, and I see a bright light on the other side and hear an angel chorus. A revelation. Too bad Jodi's not here to testify. I see the pivotal moments of our relationship through Mark's eyes. All the times he pulled away from me, and I thought he didn't like me the same way I liked him—that whole time he was fighting back urges most guys—at least guys like Greg and Mark's biological dad—give in to. When Mark kissed me at Jodi's place, he showed how he really feels about me. Maybe with Holly, he doesn't worry. She's older, and she can handle that stuff. And he thinks I can't. As much as I'd like to tell him, okay, here I am, you can have me too, I know he won't. He just won't.

"I'm lucky I got to go out with somebody like you," I say, "even if it was only for a little while."

He smiles at me. "I feel the same way, Jessie."

I get lost in his grey eyes every time. "So will you kiss me—for old time's sake?"

Mark laughs and turns the key in the ignition. "Absolutely not."

That's when I know it's not over. Someday, somewhere, I'll have another crack at him.

He drives me back to my place. I'm hoping he'll at least hug me before I get out of the vehicle, but he keeps his distance.

"See you around, Jessie."

"See you." I open the truck door. "Does this mean we're at least going to be friends?"

"Oh, you got me."

This time—I know he means it.

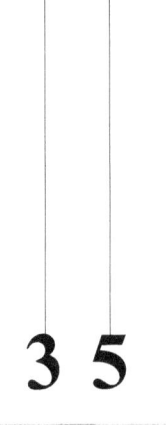

3 5

I'D LIKE TO SAY THE RAGE FINISH the season in fine style, winning our league tournament in Caronport *and* the provincial final. Truth is, we finish up fifth in the league and get blown out of the Blue Goose in the first round of provincials. The good news is—we improve a *lot*.

"Third time's the charm," says Kathy. "Maybe next year."

"Oh, next year is definitely going to be *our* year," Sue says.

I love how she says "our year." That means she'll be back, and with any luck the rest of the Rage will be too. But for some of us, hockey season isn't quite over. Near the end of February, Kathy, Miranda, and I head to Humboldt for the Saskatchewan Winter Games.

On the way to Humboldt, we stop at the crossroads where that horrible bus accident occurred. The field of crosses on the northwest side of the intersection is a sobering reminder how one simple, terrible choice can impact so many lives. It makes my own lousy choices pale by comparison. I start to take out my iPhone—which Mom gave to me before I left home—thinking I'll take a picture. But I put the phone back in my pocket right away. It seems disrespectful. Besides, there are some things you carry in your memory without needing a physical reminder—like Jodi lying on the pavement and this.

At the Games, I realize how big my hockey family is. Bailey, one of my friends from Saskatoon, is on the Zone Six team. And it's heaven to be on the same team as Shauna and Carla again.

Our team stays in one of the local elementary schools, which is a blast because we sleep together in one big room with rickety bunk beds with thin mattresses. There's always something crazy going on. Like Kathy making zoo animals out of sock tape. Theresa from Carnduff doing scenes from all the *Vacation* movies. Zoe and Emily from Weyburn singing the score from every Broadway musical ever written.

I never thought I'd say this. But girls from Weyburn are actually nice.

On Day Two of the Games, I pack up my equipment and carry it out of the Humboldt rink after our 4-2 win over Zone Three. I meet Kim coming in.

She's laughing and talking with another girl. Kim looks way different. She's wearing her hair as long as mine is short. When our eyes meet, she reacts.

"Jessie!" she screams, and she *hugs* me.

That is something Kim has never done.

It makes me want to cry because I've been feeling guilty so long about what happened to her. Now I know she's okay. Moving to Regina was the best thing for her. We don't have much time to talk, but she introduces me to her cousin Kelsey.

When I ask Kim how she's doing, she pulls down the waistband of her joggers so I can see the top of her thigh. There are scars, but the cuts have healed.

"Those aren't *that* bad," I say, pointing to the fine, pink lines.

"I know. I'm lucky," Kim says.

She tells me her aunt's a guidance counsellor in the Regina public school system. Her aunt got her to wear an elastic band on her wrist and snap herself whenever she felt the need to cut.

"It works the same way in releasing endorphins," Kim explains. "Auntie Cheryl got me to watch funny movies all the time. Laughing releases endorphins too. I guess you could say I laughed myself all the way here."

Kelsey watches Kim, smiling and nodding every so often.

I think, Kim, you got out just in time. I'm so glad you found family that know how to care for you. "Are you ever coming back to Estevan?"

Her smile fades. "I don't know."

I reach out and squeeze her hand hard. "We'll be there for you, whenever you're ready," I tell her.

When we beat Zone Two—Kim's team—in the final, Mark's there with Holly, clapping and cheering—along with his mother and my parents as well as Courtney, Evan, and Breanne. Shauna's parents and boyfriend. The Stonechilds, Parkers, and Omalus.

Jodi's there too, with Mrs. Palmer and Michelle. It means a lot because I know how much it hurts Jodi to watch us play her game.

My heart soars as the gold medal is hung around my neck. This is the pinnacle of my hockey career so far, and the future looks bright.

Afterward, Jodi finds me in the lobby. Her eyes are wet. "When we were at Notre Dame that day, it would have been my last game, and I didn't even *play* it."

I cry with her because I can't imagine how much it hurts to give up the game we love, maybe forever.

Then Kathy comes, and Kim and Michelle, and we totally have group hug.

A little *Kumbaya* never hurt anybody.

Want to find out what Jessie does next?

Read the first chapter in the third book
in the *Jessie Mac Hockey Series!*

Jessie McIntyre, 17, starts her last year of minor hockey—and high school—with loads on her mind. Her AAA team is short a head coach, her future plans are unclear, and some of her teammates aren't impressed with her new role as team captain. On top of it all, her little sister is making some lousy decisions while Jessie's parents seem unaware. But, hey, should Jessie be critical? She's made some pretty bad ones herself—especially when it comes to guys.

1

IT'S MY FIRST TIME WEARING a watermelon, the favourite headgear of a Saskatchewan Roughrider fan. "How do I look?"

Kathy Parker turns away from the mirror where she's applying an S tattoo to each cheek. "Like a warrior," she affirms. She tightens the elastic on each blonde pigtail, dyed bright green, before jamming on her own watermelon. "Let's rock 'n' roll."

Teneil Howard and Miranda Omalu await us on the Mosaic Stadium concourse. They wear green cowboy hats—not melons—and they're talking to a pair of guys in their twenties. My teammates suck on fountain drinks, and from the smug looks on their faces, I'll bet they conned their new friends into buying them alcohol. In her green crop top and white shorts, Teneil looks older than seventeen, as does Miranda with her jet-black cornbraids and halter top, which reveals way too much dark skin.

Kathy beckons to them. "Let's go! I don't wanna miss the anthem!"

Teneil and Miranda say goodbye to the guys and fall in behind us. We're like four salmon wriggling through the slow moving current of football fans. Most are decked out in the jerseys and numbers of their favourite players, but some are dressed as green nuns and priests, superheroes and villains, doctors and nurses, pirates and aliens. I feel inadequate in my green tank top and white capris. I wish I had a jersey too, so I could be a bigger part of Rider Nation.

Kathy doesn't pause to talk to the attendant outside the double doors to the ramp access. We're using her parents' season tickets, and she knows exactly where we're going. It's a scorching August afternoon. A slight breeze flutters as we head up the ramps—Kathy says there's five of them. I've been training all summer for hockey—running early every morning—so I enjoy the challenge. I'm barely puffing when we step onto the upper concourse.

I pause at the rail to take in the breathtaking view. The football field below, where the Riders and Stampeders warm up, is magnificent. A huge jumbotron at the south end encourages us to hashtag a message and picture. Beneath it is Pil Country, the standing-room-only section renowned for its rowdiness. What does it feel like to play a sport in front of so many people?

"Let's get something to eat," Miranda says, pointing at the lineup in front of the nearest concession.

Miranda's always eating. It's sinful the way she scarfs down junk food and deep-fried whatever and doesn't gain a pound.

"Later." Kathy turns into a passage between the stands and leads us to our section.

The heat and height hit me like a wave. I'm a little dizzy as I follow her down the steep stairs and along the row to our seats. The players, despite their size, look like ants from up here.

"Is it my imagination or is the air thinner?" Teneil asks.

"What if I pass out?" I ask Kathy.

She smacks my watermelon. "That's what this is for."

The roof shades the Parkers' seats, but I'm melting under the sun's relentless rays. Why didn't I wear shorts? I sit and try not to think about the moist patches in my crotch and behind my knees, the lack of oxygen in this stifling air, and the watermelon compressing my temples.

The guy in green body paint sitting next to Kathy extends a plastic cup of beer. "You ladies thirsty?"

"Sure am." Kathy takes the cup, tips her head back, and guzzles. She can really put the stuff away.

"You too?" Green Paint Guy asks, pointing at me.

"No thanks." As refreshing as that beer looks, I swore off drinking two years ago.

Someone taps my shoulder, and I shift in my seat. A short, bald man who looks like he's trying to digest a watermelon beams at me. It's Bud Prentice, my

Winter Games coach.

"Hey, Bud!" I stand up, kneel on my seat, and shake his hand. I'd hug him if I wasn't so sweaty. "Kathy never said you had season tickets here."

"He doesn't." Kathy executes a loud belch, for which she receives a high-five from Green Paint Guy.

"I bought these ones off a friend." Bud shakes Kathy's hand too, then wipes his brow, and tugs his Rider ball cap on. "Where's your fella?"

"With his homeys." Kathy gestures to Pil Country.

"The Queen of the Penalty Box and the Referee." Bud laughs. "So ironic."

Kathy gives him a patient smile. "Yeah, you're the first one to point that out."

"You got a fella, Jessie?" Bud asks.

"Nope."

"Evan's a fella," Kathy says.

"Not my fella," I say. "Who are you here with, Bud?"

Bud turns his belly, so we can see the little boy clutching a phone. "This is my grandson. Say hello, Zack."

"Hello Zack." The little guy grins at us.

"You're cute," Kathy says.

"Zack's from your neck of the woods," Bud explains. "My daughter and son-in-law moved to Bienfait this summer."

"Hi Bud," Miranda says, joining the conversation.

"Well, well, Miranda Omalu. Goaltender extraordinaire." Bud smiles broadly. "It's great to see you girls. Brings back great memories. There was something really special about that Zone One team."

"I'll say," Miranda says. "We won gold."

Bud cranes his head to look at Teneil. "I don't remember you though."

Teneil wrinkles her freckled nose and narrows her gaze. "Why would you? You cut me."

There's nothing so dangerous as a female hockey player with a grudge.

"This is Zack, Bud's grandson," I say, to lighten the mood.

"Hey, Zack." Miranda holds her hand out for a high-five.

Zack rears back and smacks it.

While Kathy and Miranda reminisce with Bud about the Winter Games, I keep an eye on Teneil. She folds her arms, turns her back and stares at the football field, where two rows of ants carry out a long roll of red and white. Must be the flag.

"What's the big deal?" I whisper to Teneil. "It happened a long time ago. Don't let it spoil your afternoon."

Teneil takes a long pull from her straw before answering. "Easy for you to say," she hisses. "You've got a Games medal. I don't."

I turn back to the others just as Zack tugs on Bud's jersey. "Grandpa, I'm hungry."

Bud rubs his round belly. "What're we having now?"

"Fries," the boy says.

Bud sighs and reaches for his wallet. "Those stairs scare the crap out of me. Would one of you girls mind?"

"Not a bit," Miranda says. "Wanna come with me, little man?"

Without another word, Zack climbs over the back of the seat and leads Miranda down our row. Teneil follows them.

"So you're getting a AAA team in Estevan," Bud observes.

I try to waft some air under my tank top. Rivulets of sweat run down my stomach.

Kathy hovers beside me, blocking what little breeze there is. "Have you seen our new rink, Bud?"

"Not yet," Bud says.

"It's amazing," Kathy says. "An oilfield construction company is donating our ice time, so we'll be the Estevan McGillicky Oilers."

"Think you'll be competitive in your first year?" Bud asks. "It's a tough league."

Kathy nudges me. A warning.

"Depends on who comes to our camp next weekend," I say.

"And Sue's coaching?" he persists. "How's she going to manage that and her engineering job?"

"She won't be head coach. Mr. Kowalski can't do it either because he's a vice-principal now. Minor Hockey's trying to find someone else."

"They better hurry," Bud says.

Kathy's phone plinks, and she stares at the screen. "It's Brett. Jessie, you sure you don't want to hang out with us tonight?"

"I don't have fake ID, remember?"

She starts texting.

And then the dreaded question.

"Last year of high school, Jessie," Bud says. "What're your plans after graduation? Are you going to try for a hockey scholarship?"

I look into his blue eyes. "Kathy and I are going to the University of Saskatchewan camp on Labour Day weekend. Do you think I have a shot at making the Huskies next year?"

"A season of AAA will certainly help," he says, looking away.

Not exactly a vote of confidence. Do I have what it takes to play U Sports hockey?

At that moment the announcer introduces the Calgary team, and thirty-three thousand fans boo, then rise and roar as the Riders take the field.

"Talk to you later!" I shout at Bud.

Miranda, Teneil, and Zack come back with the fries. I put aside my fears for my future and let myself get swept up by the anthem, opening kickoff, and crushing hits down on the field. Kathy provides a running commentary. Good thing she knows football because I don't, so I shout, cheer, and boo whenever she does. By the end of the first quarter, Calgary leads by a touchdown.

"I need to use the can," Kathy says.

"Me too."

In the washroom, we try to wash off the watermelon juice. The green Kool-Aid in Kathy's hair has leaked down her neck.

"You're bleeding green," I say, blotting my face and neck with a cold, wet paper towel.

Kathy laughs and squeezes the moisture out of her pigtails. "I'm hungry. Want a hotdog?"

"We're supposed to be in training," I argue. "There's no nutritional value in a wiener."

"Live a little, McIntyre," Kathy says.

I push the washroom door open. "You think Sue will stick around as an assistant if Minor Hockey finds us a head coach?"

"Sue loves us," Kathy says.

"Maybe she loves you," I reply. "I never know where I stand with her. I'm always afraid I'll make a mistake."

"Well, while I grab us some dogs, you wait here and think about how far playing it safe gets you."

"Can you not see the watermelon I'm wearing?" I tap the hull for emphasis. "For me, this is living on the edge."

Kathy snickers and heads for the concession while I contemplate tossing my melon in the garbage bin. Then again, what will my hair look like without it?

"Now that's what I call dedication," a female voice says behind me.

I turn around. The speaker is a tall, dark-haired girl wearing a pink, fur-trimmed cowboy hat, Rider tank top, and a short white skirt. She looks familiar, but I can't place her.

"You like wearing that?" she asks.

I try to fake it. "Sure. What are you up to nowadays?"

She laughs as if she enjoys my discomfort. "You have no idea who I am."

The laughter clicks, and I look for the rose tattoo on her ankle. "Brittni Wade."

"Of course! You honestly didn't recognize me?"

"Your hair's a different colour. And you're thinner."

"Thanks." Brittni opens the purse slung over her shoulder and removes a business card. "I'm working at a salon in Rochdale. Come see me next time you're in town. I've always wanted to do something with this." She fingers a crunchy strand of my hair.

I change the subject. "What's Cory up to these days?"

"I haven't seen her since she slept with my ex."

A tall guy holding two cups of beer comes up behind Brittni and touches one to her bare shoulder.

She starts. "Hey!"

"Hey yourself," he says.

"Jessie, this is Jamie, my fiancé."

"Hi, Jamie." My eyes dart from the rock on Brittni's left hand to the guy's crooked nose and ginger hair. He looks familiar.

"I'd shake your hand, but as you can see . . ." Jamie raises his cups.

"So when's the big day?"

"Night," Brittni corrects me. "We're getting married on New Year's Eve."

Jamie scowls. "I better not miss out on watching Team Canada. My bros won't let me hear the end of it."

"As if I'm supposed to put my life on hold for the World Juniors," Brittni says.

A light flicks. "Jamie, did you play in Humboldt with Mark Taylor?"

His scowl deepens. "Yeah, before I tore my ACL. I'm apprenticing to be a plumber now."

"I used to play hockey with Jessie," Brittni says. "Back in Estevan. Good times. Right?"

"Right." Apparently she's forgotten about calling me an "f'ing do-gooder."

"That dyke still coaching?"

I ignore her question. "So Mark's playing in Calgary again?"

He salutes me with his beer. "A toast to the Dub. Go Hitmen." He drains the cup and offers me the other.

"I don't drink beer," I tell him.

"Jessie doesn't drink at all," Brittni explains. "At least she doesn't anymore.

Isn't that right, Jessie?"

I hate it when people know your dirt.

"Look me up on Instagram." Brittni hands me her business card. "Remember what I said about your hair."

As they walk away, I think about Jamie's metamorphosis from hockey player to plumber. It's obvious he's bitter about the injury that forced him to give up hockey—and the Dream. For guys, it's the NHL. For girls, it's the National Team. Adults are always telling us, "If you want something bad enough, your dreams will come true." What a myth. Wanting isn't near enough. Take Mark and me. I want him something fierce, but I'm not any closer to that dream.

Kathy approaches, balancing a coke and two hot dogs. "You wouldn't believe the gong show I went through to get these. Help me out, will ya?"

I take one of the dogs. "Parker, you should lay off the pop."

"And you should get off my case."

At the entrance to our section, the volunteer asks us to wait for a stoppage in play in the football game. When I tell Kathy about Brittni, Kathy nearly chokes on her drink.

"Brittni was nice to you?" She coughs. "Good thing I wasn't around. She called me an 'f'ing puckhog.' Remember?"

"I remember." I start to fill Kathy in on Brittni and Jamie's career paths and wedding plans.

"Never mind that," Kathy interrupts. "We need to talk about what we can and cannot say to Bud if he asks any more questions about our AAA team."

"Okay."

"Jessie, the SHA can make or break us if we need releases for players. Don't tell Bud that Whitney's dad has been talking to the Weyburn girls."

Recruiting players from other AAA teams is forbidden, and it bothers me that Mr. Johnstone, our team manager, views this as the best way to put together the missing pieces. It's sneaky and dishonest, and I don't like to think about it. Or talk about it. I wonder if Sue knows.

The volunteer beckons to us, indicating we can go to our seats. I lead the way this time, but my mind isn't on football—or the heat—or even the steep descent.

If we don't find a head coach soon, our inaugural AAA season is over. And if that happens, where will I play? Is my dream of playing university hockey about to go up in smoke?

Acknowledgments

It is impossible to name all the people—and teams—who've have influenced me in the evolution of the #jessiemachockeyseries.

My parents taught me to love the Game when they took me to watch Canada's National Team at the Calgary Saddledome in the '70s. Soon after, Mom and Dad became season ticket holders for the Flames—at a time when Wayne Gretzky and the Oilers were the Flames' archrivals. How I loved attending those playoff games!

Later on, it became difficult to make time for the Game—and the Lampman Imperials senior men's team—in the midst of juggling my marriage, a full-time teaching career, and a young family. When my daughter Robin asked, at age nine, if she could play hockey instead of figure skate, I reluctantly agreed—as I didn't look forward to spending all my spare time at a rink.

What a fool I was.

When she evolved from playing boys hockey to girls teams, I fell in love with the Estevan Xtreme and the University of Saskatchewan Huskies. Once a women's hockey team gets under your skin, there's no going back, and so I was inspired to write a novel which reflected my love of the female game.

As I drafted *Power Plays*, I also wanted to address the issues and tough choices teens in Canada face every day—bullying, sexual harassment, low self-esteem, binge drinking, and relationships. I realized it would take more than one book to cover these subjects.

Some "beauts" have helped me realize my dream for the #jessiemachockeyseries. The members of the Estevan Writers Group have been my cheerleaders for nearly twenty years. Blaire read every word of every manuscript while Randy and Robin challenged me with their intimate knowledge of the Game. Alan Safarik, Writer-in-Residence in Estevan, gave me encouragement and constructive criticism on an early draft. I was fortunate the gang at Coteau saw the manuscript's potential and handed me over to Bob Currie who was wise, gentle, and firm in coaching me with edits on *Power Plays*. Alison Acheson was a wonderful mentor and sounding board for *Face Off* and *Breakaway*. Nik Burton, Jessie Mac would not have hit the ice without you.

My decision to reboot the series comes from reasons too numerous to mention, but how fortuitous that Jeanne Martinson and Wood Dragon Books came along at an opportune time, and that Alan should include an excerpt from *Breakaway* in his anthology *Saskatchewan Hockey: The Game of Our Lives*.

I wrestled with the manuscripts. Do I leave names, places, events, hockey rules, technology, and social media as I recorded them from 2007 to 2012? Or do I give them an upgrade? I debated this for a while, then jumped into all three manuscripts with both feet—making changes where I saw fit. I left some buildings untouched—including my beloved Estevan Junior High (even included some cameos for individuals like Mr. Saxon and Ms. Franklin)—but everything else has been tweaked. I hope the effort has been worthwhile.

Thank you to my Beta readers: Blaire, Robin, Marie Powell, and Sharon Plumb.

I'd like to give a special shout-out to the players of the U15 Estevan Bearcats and Regina Cougar Rebels, who graciously allowed me to use their images on the covers of the reboot. Thank you, Wanda Harron, for taking time out of your busy week to capture their energy, enthusiasm, and passion for the Game.

This series is truly an ode to hockey. It's for every parent who's tied a set of skates or driven a vehicle full of kids and equipment to a tournament or league game. It's for every player. Every volunteer. Every official. Every fan. This sport has so many good things to teach us. I hope you've enjoyed reading about Jessie and her peers as much as I've enjoyed giving each one a voice.

Maureen Ulrich – Author

Maureen Ulrich was born in Saskatoon, Saskatchewan but grew up in Edmonton and Calgary, Alberta. She started writing horse stories when she was eleven and historical fiction during her high school years. In 1976, Maureen returned to Saskatoon to attend university and graduated in 1980 with an education degree. Her first teaching assignment was Lampman, Saskatchewan and she has pretty much lived there ever since.

She has been writing plays for young people since 1997. Two titles *Sam Spud: Private Eye* (2007) and *The Banes of Darkwood* (2010) are available through www. samuelfrench.com. Maureen has also written and produced several professional adult productions: *Snowbirds* (2015), *Diamond Girls* (2016-2018), and *Lords of Sceptre* (2018-2019). Souris Valley Theatre in Estevan, Saskatchewan produced her full-length musical *Pirate Heart* (2018), scored by the incomparable Ben Redant.

Maureen started writing *Power Plays* in 1998. Coteau Books of Regina, Saskatchewan published it in 2007. *Power Plays* was a finalist for three Saskatchewan Books Awards and two young readers choice competitions and won a Moonbeam gold medal. *Face Off*, originally published in 2010, won a Moonbeam silver medal. Coteau released *Breakaway* in 2012.

In her free time—of which there is not a great deal—Maureen loves to read, travel, knit, hang out at rinks, football stadiums and ball diamonds, golf, ski, and ride her motorcycle. Please visit her on Facebook, Twitter, Instagram, or maureenulrich.ca.

Did you miss Book One
in the *Jessie Mac Hockey Series?*

Jessie McIntyre, 14, is new to Estevan, and she's having trouble fitting in. By signing her up with the local girls hockey team, her parents hope to give her a fresh start and help her make new friends. But bullies can be found everywhere—even in the dressing room. Will Jessie be able to find a way to protect herself and find acceptance?

New Release
Coming Spring 2021!

The fourth book in the
Jessie Mac Hockey Series!

Wanda Harron – Photographer

Wanda, whose photographs have been used for the reboot of the #jessiemachockeyseries, has been expanding a passion for photography since 2008. After taking photos of her son playing football, she was invited to shoot a high school basketball tournament. Once her photos were posted to social media, more opportunities appeared, and *Wanda Harron Photography* was born.

Wanda's experience includes shooting for the 2016 Saskatchewan Summer Games, the Regina Thunder, the Regina Red Sox and countless minor and school sports. She was invited to capture fan events at the 2017 Grey Cup in Ottawa, and one of her images was voted as the 2019 CJFL Photo of the Year. She also enjoys graduation and family photography. She thanks husband Dave and son Kyle for their support and encouragement.

When asked why she enjoys taking pictures of hockey, she said, "It is more than just striving for the perfect action shot. It's all about the emotion. It's the determination you see in the faces of the 5-year-olds out in their first session chasing the puck in a giant mob. It's the joy of a youngster scoring his or her first goal and then waving to Mom and Dad in the stands. It's the reassurance you see the defence give their goaltender when the faceoff is in their zone. It's the look of relief on the goaltender's face after the big save. Or, the look of frustration when the puck slips by. It's all about the highs and the lows. It's more than just a game."

The Players

Jaycee G. (left) has played hockey in Redvers SK, Elkhorn MB, and Estevan SK. Hockey has taught her to be a good teammate on and off the ice. The sport, which has been a part of her family for many years, lets her travel, make lifelong friends, and stay active. She is proud to keep the family tradition strong.

Megan C. (right), who wears Number 14, has been playing hockey since she was four years old. She plays center and loves to set up plays from behind the net. Her favorite player is Connor McDavid because he inspires her to try her hardest every time she's on the ice.

The Jessie Mac Dictionary

Assist – a point awarded to up to two players who have successively touched the puck immediately before a teammate scores a goal

Backcheck – return to the offensive zone and check attacking opponents

Backhand – a pass or shot made by striking the puck with the back of the stick's blade

Bag skate – when a coach tries to tire out a team by using skating drills in practice, usually for punishment

Beauty (or beautician) – slang for a talented player or, more often, a player who is fun to be around; the highest praise

Bench penalty (or bench minor) – a penalty given to the team as a whole and served by a single player, usually because the coach was "mouthing off" at officials

Bench Run – a celebration where the players on the ice for a goal skate past their own box and tap their teammates' gloves; the line is generally led by the goal scorer

Biscuit – slang for puck

Blocker – a glove fitted with a rectangular pad; a goaltender wears a blocker to protect the hand holding the stick

Blue line – one of two lines between the centre red line and the goal

Blueliner – a player who plays defence

Boarding – a penalty issued for bodychecking a player into the boards with excessive force

Body contact – a penalty issued in women's hockey or in non-contact hockey for giving a bodycheck

Bodycheck – using one's body to separate a player from the puck

Boxed – slang for a female player being hit by a puck, stick, or skate in the genital area

Breakaway – a long rush towards the goal after passing all the defenders

Breakdown – a collapse or mistake made by the opposing team

Bucket – slang for helmet

Canada West – division of U Sports which includes university teams from British Columbia, Alberta, Manitoba, and Saskatchewan

Celly – slang for goal celebration

Centre – the middle player, usually highly skilled, on a forward line

Centre ice – the central area of a rink; the spot where faceoffs take place at the start of each period and after each goal

Charging – a penalty issued for a forward attack of more than two steps against a member of the opposing team for the purpose of taking him or her out of the play

Checking-from-behind – a bodycheck in the middle of the back that sends an opposing player, sometimes head first, into the boards; the offending player is ejected from the game

Cheese (or cheddar) – slang for a puck shot into the net's top corner, or "top shelf"

Cheese Wagon – a school bus used for transporting hockey players

Cherry picker – a player who hangs out at the opposing team's blueline, out of the play, waiting for a breakaway pass; definitely not a compliment to be called one

Chicklets – slang for teeth

Chirp – slang for backtalk

Circuit Training – using weights and machines to build muscle and strength

Clearing (the puck) – moving the puck past a team's own blue line

Crease – a semi-circular area, usually in blue, in front of a hockey net into which the puck must proceed the player

Crossbar – the horizontal bar between two upright bars on a hockey net

Cross-check – a penalty given when a player holds a stick horizontally in both hands and thrusts it at an opposing player's body

D – slang for a player on defence

Defence – one of two players assigned to protect the goal from attack, also defender

Deke (or dangling) – a fake movement or shot to draw a defensive player or goaltender out of position, thereby creating a scoring opportunity

Dirty (or filthy) – an adjective of high praise, (for example, a "filthy" goal is a nice one)

Drop Pass – when a player passes the puck backwards, sometimes through his or her skates

Dub – slang for the WHL or Western Hockey League

Dump-and-chase – a strategy in which a player shoots the puck into the opposing team's end and then chases after it

Dryland – off-ice training

Faceoff – the action of an official starting or restarting play by dropping the puck between two opposing players' sticks

Faceoff dot – each of the nine circles where faceoffs may be taken, including one at centre ice and four in each end, situated to the left and right of the net

Fan (on a shot) – missing the puck entirely with the stick blade

Five-hole – slang for the gap between a goaltender's parted legs through which a puck can pass

Flamingo – when a player lifts his or her leg to avoid blocking a shot; this practice is frowned upon by teammates

Flow – slang for hockey hair; generally long and free; a compliment

Forecheck – an aggressive style of defence; checking opposing players before they can organize an attack

Forward – an attacking player positioned near the front of the team

Goal judge – a volunteer who sits behind the goal and turns on a red light if the puck goes into the net

Goalpost – either of two upright bars on a hockey net

Goalie pads – a pair of thick rectangular pads worn on the legs of a goaltender; sometimes referred to as "pillows"

Goaltender – a player stationed to protect the goal

Greasy (or garbage) goal – a loose puck or rebound shot into the net

Hash mark – one of four short lines on the edge of each faceoff circle

Hat Trick – when a player scores three goals in one game; in a "true" hat trick, the three goals are scored consecutively

Hooking – a penalty given for an illegal check where a player attempts to hold back or hinder an opposing player by tugging with the stick blade

Ice (the puck) – shooting the puck from one's own half of the rink to the far end or other half, which is permitted only while killing a penalty

Icing – an infraction for shooting the puck to the other half of the ice, in which case the referee stops the play and a faceoff is held in the offending team's end

Interference – the illegal blocking or hindering of an opposing player

Jill – clothing worn by female players to protect the genital area

Left wing (left winger) – a forward whose position is to the left of the centre

Lettuce – slang for hair (for example, a moustache might be termed "lip lettuce")

Linemate – one of three players who plays on the same forward line as another

Linesman – an on-ice official whose role is to make offside or icing calls and break up fights

Major Junior – the highest level of men's amateur hockey in Canada which includes the Western Hockey League (WHL), Ontario Hockey League (OHL), and Quebec Hockey League (QMJHL)

Offence – the act of attacking in order to score goals

Offside – an infraction where an opposing player crosses the blue line ahead of the puck in which case a faceoff is called outside the blue line

One-timer – receiving a pass and striking the puck with the stick blade at the same time

Passing lane – any open space on the ice through which a player can move the puck to his or her teammate

Penalty shot – a breakaway shot by an offensive player on the goaltender, allowed as the result of a penalty

Penalty – a punishment for breaking a rule in which case a player is temporarily removed from the game and his or her team is forced to resume play with one less player; the length of a penalty is generally two minutes, but may go as high as four, five, or ten minutes, or in extreme cases, can result in the player's removal from the game

Penalty box – an area of seating near the timekeeper's booth for players who have been temporarily withdrawn from play because of a penalty

Penalty Kill – when a team must play with one or, in some cases, two less players because of a penalty; also called PK

Penalty killer – a player, usually highly skilled, who plays while his or her team is reduced in strength due to a penalty

Pipes – slang for goalposts

Plus-Minus – a statistic indicating a player's effectiveness on both offence and defence, adjusted every time an even-strength goal is scored while the player is on the ice, with one added to the cumulative score if the player's own team scores and one subtracted if the opponent scores; ideally a player's plus-minus should be a high positive integer (for example, +30)

Point (a shot from the point) – either of two areas to the right or left of the net, just inside the blue line where it meets the boards

Poke-check – pushing the puck off an opposing player's stick with one's own blade

Power play – when a team has a one or two player advantage over the opposing team because the latter is killing a penalty; having a power play greatly increases the opportunity to score

Red line – the centre line on the ice surface midway between the two blue lines

Referee – an official, authorized to issue penalties, who supervises the game to make sure the players obey the rules; wears a black and white striped jacket with a red arm band

Right wing (right winger) – a forward whose position is to the right of the centre

Ringette – a game resembling hockey, often played by girls and women, with a straight stick and a rubber ring

Rink rat – a small child, often unsupervised, who runs amuck in the rink lobby; usually found in packs

Roughing – a penalty given for unnecessary or excessive use of force

Rubbing out – using body position along the boards to separate an opposing player from the puck; generally allowed in women's hockey

Rushing (the puck) – bringing the puck up the ice, often single-handedly

SaskFirst – an SHA program designed to provide better understanding of the game as well as promote the development of quality players, coaches, trainers, officials, and administrators.

SHA – Saskatchewan Hockey Association

Saucer – shooting or passing a puck so that it passes overtop the sticks of opposing players, also known as "chuckin' sauce"

SFU18AAAHL – Saskatchewan Female Under 18 AAA Hockey League; made up of teams from Regina, Saskatoon, Prince Albert, The Battlefords, Weyburn, Athol Murray College (Notre Dame), and Swift Current. Until 2019, Melville Prairie Fire participated in this league

Shift – a relay of players on a team; usually two defence and three forwards

Shootout – a method of deciding the outcome of a game, which would otherwise end in a tie; each team takes a specified number of penalty shots; the team that scores the most wins the shootout and the game; a shootout occurs after a sudden death overtime

Short-handed – slang for penalty killing; not having the usual number of players on the ice

Short-handed goal – when a team scores a goal while playing with fewer players, especially while killing a penalty

SJHL – Saskatchewan Junior Hockey League

Slapshot (clapper) – a hard shot taken by raising the stick blade at or above waist height before striking the puck

Slashing – a penalty given for striking or swinging at an opposing player with one's stick

Slew foot – to trip an opposing player by using one's own skates

Slot – an unmarked area in front of the net which is considered an excellent scoring position for an offensive player; low slot is closer to the net than high slot

Snipe – a skillful goal, usually top shelf, performed by a "sniper"

Special teams – a combination of players that are trained for penalty killing or for playing the power play

Split the D – when an offensive player maneuvers between the two defensive players

Stop time – when the game clock is stopped between plays

Straight time – when the game clock is not stopped between plays; often used for younger players or if the score is very one-sided

Sudden death – an extra period (overtime) to decide a tied game, in which the first team to score wins

Taco-in-a-Bag – a rink delicacy consisting of a bag of Nachos filled with taco meat, shredded cheddar, lettuce, tomatoes, sour cream, and salsa; usually eaten with a fork while sitting in the stands or talking about a magnificent goal after a game

Time out – a stoppage of play called by the coach so that the team can consider or discuss strategy or attend to an injured player

Toe drag (toey) – an evasive move where the puck carrier drags the puck along the ice with the toe of the blade faced down then pulls back to cause a defender to lunge forward while the dragger or "dangler" skates past

Top Shelf – the highest part of the net, just beneath the crossbar

U13 – a team with 11 and 12-year-old players (under 13 years old)

U15 – a team with 13 and 14-year-old players (under 15 years old)

U18 – a team with 15, 16, and 17-year-old players (under 18 years old)

U Sports – the organization of Canadian university sports, formerly CIS (Canadian Intercollegiate Sports)

Unsportsmanlike – a penalty given for unprofessional or unseemly conduct (for example, pulling the hair of an opponent or swearing at an official)

Wraparound – when a player attempts to score by coming from behind the net

World Junior Hockey Championships – an annual, international U20 male hockey tournament which begins on Boxing Day and ends in early January; players for each nation are generally selected from Major Junior and NCAA (National Collegiate Athletic Association) teams; many of these individuals have already been scouted for the National Hockey League

Wrist shot – a shot taken by sweeping the puck along the ice with a fluid motion before releasing it

Zamboni – a tractor-like machine used to shave snow off the rink and replace it with a fresh flood of water to create a smooth skating surface